THE SUSSEX DOWNS MURDER

Two brothers, John and William Rother, live together at Chalklands Farm in the beautiful Sussex Downs. Their peaceful rural life is shattered when John Rother disappears and his abandoned car is found. Has he been kidnapped? Or is his disappearance more sinister? Superintendent Meredith is called to investigate – and begins to suspect the worst when human bones are discovered on Chalklands farmland. His patient, careful detective method begins slowly to untangle the clues as suspicion shifts from one character to the next.

THE SUSSEX DOWNS MURDER

THE SUSSEX DOWNS MURDER

by

John Bude

Magna Large Print Books
Long Preston, North Yorkshire,
BD23 4ND, England.

British Library Cataloguing in Publication Data.

A catalogue record of this book is
available from the British Library

ISBN   978-0-7505-4441-2

First published in Great Britain in 1936 by Skeffington & Son
This edition published in 2015 by The British Library

Copyright © John Bude, 1936
Introduction © Martin Edwards 2015

Cover illustration © NRM/Science & Society Picture Library by
arrangement with The British Library

The moral right of the author has been asserted

Published in Large Print 2017 by arrangement with
The British Library Board

Magna Large Print is an imprint of Library Magna Books Ltd.

Printed and bound in Great Britain by
T.J. (International) Ltd., Cornwall, PL28 8RW

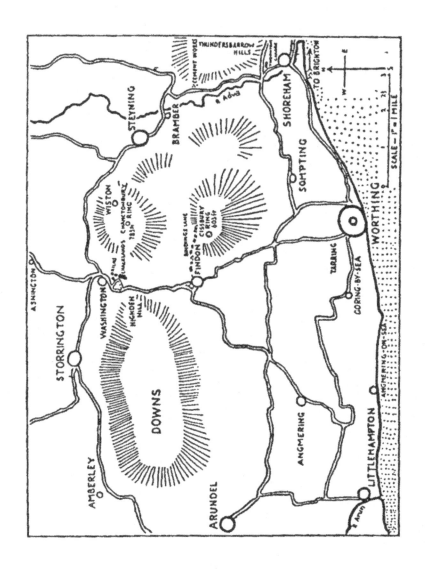

CONTENTS

CHAPTER

INTRODUCTION

The Sussex Downs Murder is an ingenious and highly enjoyable detective novel. Since its original publication in 1936, it has languished in undeserved obscurity, and affordable copies have been almost impossible to track down, even though the author, John Bude, carved a successful career as a full-time crime writer for more than two decades. Bude's first two detective stories, *The Cornish Coast Murder* and *The Lake District Murder,* which had been equally rare, have found an appreciative new public in the twenty-first century thanks to their reappearance as British Library crime classics. I suspect that Bude has more readers now than he did during 'the Golden Age of murder' between the two world wars, and his new fans will surely relish *The Sussex Downs Murder,* which shows a youngish writer quietly mastering the craft of entertaining mystification.

This story is, to my mind, a conspicuous advance on his previous work, because of the range and quality of the ingredients. First comes the setting. Throughout his career, Bude's careful depiction of place was one of his strengths. Here, the Rother family farmhouse, Chalklands, and the surrounding area, are convincingly realized, and in keeping with Golden Age tradition, we are supplied with a map to help us follow the events of the story after John Rother goes missing, in circumstances which at first (but deceptively) seem reminiscent of the disappearance of Agatha Christie.

Second comes the plot. Bude's growing confidence as a novelist is on display as he offers a pleasing sequence of twists and turns, dextrously shifting suspicion from one character to another, despite the relatively small cast list. A clever touch sees a significant clue planted at a very early stage in the story, while even the title of the book is significant. In common with many other Golden Age novelists, Bude borrowed plot elements from real life. The message which lures William Rother to Littlehampton General Hospital calls to mind the hoax at the heart of the legendary Wallace case, five years before this book was published. Crime writers ranging from Dorothy L. Sayers and Margery Allingham to Raymond Chandler and P.D.James have been fascinated by the Wallace mystery, and several good books have drawn on it. A sign of Bude's skill is that the mysterious message forms only one of a host of complications facing Superintendent Meredith. Here, as in his previous book, Bude shows himself to be a disciple of Freeman Wills Crofts, most famous of the meticulous detective novelists of the Golden Age whose elaborately constructed puzzles tested the wits of countless readers.

Third comes the detective. Meredith was introduced in *The Lake District Murder,* and proved such an appealing character that Bude not only relocated him from Cumberland to Sussex for this story, but also went on to feature him in most of his later novels. Meredith is modelled on Crofts' Inspector French, both in his diligence and his love of a good meal, but has a stronger sense of humour, as well as a cheeky son who makes a telling contribution to the detective work. Meredith is no undisciplined maverick, and unfashionably (by modern standards) lacks both a drink problem and a tormented emotional life. But he is portrayed credibly – some of his early guesswork proves mistaken, but he keeps battling on – and with genuine affection.

Fourth comes the manner of writing. There is nothing pretentious about John Bude's work. He did not have the high literary ambitions of Sayers or Allingham, but his characterization is neat, and his touches of humour deft – one witness who claims to have 'a psychic eye' illustrates both qualities, while the brief final chapter is a nice touch. Bude's humanity – evidenced here by Meredith's reflections at the end of the story – also helps to lift this book out of the 'humdrum' category to which so many Golden Age mysteries have been consigned, often without much critical thought.

The Sussex Downs Murder may not have made Bude rich, but it confirmed the promise of his earlier books. Bude's real name was Ernest Elmore, and sound research was his hallmark. Sometimes he used personal experience as the basis for his settings; a spell as a games master at a school provided background for the wittily titled *Loss of a Head*, while holiday trips inspired *Death on the Riviera* and *Telegram from Le Touquet*. Like Crofts (and unlike most modern crime novelists) he made effective use of industrial backgrounds in novels such as *Trouble-a-Brewing, Death on Paper,* and *When the Case was Opened.*

A quiet, sociable family man with a son and a daughter, he ran the local Home Guard during the Second World War, having been deemed unfit to serve in the forces. He enjoyed golf and painting, but never learned to drive (although his daughter Jennifer recalls that this did not deter him from pointing out to his wife when she should change gear). In 1953, he became a founder-member of the Crime Writers' Association, and was a co-organizer of the Crime Book Exhibition which was one of the CWA's early publicity initiatives. He lived near Rye, and was a popular and hard-working member of the CWA's committee from its inception until May 1957. The following November, having just delivered the manuscript of what proved to be his final novel to his publishers, he went into hospital for an operation, and died two days later. He was only fifty-six, and one speculates that, had he lived another fifteen years or so, his body of work might have been impressive enough for his name to have remained reasonably well known to crime fans. It was not to be, and until the British Library took the initiative in reviving his early work, the merits of John Bude were remembered only by a select number of connoisseurs. Now, the reappearance of *The Sussex Downs Murder* should help to secure his reputation as one of traditional British crime fiction's more accomplished craftsmen.

Martin Edwards

CHAPTER 1

THE OPENING OF A PROBLEM

Dominating that part of the Sussex Downs with which this story is concerned is Chanctonbury Ring. This oval cap of gigantic beeches may be seen, on fine days, from almost any point in the little parish of Washington. It is a typical village of two streets, two pubs, a couple of chandlers, a forge, an Olde Tea Shoppe, and a bus service. Although the parish is bisected by the main Worthing–Horsham road, it has managed to retain in the face of progress all those local peculiarities which have their roots in the old feudal system of government. There is still a genuine squire at the Manor House to whom the group of idlers outside the 'Chancton Arms' whatever their politics, instinctively touch their hats; whilst the well-being of the church rests in the conservative hands of the Reverend Gorringe, as typical a parson as ever trod the pages of Trollope. Farming is the main topic of conversation and most of the able-bodied men have taken to the plough as a kitten takes to milk. Scattered round the limits of the parish are farms whose owners have borne the same names for a score of generations.

Three generations of Rothers had inhabited the long, low farmhouse known as Chalklands, which lay under the Ring. The upper arable land petered out on to the short-turfed slopes of the down, where John and William Rother, the present occupants, grazed their shorthorns. The Rothers had not always lived at Chalklands. Before the shrinkage of a considerable family fortune, the Rothers had owned Dyke House, and a number of John's and William's ancestors had been buried in a vault at Washington Church. It was claimed, on the evidence of family portraits, that the present John Rother was the spit and image of his great-grandfather, old Sir Percival Rother, who had died in the North Room at Dyke House and occupied the last remaining space in the family vault. Since that event the Rothers had contented themselves with a farmhouse and a rectangle of good earth in the churchyard.

John and William were brothers, a fact which astounded strangers because they appeared to have nothing in common save their ancestry. John was bluff, rubicund, a stocky, rather loud-voiced, hail-fellow-well-met type of man; William slim, tall, and sensitive. John was practical, William imaginative. John was content to farm as his father had farmed and his grandfather before him; William, the younger brother and partner, was a theorist who believed in experiment. It was natural that a certain antagonism should have sprung up between the brothers. And the village had been quick to note that this dissension was not lessened when William suddenly married Janet Waring, daughter of a retired colonel, who had recently died at East Grinstead. Had William's finances been healthier it was rumoured that he would not have taken his wife back to Chalklands. But John was the capitalist of the concern and William had to cut his cloth accordingly.

The Rothers did not rely entirely upon farming for their income. They were lime-burners. Behind the house was a great white horseshoe of chalk, some forty feet high, into which the picks of diggers were for ever eating. To the side of the farmhouse were three lime-kilns, the creamy smoke of which eddied through a belt of shrubs and thinned out before reaching the gravel drive.

On July 20th, 193–, a Saturday, a Hillman Minx was drawn up before the long, white-trellised verandah which projected over the lower windows of the house. John himself, with a suit-case in his hand, stood at the front door talking to Janet and William.

'So it's no use,' he was saying, 'forwarding letters until I reach Harlech. I may break my journey at any point *en route*. I can't stick being bound by an itinerary when I'm on holiday.'

Janet smiled. 'Like me, John. Have you packed everything?' Adding, 'You know I don't like to interfere on these occasions.'

John nodded, stuck a tweed cap on his head, kissed Janet on the cheek, and held out his hand to William.

'Well, you're all set for three weeks, Will. Don't forget Timpson's order for that yard and a half, or Johnson's load for Tuesday. See that he keeps up to scratch, Janet, and doesn't meander about talking theories. There's only one way of making lime, you know, Will, and that's burning chalk. Well, good-bye.'

William nodded and muttered something con-

17

ventional about having a good time, as usual ignoring his brother's slights, realizing that John was always disappointed if he didn't rise to the bait.

'Plenty of petrol?'

'Four gallons, thanks – in a clean tank. I want to make a test run.'

'Good – and you'll reach Harlech...?'

'Wednesday, at the latest,' said John as he climbed into the driving-seat. 'So you'll have to wait until then if you want any good advice.'

Then, after several more clamorous good-byes and a great deal of waving, the Hillman shot off round the curve of the drive and vanished behind a hedge of clipped laurel.

At that moment two other disconnected events took place. The parish clock chimed the quarter past six, and Pyke-Jones, the eminent Worthing entomologist, threw himself with a sigh of content into an arm-chair at the vegetarian guesthouse known as the Lilac Rabbit. Pyke-Jones had just returned from a gruelling ramble with his net and specimen-case over the downs near Findon. It was his wont to patronize the Lilac Rabbit during week-ends, making Findon – a village about half-way between Worthing and Washington – his headquarters for these spirited attacks upon the local butterflies and beetles. He little realized as he sat there sipping his tonic-water, preparatory to his evening meal of nut-cutlet, salad, and raw carrot, that John Rother's departure from Chalklands was to interfere with his plans for the following morning.

He little realized as he set out at nine o'clock on the morning of Sunday, July 21st, that he was

18

walking slap-bang into the middle of a tragedy. He was making for Cissbury Hill along a winding, sun-bleached lane which ran under the foot of the downs and eventually petered out in a lonely farmyard some four miles from the village. About half-way along this glorified cart-track, Pyke-Jones unlatched an iron gate which gave on to the open downside and began the gentle ascent, at that point dotted with thick and haphazard clumps of gorse. A hundred yards from the lane, much to his astonishment, he came upon a parked car. It had been shunted back between two large gorse bushes. The nearside door of the saloon hung open, and a few paces from the running-board a tweed cap lay, lining upward, on the turf. Impelled by curiosity Pyke-Jones stopped a minute to investigate, rather puzzled that the owner of the car should have been so careless as to leave the door open and his cap on the ground.

Then a few feet away he stopped dead, uttered an exclamation of alarm and horror and went down on one knee. The inside of the tweed cap was covered with blood! There was blood on the running-board of the car, on the upholstery of the driving-seat, on the wheel itself. The triplex windscreen was starred in several places, whilst the floor of the saloon was littered with glass from the shattered dashboard dials. Not daring to touch the cap, he rose and called out in a high, quavering voice:

'I say – is there anybody about? Is anybody there?'

There was no answer.

Thoroughly shaken, fearful of what might have

taken place, Pyke-Jones hesitated a moment, wondering what he ought to do. Then pulling out a notebook he hastily jotted down the registration number of the car, and started off at a jog-trot for Findon.

Two hours later Superintendent Meredith, who had recently been transferred from Carlisle to Lewes, was closeted with William Rother in the old-fashioned drawing-room at Chalklands.

'There's no doubt about it, Mr. Rother,' Meredith was saying, 'it's your brother's car right enough. Your identification of this cap makes it even more certain. Have you any idea how the car could have got there, or where your brother is now?'

'None whatsoever. I can't understand it. My brother left here about six o'clock yesterday evening on his way to Harlech in Wales. He was intending to break his journey at one or two places of interest on the way. You say the car was found under the north side of Cissbury?'

Meredith nodded.

'Just off a *cul-de-sac*, Mr. Rother, which ends at Bindings Farm – four miles from Findon.'

William, paler than usual, was obviously suffering under the stress of the unexpected events.

'I know the place, yes. But why John should have taken his car down that lane is beyond my comprehension. You say the police have searched the surrounding part of the down and have found no sign of my brother?'

'None. Nobody had noticed anything at Bindings Farm either. The Findon sergeant made inquiries there at once. The search is still going on, of course. The usual police broadcast will have to be issued, so I should like to have a description of your brother, Mr. Rother – height, build, complexion, clothes, distinguishing marks, and so on. Can you let me have these details now?'

After the description had been taken down, Meredith closed his notebook and went on: 'I know this must be a painful interview for you, Mr. Rother, but I'm afraid we must face up to facts. On the evidence to hand you can guess what we're bound to suspect?'

'Foul play of some sort?'

'Exactly. There's the possibility, of course, of attempted suicide, but I've a very strong reason for ruling out that explanation.'

'Confidential I take it?'

'I'm afraid so, Mr. Rother. There are certain bits of evidence which the police, you know, like to keep hidden in their pockets. At present everything points to assault. Though so far it's impossible to say when and why your brother was attacked. You know of nobody, I suppose, who might have done him injury? Anybody, for example, who bore him a grudge or so on?'

William, after a second's deliberation, shook his head.

'My brother was, I think, pretty popular in the locality. He was reserved over his private affairs. I was never really in his confidence. As a matter of fact we didn't quite see eye to eye over things – farming in particular.'

'You're in partnership here?'

'Yes – both in the farm and the lime-burning business.'

21

Meredith jotted down a couple of notes, looked up, and said after a moment's thought:

'You realize that there is one rather confusing factor in this case, Mr. Rother?'

'I don't quite–?' began William.

'If we assume that your brother was assaulted – where is he now? A wounded man would not get far without causing attention, particularly in a country district.'

'Perhaps he was attacked late last night,' suggested William, 'and then wandered off and collapsed somewhere on the downs.'

Meredith shook his head.

'I thought the same thing at first, sir – but the trail of blood ends a few paces from the car. That's pretty pointed, isn't it?'

'Why? I don't quite see–?'

'Surely it suggests the assailant worked with a second car and possibly a confederate. Your brother must have been driven off, unconscious perhaps, in order to remove him as far as possible from the scene of the attack.'

'But for what reason, Mr. Meredith?' William had grown more and more agitated as the Superintendent's level voice dealt with the official possibilities of the tragedy. 'The whole thing seems senseless! Why was my brother attacked? Who attacked him? How the devil did his car get under Cissbury Ring when it should have been *en route* for Harlech?'

'If I could answer those questions, sir, the police investigation would be at an end. There is one fairly feasible explanation of his removal by a second car. Kidnapping, with the idea of extracting ransom-money.' Meredith gave a crooked smile. 'An unfortunate criminal habit which has been imported to this country from the United States. But that's theory only. There's nothing so far to suggest that this is the case.'

There was a long pause during which William rose uneasily, strode to the french windows and stared out over the lawn.

'Tell me, Superintendent,' he asked, obviously finding it difficult to control his emotion, 'what are the chances?'

'Of what, sir?'

'Of my brother still being alive?'

Meredith hesitated, shrugged his shoulders and then said with typical caution: 'It's too early, sir, to say anything definite. I suppose it's about fifty-fifty. We may know considerably more inside the next twenty-four hours when these particulars of your brother have been issued to the police. There'll probably be an S O S broadcast as well, if nothing comes to light within the next few days. Until then, Mr. Rother, I should hang on to the old saying: "No news is good news."'

He rose, took up his peaked cap from the piano, and added: 'By the way, Mr. Rother – what was your brother's mood when he left you last evening? Did he seem depressed, apprehensive, nervous?'

'No – I should have said he was in a perfectly normal frame of mind.'

'What did you talk about – anything in particular?'

'Oh, just trivial matters – about some orders for lime which had to be sent off. I remember asking

John if he was all right for petrol.'

Meredith registered this detail, pondered, and then suddenly demanded: 'Did he answer that question?'

'Yes.'

'You remember what he said?'

'Perfectly. He said, "Four gallons, thanks – in a clean tank."'

'Meaning, I suppose, that he had emptied his tank and filled up with exactly four gallons?'

'That's the idea. It was a fad of his on long journeys to estimate his exact mileage per gallon.'

'Have you any idea what his car did to the gallon?'

'About forty, I think. Perhaps less.'

'Thanks,' said Meredith. 'I won't keep you any longer, Mr. Rother. You may depend on me to let you know the results of our investigations at once. Are you on the 'phone?'

William shook his head.

'We're rather off the beaten track here, I'm afraid.'

'Well, I'll ring through to your local station and the constable can cycle up if anything comes to light.'

William took the proffered hand and shook it warmly.

'Thank you, Mr. Meredith,' he said as he escorted him towards the door. 'I'm naturally worried to death over this affair. Your consideration is a great help. I don't know how I am going to break the news to my wife. She'll be back from church at any minute now.'

'She was fond of your brother?' inquired Mere-

24

dith as he edged diplomatically through the door.

'Very,' said William dryly. 'They had a great deal in common. In fact I've always upheld–' He broke off with an apologetic laugh. 'But, look here, Superintendent, I mustn't waste your time with family affairs. This way – to the left.'

As Meredith sat beside the police chauffeur on his way back to Findon, he felt he had gained little from his interview with William Rother. He hoped that the missing man would turn up within the next twenty-four hours and thus put an end to an annoying routine case. The only original factor present at the moment was Rother's disappearance, and should he turn up, the case and the mystery would automatically come to an end. If he didn't turn up – Meredith smiled to himself – but that was ridiculous! You couldn't spirit a man away, alive or dead, with the ease of a conjuror disposing of a rabbit in a top-hat. Rother would turn up right enough, and the case would resolve itself into the usual 'assault by a homicidal maniac' or something of the sort – a motiveless, callous crime, yet all the more unpleasant because accidental in origin.

'On the other hand,' he thought, 'that wouldn't explain away the presence of John Rother's car under Cissbury Ring. Four gallons of petrol in his tank, eh? Exact. That's about the one valuable bit of evidence I've got from this interview, I reckon.' He turned to the constable at the wheel. 'I want you to take me back to the scene of the crime, Hawkins. Can you empty a petrol tank for me and measure the contents?'

'Easy sir – if we pick up some two-gallon cans

25

at the Findon garage.'

At the Findon Filling Station the cans were placed in the car and the two men turned off the main road, swung left into what was known locally as Bindings Lane, and drove along under the downs. A constable was standing guard over the Hillman, and already a small knot of sensation-seekers, mostly children, was grouped round the car. There was nothing further to report and so far all the searchers in the locality had drawn a blank. Hawkins loosened a union-nut on the carburettor feedpipe, therefore, and carefully drained off the petrol into the cans.

'I'll take an accurate measure of that back at headquarters,' said Meredith. 'How much is there roughly?'

'About a can and a half, sir,' said Hawkins.

Meredith, after arranging with the constable for the Hillman to be taken to the Findon garage, jumped into the police car and was driven back to Lewes – a matter of some twenty-five miles.

Once in his office he got to work with a gradu-ated beaker and made an accurate measurement of the petrol from Rother's tank. Just as he had completed the job, there was a brisk rap on the door, and the Chief Constable, Major Forest, stumped into the room. He stumped everywhere – a brusque, stocky, energetic little man with a bristly moustache and semi-bald head. Although curt to the point of rudeness he was liked by his staff, who recognized his almost demoniac effi-ciency.

'Hullo, Meredith. What's the game? Don't you ever have a day off?'

'It's this Rother case, sir.'

'Oh, that abandoned car affair. I saw your report on my desk. Make anything of it?'

'Not yet. It looks like assault.'

Major Forest agreed.

'And what the devil are you up to here? The whole place reeks of petrol. Trying to burn down the station as a protest against long hours, eh?'

Meredith explained what he had learned from William Rother at Chalklands.

'Well – what's the result? Come on, Meredith, don't look cunning. You've found out something.'

'There's about three and a quarter gallons unused, sir. Rother left Chalklands with exactly four in the tank. His car does about forty to the gallon. So by a simple deduction–'

'All right! All right!' cut in the Chief. 'You can cut out the mathematics. What you're trying to tell me is that Rother had done about thirty miles before he parked his car under Cissbury.'

'Exactly, sir. And it's about four and a half miles direct from Chalklands.'

'Which proves?'

'Nothing, sir.'

'Umph – that's a great help!'

'Nothing at the moment. The data may be useful later on. You see, sir–'

'Oh, well, go about the job in your own pig-headed way. I never could understand your methods. You're thorough but finicky. Like a bally woman over details. But far be it from me to interfere. It's your case. If Rother doesn't turn up within three days we'll have his description broadcast from London.'

'Right, sir.'

Three days later the unemotional voice was announcing:

'Before I read the general news bulletin, here is a police message. Missing since Saturday, July 20th, John Fosdyke Rother, aged thirty-nine, height five feet eight inches, of stocky build, ruddy complexion, hair greying at the sides, blue-grey eyes and clean shaven. When last seen Mr. Rother was wearing a light brown plus-four suit, light brown hose, and brown brogue shoes. Probably hatless. His car was found abandoned under Cissbury Ring a few miles inland from Worthing early on Sunday, July 21st. It is believed that Mr. Rother may be wandering with loss of memory. Would anybody who can give any information as to his present whereabouts please communicate with the Chief Constable of the Sussex County Constabulary – Telephone Lewes 0099 – or with the nearest police station.'

That was Wednesday, July 24th.

A week later John Fosdyke Rother was still missing and the Superintendent had not advanced a single step along the path of his investigation. It seemed, for all Meredith's ridicule, that the missing man's assailant had achieved the impossible – the rabbit had been spirited away out of the top-hat.

'And that,' thought Meredith, 'scarcely argues the work of a homicidal maniac.'

Already it looked as if the police were up against a carefully planned and cleverly executed murder, and, what was more, a murder without a corpse!

CHAPTER 2

BONES

'Well, whatever it is, mate,' said Ed with a profound air of conclusion, 'it didn't ought to be there.'

'You're right,' nodded Bill. 'Spoils the mixing when you finds lumps of what didn't ought to be there in the lime. Spoils the slack – to say nothing of the mortar.'

'I wonder what the 'ell it is anyway,' said Ed, holding up the piece of foreign matter which had been tipped out of the lime-sack into the big bowl of sand made ready for mixing the mortar. '*Looks* like a bit of bone, don't it?'

''Ooman bone,' added Bill with a gruesome twist of the imagination.

'Dog's bone more like,' said Ed as he tossed the object in question on to a near-by heap of rubble. 'Now don't stand there growing old – 'and me that can of water and let's get this lot mixed.' Adding with a look of scorn: 'You and your 'ooman bones. You got a criminal turn of mind, you 'ave.' Then brightening a little: 'Mind you, Bill, things – relics as you might say, *'av* been found in queerer places than a bag of lump-lime afore now. I once 'eard of a chap out Arundel way 'oo found a 'ooman skull in an old chimney what 'ee was pulling down. Norman they reckoned it

29

was – though 'ow the 'ell they knew the poor devil's name on the evidence of 'is 'ead only, Gawd knows!'

Ed expectorated into the seething pool of lime which he was now slaking with water, and his mate began to stir in the sand. They were laying the foundation of a new wing which was to be added to Professor Blenkings' 'desirable mansion' facing the sea-front at West Worthing. This gentleman, a retired professor of anatomy, was at that moment crossing the lawn from the summerhouse, where he had been indulging in a postprandial nap. The raised voices of the bricklayer and his mate drew him back to the realization that, after months of argument with his architect, the new wing was actually under way. He felt affable and, in consequence, talkative.

'Afternoon, men.'

The two labourers touched their caps.

''Noon, sir.'

'Getting along all right?'

'As well as may be,' said Ed with a wink to Bill. 'Though my mate 'ere claims to 'av found a 'ooman bone in the last lot of lime what's come from the builder's yard.'

'A human bone!' The Professor twiddled his green sun-glasses. 'That's interesting. Very. I happen to have made a lifelong study of bones. I should like to see it.'

'I was only pulling your leg, sir. It's just the tail-end of a dog's dinner if you really want to know. I threw it on that 'eap.'

The Professor followed the line of Ed's outstretched hand, took a pace forward, peered, and let out a sharp exclamation.

'But good gracious! How extraordinary! Your friend's right. It *is* a human bone.' He reached down, picked up the specimen and turned it over apprisingly in his hand. 'A full-grown male femur. Almost intact too. Most interesting.'

'Femmer?' inquired Ed, pushing back his cap and scratching the top of his ear. 'What's that, eh?'

'Thigh bone – the longest bone in the human frame.'

'And 'ow the devil did a 'ooman thigh bone get into that bag of lump-lime? That's what I'd like to know,' said Ed in a profound voice. Adding darkly: 'And that's what we *ought* to know, sir. You can see that.'

'It's certainly unusual, I agree.'

'It's more, sir – it's more than that. A lot more. Don't you see?'

Ed was now thoroughly agitated.

'See what?' The Professor was a little bewildered by the other's vehemence.

'That it's a matter for the police,' contested Ed. 'Maybe there's a natural explanation. Maybe there's not. Maybe that there femmer was not put in that lime-bag by accident. Maybe it's–'

'Yes – maybe it's murder!' cried Bill, determined to take all the wind out of Ed's dramatic dénouement.

'Murder!' exclaimed the Professor incredulously. He had been dealing with human bones for so many years that he had almost forgotten that, clothed in flesh, human bones walked and talked and breathed.

31

'Yes,' nodded Ed. 'When a chap's done another chap in 'ee's got to get rid of the corpse, ain't 'ee?'

'Then in that case–' began the Professor, now really upset. 'You think I ought to inform the police?'

Ed was emphatic. 'I do, sir. And at once. We don't want no trouble to come our way over this, do we, Bill?'

'Then I'll 'phone! I'll 'phone the station at once.' Already the Professor was trotting up the path, with the thigh-bone tucked under his arm like an umbrella. 'Dear me! Murder. Most interesting.' He met his housekeeper in the hall and waved the bone in her face. 'It's murder, Harriet. So the workmen say. I must 'phone the police. We don't want trouble to come our way over this.'

Twenty minutes later Sergeant Phillips of the Worthing Borough Police was interviewing the little group in the garden. His questions were brief and to the point. In five minutes he had collected all the necessary data and jotted it down in his notebook. The men worked for Timpson & Son, Builders and Contractors, in Steyne Road. They had no idea from whom Timpson's bought their lime, but Fred Drake, the yard foreman, would be able to supply the information. The Professor explained that he had recognized the bone, at once, to be a femur. In his opinion the bone had been sawn through at either end with a surgical saw, probably to sever it from the rest of the body. He had no idea how old the bone might be, but it was certainly that of an adult male of average height. It was difficult, of course, to gauge the original build of a man with any accuracy from the bone-structure alone. It did not necessarily mean that the femur of a fat man would be bigger than that of a thin man. It was a most extraordinary affair – unprecedented, the Professor imagined, and he sincerely hoped that there had been no crime to account for the bone's presence in the bag.

At Timpson's the sergeant found the yard foreman washing his hands under a tap.

'Fred Drake?'

'That's me.'

'I want a little information.'

'Go ahead.'

'That bag of lime which was delivered this morning at Professor Blenkings' place on the front – where did it come from?'

'Rother's,' said the foreman. 'Rother's of Washington. Know 'em?'

The sergeant nodded. He knew, what was more, about the disappearance of John Rother. To his mind it already seemed that the thigh-bone, wrapped up in brown paper under his arm, would have to be handed over to the County Police. Light was already dawning. He had clasped the link almost by instinct.

'When did this particular load come in?'

'Yesterday. A yard and a half.'

'Delivered in bags?'

'No – our chaps put it in the bags as it's wanted. We dump it in that big shed down there.'

'Any other been sent out from that dump?'

'No.'

'Right – then see that the shed is locked up and the lime not interfered with until we pay you

33

another visit, Mr. Drake. They'll explain to Mr. Timpson in due course from the station. Thanks for the information. Good day.'

Superintendent Meredith whistled into the 'phone when the news came through from Worthing.

'So that's the way the wind's blowing, is it? Well, look here, Sergeant, I'll be right over to collect that thigh-bone. In the meantime get that dump at Timpson's sifted by one of your men. If anything further turns up ring that professor fellow and arrange for him to meet us at your place at six o'clock.'

Once settled into the police car on the way to Worthing, Meredith ignored Hawkins and began to readjust his outlook to this new slant on the case. That the thigh-bone was John Rother's he did not doubt – it was quite inconceivable that these two extraordinary, even sensational factors connected with the Rother ménage should bear no relation to each other. A man named Rother is attacked in a lonely spot, killed, and the body removed from the scene of the crime. A male femur is found about ten days later in a load of lime which had come from the Rother kilns. Surely the intermediate events could be construed something in this manner: The murderer or murderers having killed their victim were faced with the necessity of ridding themselves of the body. They believed, no doubt, that it would be some few days, even weeks, before the abandoned Hillman would be found in that isolated spot under Cissbury Ring. If in the meantime, therefore, they could dispose of the body, there was a good chance of them making a get-away, probably to the Continent, before the crime was discovered. Secondly, the body in a murder case may render up clues to the police, quite unanticipated by the murderer. But dispose of the body and these clues would be, *ipso facto,* unavailable.

Now a human corpse may be concealed in various ways, some more efficacious than others. It may be buried, dissolved in acid, thrown into the water, or burnt. As Meredith was now beginning to think, Rother's murderer had resorted to the last expedient. In some safe place the body had been dissected, according to Professor Blenkings, with a surgical saw, and the limbs and trunk burnt, either in part or whole, in the lime-kilns at Chalklands. In this manner, no doubt, the murderer intended to hide the identity of his victim and possibly broadcast the bones piecemeal so that the crime might never be discovered at all. As Meredith reasoned, portions of the sawn-up body would have been placed at intervals during the last ten days, obviously at night, on the kiln or kilns. With lime being sent out to various builders in the locality there was quite a chance that an odd bone or two in a fair-sized load would rouse no comment. The average workman would think they were animal bones and, if the Professor had not been on the spot, the thigh-bone would have been cleared up with the rubbish.

'Pure theory at the moment,' Meredith argued with himself, 'but at any rate a workable basis for investigation.'

He realized, as the car drummed through the crowded streets of Worthing, that an immediate visit to Chalklands was imperative. He wanted to acquaint himself with two things – firstly the method employed in lime-burning, and secondly with a complete list of orders dispatched from the farm since July 20th. In the meantime he hoped Worthing would be able to supply him with a little more evidence.

In this he was not disappointed. Sergeant Phillips, Professor Blenkings, and an inspector were waiting for him in the latter's office. On the table was a brown-paper parcel.

'Well,' said Meredith after introductions, 'what luck at Timpson's?'

'The devil's own,' answered the Inspector. 'Take a look at this little lot.'

And with the air of a salesman displaying a tasteful line in neckwear, the Inspector opened out the parcel. In the centre of the paper was a heap of bones – some big, some small, some thick, some thin, some straight, some curved.

'Good heavens! I suppose there's no doubt that they are parts of a human skeleton, Professor?'

The Professor stepped forward and peered through his spectacles which he now wore in place of his green sunglasses. After a quick examination he shook his head.

'Dear me, no – there's no doubt about their origin.' He picked up a couple of the smaller bones and held them out on his palm. 'Now just look at these, gentlemen. Two beautiful examples of metacarpal from the hand of an adult male. And here' – he held up another specimen. 'The upper half of a sawn-off tibia. Whilst this curious-looking object is what we call the sesamoid patella. You may be aware of what that is in common speech, eh, gentlemen?'

'A knee-cap,' hazarded Meredith with a wink at the Inspector.

'Quite right,' beamed the Professor, as if congratulating a student on an unexpected piece of bone-lore. 'A human kneecap. This really is a most comprehensive collection, isn't it? First a femur, then a tibia – ah, and here's a pretty portion of fibula, to which must be added our sesamoid patella. In other words we could almost construct the framework of a right-hand male leg from the hip to half-way down the shin. Most interesting, eh?'

'Very,' said Meredith dryly. 'And extremely helpful, too, sir. Now suppose by any chance I am able to collect the ... well, let us say the missing pieces of the jig-saw, could you fit the puzzle together for me, Professor?'

'Most certainly. I could make you a really lovely skeleton, provided all your bones belong to the same adult.'

'Do these seem to fit?' asked Meredith patly.

'At a casual glance I should say "Yes" – but if I may take them with me I could–'

'Do. And let me know the result as soon as possible.'

'To-morrow at the latest.'

'Good. Would you get in touch with me direct – Lewes 0099?'

The Professor beamed again. 'It's all very unusual, isn't it? Dear me! I never suspected that one day I might be called in to help to solve a murder. Most interesting. Most interesting.'

37

And collecting up the relics, the Professor bade the officials good day and disappeared humming a little tune.

'That old fellow's going to be useful,' was Meredith's inward comment as he left the police station. 'If we get anything like what he calls "a comprehensive collection" there'll have to be an inquest. But it will take an outsize piece of luck, I reckon, to prove the identity of the skeleton!'

As it was then very late he decided to visit Chalklands the following morning.

Just after nine o'clock, therefore, his car turned up the lane which led to the farmhouse from the main-road and a little later drew up in front of the long white verandah. A girl was watering some potted geraniums, ranged in tiers, between two enormous sash-windows. On seeing the car draw up she put down her can and came forward to greet the Superintendent.

'Good morning, ma'am. Is Mr. William Rother around anywhere?'

'My husband? Yes, I think he's out by the kilns somewhere.'

'Thank you, Mrs. Rother. Perhaps, as I'm not in uniform, I ought to explain that I'm a police superintendent investigating the disappearance of your husband's brother. My name's Meredith.'

The girl looked startled for a moment, then, with an uneasy glance round, said in a low voice:

'My husband's worried to death over this dreadful affair, Mr. Meredith. It seems to be preying on his mind. Although he says little about it, I know he's thinking and thinking all the time about John. Tell me honestly – what chance do you think there is of John ever turning up?'

Meredith hesitated, appraised the agitated young lady with a judicious eye and for some instinctive reason decided to equivocate.

'It's quite beyond me to say. Missing people have sometimes turned up years after their disappearance.'

'But hurt like that – surely it's inconceivable that he could have wandered far?'

'But we've no idea how badly he was hurt, Mrs. Rother. What makes you say that? I never mentioned the details of what we found to your husband.'

'But ... but I've been reading the newspaper reports,' answered the girl, obviously ill at ease on being picked up on this point. 'They mentioned the terrible blood-stains.'

'Exaggeration.'

Meredith dismissed her fears with a shrug and took closer stock of Mrs. William Rother. He noticed that her natural prettiness was partially cancelled out by the drawn lines of her mouth and the dark smudges under her clear grey eyes. It was obvious that her husband was not the only one worrying about John Rother's disappearance. She was younger than he had anticipated – twenty-five or -six perhaps, at least ten years younger than her husband. Her vivacity, he thought, was her greatest charm – a vivacity that sent shades of expression coursing through those clear grey eyes and lent to her youthful figure an air of delicate vigour.

'Fine-drawn,' was Meredith's inward comment. 'With a brain behind her good looks.'

39

'Can you tell me,' he went on aloud, 'which way I have to go to the kilns?'

She came down to the gate and directed him.

'Look – behind those bushes to the right. You can see the smoke rising.'

Meredith touched his hat and set off on foot to where the great white belches of smoke were rising and thinning away down the wind. Clear of the bushes he came suddenly on the kilns.

A wide sweep of downland lay in the distance beyond the natural wall into which the kilns had been sunk. An extensive though deep valley, divided by the unseen main road, dropped from the farm level and up again to the tree-crested hump of Highden Hill. To the right, only just glimpsed in the clumps of summer trees, huddled the tiled and thatched roofs of the village. On a higher level, its grey stone sombre against the blue sky, stood Washington Church, with the Vicarage crouching under the lee of its northern shadow. Directly below the kilns ran a continuation of the lane up which Meredith had driven, obviously linking up again with the main road. A low flint wall edged the thirty-foot sheer drop between the kiln-level and this lane, which at that point was bordered by stables on the far side and on the near side by a sort of yard where the lime was loaded on to the wagons. Standing below in this yard, watching a carter harnessing his horse, stood William Rother.

Meredith leant over the little wall and let out a call.

'Excuse me a moment, sir. Can you come up?'

Rother looked up quickly, recognized the

Superintendent, nodded, and started off up the lane on a detour which would eventually bring him on to the higher level. Arriving there he held out his hand. Meredith was shocked by the man's appearance. In ten days his entire face had altered. From a thin, white mask, hollowed here and there as if by a sculptor's chisel, burnt the dark, over-bright eyes of a man who is on the verge of a nervous collapse.

'My God, sir!' was Meredith's involuntary exclamation. 'You look ill.'

'I am ill,' replied Rother in level tones, with expressionless eyes. 'Do you wonder at it? Tell me' – he placed a thin, nervous hand on the Superintendent's sleeve – 'tell me – have you brought any news?'

'I'm afraid not, Mr. Rother. I'm out here on another line of inquiry. Connected with your brother's disappearance, I admit, but at the moment a private matter. You understand?'

'Perfectly.' The voice sounded totally disinterested. 'What exactly do you want to know?'

'I want to know how you make lime?' said Meredith bluntly.

Rother eyed the Superintendent suspiciously, as if uncertain whether he had heard aright.

'But what has that got–'

'Please, Mr. Rother, I explained before, this is a private police investigation. All I'm asking for is information, and it's for your own peace of mind if you let me have it.'

'Very well.' Rother lifted his narrow shoulders. 'I'll restrain my natural curiosity. Well, the process is simple enough. Here are the kilns –

41

three of them – twenty feet deep or thereabouts. The fires are lit in the first place at the bottom of the shaft, and after that, except for purposes of repair, the kilns are never let out.'

'How do you keep them alight?'

Rother pointed to two heaps – one black, one white – on each side of the kiln's circular mouth.

'Chalk and powdered coal – cullum, we call it locally. When the kilns are banked up, usually twice a day, we shovel on one layer of chalk to one layer of cullum. By the time the red-hot chalk reaches the base of the shaft it has been transformed by combustion into lime. Down below there are brick arches terminating at the bottom of each kiln. The men use these arches to dig out the lime, the chalk level automatically falls at the top, and the kiln is restoked with more layers of chalk and cullum. To put it as simply as possible, when a kiln is functioning properly, it consists of three layers. At the bottom pure lime, in the middle red-hot chalk in the process of being changed into lime, at the top pure chalk alternating with layers of unburnt cullum. You follow me, Mr. Meredith?'

'Perfectly, sir. You've told me exactly what I was after. When are the kilns usually banked up?'

'Early morning and late afternoon.'

'Would the level have fallen at all during the night?'

'To a certain extent – yes – due to the crumbling process of combustion.'

'A couple of feet?'

'Yes, quite that.'

'Thanks. And now I wonder if you could let me have a glimpse of your order-book?'

42

CHAPTER 3

MORE BONES

Whatever William Rother may have thought about Meredith's strange request for a glimpse of the order-book he allowed no hint of it to show on his haggard features. He just muttered, 'Very well,' in the toneless voice of a man who makes no resistance to a whim, however queer he thinks it, and led the way back to the farmhouse. This time they entered it from the back, first through a small courtyard sporting a fir tree and a square of unkempt grass, then across some uneven flags into an airy stone-floored kitchen, the centre-piece of which was an enormous, well-scoured deal table. At the far end of the kitchen, under a low window, was a second, smaller table covered with a red cloth and loaded with ledgers, files, letters, reference-books, inkpots, pens and paper. On the broad window-sill stood a portable typewriter.

Rother smiled wanly.

'The office,' he explained with a side-jerk of his head. 'Such as it is. We don't boast a study up here at Chalklands. Now what exactly are you after?'

'I want a list, if possible, of all your customers supplied with lime during the last ten days – that is to say since the night of your brother's disappearance.'

'With the amounts delivered?'

43

'Yes.'

Rother picked up an ordinary black exercise-book and handed it to Meredith.

'You'll find everything you want there, Mr. Meredith. It seems an extraordinary request to me, but you know your own business best. I'd do anything to help solve the mystery of John's disappearance, and if he's dead – which I'm beginning to suspect – to hang the man who murdered him. But what you imagine you'll get out of that order-book beats me!'

'May I take a copy?'

Rother nodded.

'And in the meantime I want to walk out to the chalk-pit. If there's anything further you want you'll find me there. It's directly behind the house.'

'Thanks – that's all I want to bother you with at the moment, Mr. Rother. I'll just copy these data into my notebook and then I'll be off. One other question before you go. Had your brother any particular friend with whom he was really intimate?'

'Yes – Aldous Barnet, the novelist.'

'The detective-story writer?' asked Meredith with a grin.

'That's him. He lives at a house called Lychpole near the church. He and John were at school together. You may know him?'

'Well, I've read a couple of his books. I must say his Inspector Jefferies gets a darn sight more luck in his investigations than usually comes my way! The chap seems so brilliant that he doesn't need to worry over the details of routine work. I envy him.'

With a half-smile to show that he had registered Meredith's amusement, William nodded, and with a preoccupied expression on his pale features wandered out of the door.

Sitting at the window-table Meredith examined the order-book. It was much as he had expected. Column 1: Date when Order was Received. Column 2: Name and Address of Firm. Column 3: Amount of Lime Ordered. Column 4: Date of Delivery. Between Monday, July 22nd and Wednesday, July 31st (that was to say the previous day), twelve different firms had been supplied. The amounts varied between a yard and two and a quarter yards, which Meredith knew constituted what was commonly termed a 'load' of lime. In most cases a full 'load' had been ordered. Five of the firms were in Worthing, including Timpson's; three in Pulborough; one at Steyning; one at Storrington; one at Ashington, and the remaining consignment, a yard, to the Washington Vicarage.

As he was closing his notebook and replacing the order-book, a plump, red-cheeked woman bounced into the kitchen. Good nature exuded from every pore in her body. She wore a lilac printed frock with the sleeves rolled up to reveal a pair of brawny, sunburned arms, and a large, blue, serviceable apron was tied round what should have been her waist.

'Oh Lawks!' she exclaimed, startled out of her normal composure by the unexpected intruder in her kitchen. 'I beg 'ee pardon, I'm sure. I had no idea as to there being a stranger 'ere, surr.'

'That's all right, Mrs...'

'Kate Abingworth's my name. I'm housekeeper

45

up 'ere, surr. 'Av been for the last fifteen years.'

'Mr. Rother was just letting me copy out something.'

'Ah, that'll be Mr. Willum, poor feller.' And she shook her head in motherly commiseration. ''Ee's eating less than enough to keep a sparrer on the wing these days, surr. It's turrible to see 'im wasting away like 'ee be. Delicate 'ee always was, but this trouble what's descended on this household 'as changed that young feller complete.'

'Mrs. Rother seems upset too?' commented Meredith, always on the alert for possible information.

'Ay, she's took it 'ard, too, surr, 'as Mrs. Willum. But I don't wonder, I don't, seeing 'ow fond she were of Mr. John. Like 'usband and wife they were – if you'll pardon my simple way of putting it. Not that things had gone as far as that, o' course, but in their manner of fussin' over each other. Like a 'en with 'er chick was Mrs. Willum with Mr. John – not that she 'asn't done right and fair by Mr. Willum, but I've always up'eld–' And here Mrs. Abingworth lowered her voice and stepped closer to the Superintendent, almost speaking into his ear. 'I've always up'eld as Mrs. Willum *married the wrong man!*'

Her emphasis on these last words was so heavy that Meredith immediately assumed a look of startled incredulity. He realized that Kate Abingworth was one of those simple-minded souls who find their greatest pleasure in life in gossiping about their employers.

'You've noticed things, eh?' asked Meredith in a conspiratorial voice. 'Happenings, so to speak?'

'I 'av,' beamed Kate Abingworth, delighted to share these intimacies. Her voice dropped to a whisper. 'One night, as sure as I draw breath, I saw Mrs Willum creep out of the house with a suit-case in her 'and, and join Mr. John on the front lawn. You see 'ee – meaning Mr. Willum – don't sleep with 'er – not nowadays. She sleeps in the North Room now, and what I say is, any woman 'oo could sleep in such a cold, draughty barn of a room, must 'av a gurt strong reason for not sleepin' with 'er man.'

Meredith nodded in agreement, and Mrs. Abingworth, suddenly realizing that she had unburdened her secrets to a complete stranger, drew herself up, did something emphatic to her back hair, shook out her apron and lifted the lid of a huge saucepan which was simmering on the old-fashioned range.

'Not as I *knows*,' she added. 'It's only as I *suspects*.'

'Quite,' said Meredith; adding as he gathered up his cap: 'That smells good, Mrs. Abingworth.'

'And it should do, surr. Quince jam that is, made according to my dear old grandmother's recipe, 'oo died only a day short 'o ninety-six. A wunnerful old woman was my grandmother. Well, good day to 'ee, surr.'

Meredith found his way back to where he had parked his car on the drive and, without seeing Janet Rother again, climbed in and drove in a reflective mood down to the village. Kate Abingworth's voluntary information had stimulated his curiosity. He wondered, for example, why the girl was carrying a suit-case that night she was

47

reputed to have met her brother-in-law on the lawn. Why a suit-case when she had obviously sat down to breakfast at Chalklands the next morning? Mrs. Abingworth did not suggest that William suspected his wife of unfaithfulness, so that she could not have stayed the night anywhere with John. Besides, the housekeeper wouldn't have missed putting two and two together if Janet and John had not turned up to breakfast the next morning. Why was she on the lawn at all? Meredith sighed. A romantic infatuation for her brother-in-law, he supposed, the fascination of tasting forbidden fruit. He wondered if the missing man had been in love with the girl, or merely obliging enough to respond to her infatuation. Perhaps Aldous Barnet might have something to say on the matter, and he decided to visit Lychpole as soon as he had put through a few 'phone calls from the local police station.

He then methodically got in touch with Worthing, Pulborough, Steyning, Storrington, and Ashington. He pointed out the necessity for tracing the where-abouts of every bit of lime which had come from the Rother kilns. The local authorities were to get in touch with the builders concerned and have all stocks of lime meticulously sifted. In cases where bags had already been sent out on jobs, the places were to be visited and the workmen questioned as to whether they had found anything in the shape of a bone or bones in the lime used. Reports were to be sent through to Lewes at the earliest possible moment. He then sent the Washington constable up to the Vicarage, where a new bay-window was being pushed out on the south front. A local builder by the name of Sims was doing the job, and the constable was to get in touch with the man and have the whole yard of lime sifted.

Satisfied with this careful piece of staff-work, Meredith drove up the curving and hilly main street of the village, passed the local emporium and the school, and stopped at a white gate bearing the inscription 'Lychpole'.

On explaining to the maid that he was a police superintendent, Meredith was ushered into a long, low-raftered room, where he was joined a few minutes later by Aldous Barnet. He was a tall, cadaverous, intellectual-looking man with horn-rimmed spectacles and a slight stoop. He looked about fifty-five.

'We've never met, but I've heard of you,' he said as he held out his hand. 'Major Forest is an old friend of mine. He's helped me a lot with the technical side of my detective books. Won't you sit down?'

'Thank you, sir,' said Meredith as he sank into a big chintz chair. 'I don't want to bother you if it's an awkward moment, but it's about the disappearance of Mr. John Rother. I'm working on that case.'

'A rotten show,' murmured Aldous Barnet with a shake of his head. 'A rotten affair, eh? I know it's not exactly politic to ask the police leading questions, but, tell me, have you got any further? I know only the bare details of what was discovered.'

'We've nothing definite ... yet. That's why I've come to you. You were John Rother's best friend, weren't you?' Barnet nodded. 'Then you know something about his personal affairs.'

'A little – yes,' acknowledged Barnet with obvious caution. 'He was a reserved sort of chap. What precisely do you want to find out?'

'Well,' went on Meredith with assumed reluctance, 'you know how it is – a man is forced into the limelight and people chatter. Often we hear a lot of unpleasant gossip – most of it untrue. Now I've come to you because I know I can rely on your information, Mr. Barnet. Tell me, is there anything at all in the rumour that John Rother was having – an affair, shall we say – with his brother's wife?'

Barnet rapped out sharply: 'Who told you that?'

'I'm afraid I can't answer that question – but is it true? Was there anything between them?' Meredith glanced up and caught the wary expression on the other man's face. 'Come, Mr. Barnet, you won't gain anything by being secretive about the matter. I'm investigating the case of your friend's disappearance. For the sake of argument let us suppose he *was* murdered under Cissbury – what then? Isn't it up to you to help me all you can?'

'I'm sorry,' said Barnet in quiet tones. 'You're quite right. Much as I abominate hanging out other people's dirty linen in the daylight, I suppose for the sake of justice it's got to be done. I can't tell you much – that was one side of John's life over which he was exceptionally reticent. I only know that he and Janet were reputed to be a little more than just ... friendly. They had been seen about together on the downs, walking or riding – it was common property in the village, I'm afraid.'

'You mean they were brazen about it?'

'No – not that,' said Barnet hastily. 'Just blind to other people's curiosity, I imagine.'

'And William Rother?'

'He knew, of course. How could he help knowing?'

'And yet he did nothing?'

'How could he? There was nothing definite enough to create a scene over. He was angry, of course – but then he and John had always been at loggerheads. Not only over this particular trouble but everything. I have an idea, too, that Janet was passive rather than active in the affair. I don't for a moment think that she was really in love with John.'

'To your knowledge, Mr. Barnet, did John and Janet Rother ever stay the night anywhere together – I mean slip off to an hotel or anything?'

Barnet looked incredulous, then shocked.

'Never! At least as far as I know personally. I think you're laying rather too much stress, Superintendent, on what may have been merely a romantic flirtation.'

'Perhaps,' agreed Meredith with his usual tact. 'You know the couple and I don't. That's why I've come to you. Do you know anything about the financial arrangements up at Chalklands?'

'Really!' growled Barnet. 'Is it necessary for me to answer these questions?'

'Not necessary,' replied Meredith with a placatory smile; 'but you must realize, Mr. Barnet, that if there's a coroner's inquest you'll probably be subpoenaed as a witness. Surely it's better to talk over Rother's private affairs *in* private than broadcast them all over the village?'

Barnet acquiesced with a gesture of hopelessness.

'Oh, very well. Go ahead. It's your job to ask questions, but why not tackle Rother's solicitor? I imagine he'd know more about his finances than I do.'

'I only want one bit of information, and it would save me a lot of time and trouble if you could supply it. In the event of John Rother's death who would be the chief beneficiary under his will?'

'His brother.' Then registering Meredith's look of surprise, he added: 'You see, for all his dislike of William, John had an almost fanatic regard for the well-being of the family name and estates. As a matter of fact, only a short time back we discussed this very matter. That's how I know.'

'And the approximate benefits?'

'The estate, of course, some property, and about ten thousand pounds' worth of investments.'

'Quite a nest-egg,' commented Meredith. He tackled his informant from a new angle with an abruptness that was characteristic. 'William Rother is a hot-headed sort of fellow, isn't he?'

'Hot-headed?' Barnet shook his head decisively. 'Slow to anger I should have said, but a madman when really roused. A misunderstood mortal, Superintendent – an idealist hiding his sensitiveness under a placid disregard for other people's opinions. I've known him, when one of his pet principles was attacked, to lash out with his tongue as if he had a devil inside him. An awkward customer to handle then, believe me. I've had him on local committees.'

'He seems terribly upset about his brother's disappearance.'

'So I've heard. I haven't seen him since that Sunday. But there's nothing strange in that, is there?'

'Only this,' said Meredith in measured tones, 'that his brother's disappearance clears up the trouble over his wife and puts a small fortune in his pocket!'

Barnet glanced disdainfully at the Superintendent through his horn-rims and said in icy tones:

'You police fellows get a pretty warped idea of humanity, don't you? John *was* his brother, you know, however much they disagreed.' Then suddenly: 'Good God! – you're not suggesting–?'

'I'm not suggesting anything. I'm merely trying to get a proper view of the facts. In any case Rother may turn up. Why are you so certain that he won't?'

'I'm not! I'm not!' protested Barnet hastily, adding, as the maid entered the room: 'Well, what is it?'

'Please, sir, the constable is in the hall and would like to speak urgent with the gentleman here. He noticed his car outside as he was going by.'

'Will you excuse me a moment?' asked Meredith as he rose and followed the girl into the hall.

Two minutes later he re-entered the drawing-room and crossed over to the window. As he examined more closely what lay in the palm of his hand, he called Barnet over to join him.

'A moment, sir, if you will. I want your opinion on something. Take a look at these.'

Barnet stared intently for a moment, picked up the objects one by one, and turned them over in

53

the light.

'Well?' demanded Meredith eagerly, irritated by the man's deliberation.

'Where did you get these?'

'The constable found them.'

'They're Rother's. Tell me, Superintendent, how the devil did you get hold of these things? What does it mean? For heaven's sake, man, don't keep me in suspense – what exactly does it mean, eh?'

'It may mean murder, Mr. Barnet,' said Meredith quietly, as he slipped the little objects into his pocket. 'I can't say anything for certain yet. Now, if you'll excuse me, I've got several visits to make. Thank you for your information – you may be sure that I shall treat this interview as confidential as far as I am able.'

As his car raced back up the steep slope to Chalklands, Meredith thought: 'So it *is* murder after all! A second identification of this little lot in my pocket will make it certain. Somebody had a motive too. I wonder if...?'

William Rother was having lunch when Meredith put in his second appearance at the farmhouse. He came into the drawing-room with a look of inquiry on his thin, drawn features.

'You want me?'

'Yes, sir. I want you to identify these articles for me.' And clearing a space on an occasional-table Meredith set them out in a line – the belt clasp, the slender metal chain, and the little brass disc such as was worn by soldiers in the war. He noticed that William's hand was shaking like a leaf as he picked up the various articles and scrutinized them.

At length he said in a constrained voice: 'These

things are my brother's. He used to wear the disc on this chain round his wrist. You notice his initials are on it – J.F.R. – and that the date of his birth is inscribed underneath? After the war he had that disc made out of a piece of shell-case which he had picked up in France. He always wore it on his right wrist. A sort of talisman, I suppose.'

'And the belt-buckle?'

'It corresponds to the clasp on the belt John was wearing the afternoon he set off for Harlech. It was one of his peculiarities that he always wore both belt and braces.'

'You could swear to these articles being your brother's?'

'Unless an exact replica has been made of each object,' said William. Then suddenly lowering his tall frame into a chair he asked in a shaken voice: 'I suppose it is too much to tell me *where* you found these things, or what it means, Mr. Meredith? As his nearest relative I ought to know ... I'm quite prepared to know the worst. Tell me, does it mean...'

And he left his unfinished sentence hanging like a query-mark over Meredith's head.

'I'm afraid so, Mr. Rother.'

William buried his tired grey face in his hands.

'Oh, my God!' he muttered brokenly. *'Murder!'*

'I had hoped you might have been spared this news, but there's no doubt about it now. I'm sorry. I'll let you know, of course, how the police investigations proceed. This opens out a new line of inquiry. It now gives us something definite to work on.'

'How definite?' was Meredith's self-demand as

55

he sat over lunch in the 'King's Arms' at Findon on his way back to Lewes. Well, the Washington constable had sifted the buckle, chain, and brass disc out of the lime which had been delivered at the Vicarage three days after Rother's disappearance. The constable had also discovered some more gruesome relics which Meredith had failed to show either Barnet or William Rother. Bones. More bones. And on reaching headquarters there were messages already forwarded from Worthing, Pulborough, Steyning, Storrington, and Ashington. In every case except one (Ashington) bones had been discovered by the local police in the various consignments of Rother lime. These were being sent over to Lewes at once.

Meredith had scarcely completed the reading of these messages when the 'phone-bell rang. It was Professor Blenkings speaking from West Worthing.

'Ah, yes – dear me – the Superintendent. I've come to a decision about that little matter. Mind you, only after the most careful consideration. I feel one can't be too meticulous in a case of this sort – I mean it would be unforgivable if my evidence hanged an innocent man. You follow me, my dear fellow?'

'Quite,' said Meredith, admirably concealing his impatience. 'Well, sir?'

'The bones are undoubtedly those of the same adult male. I've wired together the few specimens available and they make quite a presentable framework of a human leg. But with a more extensive supply ... dear me, yes ... I could–'

'To-morrow,' cut in Meredith, 'you shall have more bones. A lot more. We're collecting them from various sources. I'll have them sent direct to your place, sir.'

'Thank you. Thank you. Most kind. I'll get to work and see if I can build that skeleton you asked for.'

'That's very helpful of you, Professor. I'll keep in touch with your progress. Good-bye.'

'Good-bye, and, if you'll allow me to say so, I'm quite enjoying this unexpected piece of work, however elementary its nature. Most interesting.'

'Elementary!' thought Meredith as he hung up on the fussy, high-pitched voice. 'In his case, yes – but it looks as if I'm going to have a devil of a job to make this investigation *move!*'

He sat at his desk, legs sprawled, pipe drawing well, reviewing the evidence, turning the case over and over in his mind.

The first point to be considered was motive. Why had John Rother been lured to that lonely spot and murdered? Who would have had any vital reason for wanting him out of the way? Meredith had already half-answered this question in his talk with Aldous Barnet. He had not been joking when he had hinted that William Rother had two very strong reasons for wishing his brother dead. Moreover, William was well situated for placing those portions of the sawn-up body on the kiln. Again, why was the man so violently keyed-up? His highly strung condition surely, arose from something more abnormal than mere grief for the loss of his brother? Particularly as they had never wasted much affection on each other. His wife's undivided loyalty and ten thousand pounds – these were the stakes.

Had William Rother chanced the gamble?

As usual Meredith then attacked this theory from the opposite view-point. William could not have murdered his brother because any man in his senses would not be such a fool as to rid himself of the remains on his own door-step, so to speak. Why go to the trouble of portering the corpse from the scene of the crime back to Chalk-lands? Why not dig a hole somewhere in the gorse bushes on Cissbury Down and bury the body there? Again the motives were too obvious. Every-body would immediately suspect William of the crime because they knew about the trouble with his wife, and would soon know, if they didn't know already, that he was the sole beneficiary under his brother's will. Further, the whole village knew that he was antagonistic to his brother. Wouldn't the risk of murder be too great?

On the other hand, who was left? Janet Rother, Kate Abingworth, one of the farm-hands, Aldous Barnet ... oh, damn it, the list, thought Meredith, could be prolonged indefinitely! If William hadn't killed his brother then anybody might have done so.

He switched over to the known facts. Rother had been hit on the head with a blunt instrument – perhaps a spanner – a fact easily deduced from the blood-stains on the inside of the tweed cap. The body had been removed – obviously by a second car – from Bindings Lane to some point where it could be dissected and hidden, ready for being placed piecemeal on the kiln. Footprints and car tracks were unavailable as evidence because of the three weeks' drought preceding

July 20th. Rother had been set upon some time between Saturday evening, say 7 o'clock, and 9.30 on Sunday morning when the tragedy had been discovered by Pyke-Jones. Had William Rother an alibi during those hours? And where was Janet Rother? And why the devil had Janet Rother been on the lawn that night with her brother-in-law with a suit-case in her hand? How had John Rother been lured to that lonely spot under Cissbury? Where had he run the car after leaving Chalklands for his holiday in Harlech? Why thirty miles instead of four and a half, which was approximately the distance between the farm and the scene of the assault?

Questions! Questions! Questions!

A constable knocked on the door, lumbered in and dumped a sack on the floor.

'From Worthing, sir.'

'Bones,' thought Meredith. 'More bones. I bet John Rother never thought that part of his mortal body would be tied up in a sack and chucked on to the floor of a police office.'

He rose abruptly, stretched himself, glanced at his watch and suddenly remembered that his wife had ordered a cut of fresh salmon for his high tea. Confound this murder – he was hungry! He reached out for his peaked cap.

CHAPTER 4

THE LITTLEHAMPTON AUNT

On Tuesday, August 6th, the day after Bank Holiday, an inquest was held on the remains of John Fosdyke Rother, and the Coroner brought in a verdict of Murder by Person or Persons Unknown. There had been quite a lively discussion in police circles as to where the inquest should be held, since the body, or portions of it, had been discovered in so many widely different localities. Worthing seemed a reasonable place since most of the bones had been discovered in the borough, but in the long run it was decided that the Professor's masterpiece, the skeleton, should be removed to the County Police headquarters, and the inquest was consequently held in Lewes.

The skeleton was not complete by all means; several of the smaller bones were still missing and, what was more vital, the skull so far had not been discovered. Why the head had not been passed through the kiln with the rest of the dismembered body remained a mystery to Meredith. After all, the skull would be the most incriminating section of the bone framework, since any fracture in the cranium would corroborate the fact of the blow or blows with the blunt instrument. Perhaps the murderer had been unable to divide the head into small enough pieces, for it was obviously out of the question to pass the complete head through the kiln without discovery. For one thing it would be too big, and for another, even a village idiot would recognize a human skull when he saw it. The probability was that it had been taken to some out-of-the way spot and buried.

The Professor's exhibit made an interesting study. At every point where the framework had been sawn through he had marked the bone with red paint. One was thus able to see at a glance into how many pieces and where exactly the body had been severed. Meredith was amazed by the care, patience, and even skill, exercised by the murderer in so dividing the corpse that the bones would stand a minimum chance of discovery in the lime. It argued time and a good margin of safety while the gruesome job was being done. It must have taken hours for the murderer to have completed the task. There was, however, one unusual point which struck Meredith at once. He spoke to the Chief Constable about it.

'Where do you think he got rid of the clothes, eh, sir?'

'In the kiln, of course,' barked Major Forest. 'What a dam'-fool question, Meredith! We shouldn't have found the belt-buckle in the lime otherwise, should we?'

'No, sir – but what about his braces?'

'His braces?'

'Yes, Rother wore both belt *and* braces.'

'Nothing funny about that, is there? I often do myself. It's a recognized symbol of pessimism.'

'Then where are the metal clasps off the braces? We found the belt-buckle.'

'Couldn't they have been made of leather and webbing – no metal at all?'

'Possibly. Then what about his buttons? I reckon an ordinary coat or trouser button would go through the kiln without melting. Then there's boot-nails, cuff-links, studs, and, possibly, a tie-pin. Why haven't we found these, sir? It strikes me there's still a good bit of mystery hanging around this case.'

'Something in what you say.' Major Forest eyed Meredith with a twinkle of unspoken approval. 'You're not such a dam' fool as you look, are you? But thank heaven you didn't start splitting these hairs in front of the Coroner, else we should never have got a verdict. And I don't like untidy ends hanging around. After all, that buckle and disc left no loophole. Combine them with the poor devil's bones and there was no question either of his identity or of how he met his end. What's your move now? Interview William Rother, I suppose?'

'Yes, sir. I've got to find out what he did on that Saturday night and the early hours of Sunday. The case against him looks pretty black, you'll agree, sir?'

'Very, and you'd better find out what that young lady was up to as well. I saw her after the inquest today with Barnet. She looks intelligent and happens to be extremely pretty. An almost criminal combination, Meredith.'

Out at Chalklands, William Rother and the Superintendent sat on the verandah, gay with its pink and scarlet tiers of geraniums. To a casual passer-by there was nothing to indicate the serious and even sordid trend of their conversation. Over

62

the lawn a peacock butterfly was zigzagging and the drone of bees in the verbena clumps was as drowsy as the heat of the August afternoon. A chalk-waggon rumbled sleepily down foot-deep ruts, unseen from the house, where a high, clipped laurel hedge shut out all save the brown-flanked slope of Highden Hill, and the rolling ridge of downland which receded behind it. A cluster of cream roses ran up one of the latticed pillars of the verandah, disturbingly fragrant.

'You understand, of course,' Meredith was saying in his politest tones, 'that all this questioning is a mere matter of routine. Police red tape if you like.' He noticed that the expression on the man's face never altered. 'First of all, can you give me the exact time that your brother left here for Harlech?'

William considered the question for a moment and then said:

'Within a minute or two of 6.15. I remember noticing the time on his dashboard.'

'And he always kept his car clock correct?' William nodded. 'What exactly did you do after your brother left, Mr. Rother – I mean, were you up here at the farm all the rest of that evening?'

'No,' said William. 'I went to Littlehampton.'

Meredith felt a sudden twinge of interest run through his veins:

'May I ask why?'

'Yes. I had a telegram to say that my aunt had met with an accident and was seriously injured in hospital there.'

'And the telegram was sent by?'

'A Dr. Wakefield. At least,' William corrected himself, 'it was *signed* Wakefield.'

Meredith asked sharply: 'What on earth do you mean? Wasn't it sent by the doctor?'

William slowly shook his head and went on in a toneless voice: 'I'll tell you exactly what happened, Superintendent. At about twenty past seven this telegram arrived to say that my aunt was in hospital. It was addressed to John, but as he was out of reach I naturally opened it myself. I took out the car at once and drove as fast as I could to Littlehampton. When I arrived at the hospital nobody knew anything about my aunt. I next called on Dr. Wakefield, whom I knew slightly, and he denied emphatically that he had sent that telegram. On reaching my aunt's flat I found her perfectly well – in fact in better health than she had been for some time. I stayed chatting with her for a space and then drove back here. From that moment to this I have no idea who sent me that telegram or why it was sent.'

'Have you kept the form?' asked Meredith anxiously.

'Yes – it's here in my wallet. I expect you would like to see it?'

Meredith thanked him, took the proffered slip of paper and studied it closely. It read: *Please come at once your aunt seriously injured in accident taken to Littlehampton General Hospital – Wakefield.* It had been handed in at the General Post Office, Littlehampton, at 6.50 – received Washington Post Office at 7.3 p.m.

'Do you mind if I keep this?'

'Not a bit,' concurred William, without interest.

'What time did the telegram reach you here?'

'About a quarter past seven, I imagine. You

probably noticed that it was handed in at 7.3 at Washington. The boy then had to cycle up here with it.'

Meredith made a quick note.

'And what time did you leave in the car?'

'Oh, ten minutes or so later – between twenty and twenty-five minutes past seven as far as I can remember.'

'Thanks. And which way did you go to Littlehampton?'

'The direct route – turning right just before Findon and then on through Angmering.'

'Did you stop on the way at all?'

'Yes – I went right into Findon because I was short of petrol. I had two gallons put in at Clark's Filling Station. I then drove back and took the fork I mentioned.'

'This is your own car, of course?'

'Yes – a Morris Cowley.'

'Have you any idea of the time you arrived in Littlehampton?'

'Yes – just as it was striking eight.'

'And you left?'

'Some time before nine – but I can't say for sure.'

'Arriving here?'

'Ten, a quarter to – I really can't say with any accuracy.'

'You returned direct without stopping?'

'Yes.'

'And you've no idea at all why this faked telegram was sent?'

'No – none whatever.'

'And after you arrived home I suppose you

65

went to bed?'

'After a drink and a look at the paper – yes,' said William, adding dryly: 'I have no doubt that both my wife and Mrs. Abingworth will corroborate the time of my going to bed. Once in bed, Superintendent, I'm afraid you'll have to take my word for it that I didn't go out again until after breakfast on Sunday!'

Meredith laughed.

'Good heavens, sir – there's no need to take that attitude to this perfectly usual cross-examination. I shall have to put your wife and Kate Abingworth through the same hoop. Your wife knows about this telegram?'

'Of course.'

'By the way,' added Meredith as he got out of his deck-chair and knocked out his pipe, 'did you return from Littlehampton the same way as you went?'

'Yes.'

'Well, that's all, Mr. Rother, thanks. It's been very kind of you to give me these details. No evidence is irrelevant in a murder case, you know. This faked telegram, for example, I shouldn't have heard of it, perhaps, if I hadn't put you through the routine questions.'

'You think the telegram may have something to do with the tragedy?'

'It would be curious if it hadn't, wouldn't it?' replied Meredith with an evasive smile. 'Now could I have a word with your wife?'

Janet Rother, when she appeared on the verandah and took the deck-chair vacated by her husband, seemed to have regained some of her

66

normal colour and vivacity since Meredith had last seen her. She offered no objection to the cross-examination and seemed quite ready to give detailed answers to all the Superintendent's questions. Her evidence, however, was of a negative rather than a positive nature. Only two points seemed to have any direct bearing on Meredith's investigations. The first was that, in her opinion, William had not reached Chalklands from Little-hampton until nearly half past ten. The second that she herself had taken a walk up to Chancton-bury Ring after John's departure, and had not returned to the farmhouse until after dark. Probably, she said, about a quarter to ten. She upheld that it was quite usual for her to go off on long tramps like that as she was passionately fond of both walking and the downs themselves. Meredith then asked for a recent photograph of John Rother and brought the interview to an end.

Kate Abingworth, whom Meredith tackled in the kitchen over a cup of strong tea and a slice of homemade cake, had no concise idea of the time 'Mr. Willum had returned that luckless night of Mr. John's doing-away'. It might have been ten or half past. She remembered, however, that her mistress had come into the house just after the stroke of half past nine. Judy, the maid-of-all-work, left at six, and as she didn't 'sleep in' Mrs. Abingworth didn't think 'as she could give any h'evidence as could be *called* h'evidence like, her being a stupid girl anyhows and about as much good in the house as a bundill of faggits'!

'And what about the night when you saw Mrs. Rother on the lawn with Mr. John – when was that exactly?'

'A Saturday,' said Kate Abingworth promptly.

'Yes,' smiled Meredith, 'but which Saturday?'

'The Saturday after Em 'urt her leg over at Arundel on a Thursday. I had a letter from my sister that same morning. Em's her eldest and a 'andful of mischief at that, surr. Climbing she was over the cow-shed roof and the guttering come away from under her very feet. Lucky she weren't–'

'Quite,' cut in Meredith, 'but what was the date?'

'The date? Now that I don't rightly recall, surr. But I still 'av Martha's letter in my bag. I keep all 'er letters I do, for she writes that funny it's like a book. She fair makes my ribs ache what with 'er–'

'Have you the letter handy?'

Kate Abingworth went to a sideboard on which lay a voluminous black hand-bag. After running through its overflowing contents, she drew out the letter and handed it to Meredith. He glanced at the post-mark – July 12th. After a quick calculation he realized that the 12th was a Friday and that the letter had reached Mrs. Abingworth on Saturday, July 13th. So this nocturnal, secret meeting between John and Janet Rother had taken place exactly a week before John set off on his holiday.

He went on: 'You're quite certain Mrs. Rother had a suit-case in her hand?'

'Yes, surr. 'Twas bright moonlight and I saw her 'and it over to 'im as clear as if it had been day.'

'How was it you happened to be looking out of the window?'

'Touch of newralgy, surr – which comes on me like a visitation off and on, so that what with trying one thing and another I'm always putting my 'and in my pocket to–'

At that point Meredith felt it politic to draw the interview to a conclusion and, after thanking the housekeeper for his cup of tea, he jumped into his car and set off for Findon.

Things certainly looked blacker than ever now against William Rother. That faked telegram was obviously his clumsy idea of obtaining an alibi whilst the murder was committed. Granted he *went* to Littlehampton, visited the hospital, the doctor and his aunt; but between the time of his departure from Littlehampton and his arrival at Chalklands he had committed the crime. Those were the two 'times' over which he was uncertain, and his wife's evidence tended to make his arrival at the farm appear *later* than he had suggested. Perhaps this aunt would be able to give a more concise idea of the time he had left her flat. William thought he had departed somewhere about nine. Janet Rother declared he had not arrived at the farmhouse until 10.30. He had, therefore, taken approximately an hour and a half to cover the distance between the coast-town and Chalklands.

Drawing into the side of the road, Meredith felt in the door-flap of his car and pulled out his inch-to-the-mile map of the district. With a flexible steel rule he carefully scaled the distance. Thirteen miles at the most! An hour and a half to cover thirteen miles? It was incredible, absurd! William had assured him that he had returned by

69

the direct route and had not stopped on the way.

Meredith experienced a thrill of satisfaction, a customary sensation when a ray of light penetrated a particularly murky problem. If only he could make certain of the time John Rother had been killed – that would drive the nail further home. He had left Chalklands at 6.15 by the clock on the Hillman's dashboard. He had then driven about thirty miles, somewhere, for some unknown reason, before reaching the point under Cissbury Ring. Not that Meredith could calculate anything from that. Rother might have stopped for an hour, two hours, at any place *en route* while covering those thirty miles. Or he might have reached his fateful rendezvous and waited there for several hours before his murderer turned up and attacked him. He might have–

Meredith suddenly felt his heart quicken, whilst a surge of blood rushed through his ears. A quick excitement took hold of him. He pressed his foot on the accelerator. Fool! Blind fool that he was! He was cracking up in his old age. Fancy missing a point like that! He could imagine the withering scorn of the Old Man if ever he learnt the details of this piece of crass short-sightedness.

The clock on the Hillman's dashboard was correct. During Rother's last struggle in the car the dashboard dials had been smashed in and Meredith remembered now that the clock was not ticking. Which meant – *that the clock would have stopped at the exact time the murder was committed!*

Reaching Findon he drew up at Clark's Filling Station, where John Rother's car had been garaged since Pyke-Jones' discovery. But before examining the car there was one other point about which Meredith wanted information.

Clark himself recognized the Superintendent and touched his forelock.

'How-do, sir. Anything you want?'

Meredith nodded.

'A spot of information, Mr. Clark. On the night preceding the discovery of Rother's Hillman under Cissbury, I understand that his brother, William Rother, called at your place for some petrol.'

'That's right, sir – he did. He said he was off to Littlehampton, where his aunt had met with an accident. He drove back up the road after I'd run in a couple of gallons and took the Angmering-Littlehampton turning. You can see it from here – about a hundred yards or so up on the left.'

'What time was this?'

Clark considered this point for a moment, running a forefinger through his hair.

'Half past seven – twenty to eight. Somewheres around then.'

'Thanks – now could I have a look at Rother's Hillman? It's still here, isn't it?'

'Yes, sir – this way. We've not done anything to her yet, though Mr. William has left instructions for the windscreen and dashboard dials to be repaired. It's been a bit of a rush of late. It always is in the holiday season.'

'Thank God for that,' thought Meredith as he followed Clark down the length of a big corrugated-iron garage to where the car was backed away in a corner. It would have been a nasty jar if Clark had already repaired the damage and thrown away the old clock.

Wasting no time in explanation, he pushed his head in through the open window of the driving-seat and fixed his eyes on the battered face of the clock. The hands, which providentially had suffered no damage, had stopped at exactly five minutes to ten. 9.55 p.m.! What time could have fitted in better with his theory that William was the murderer? If he could have chosen a time to illustrate his suspicion it would have been within five minutes one way or the other of ten o'clock! Did it mean that he was now in a position to make an arrest?

CHAPTER 5

THE CLOAKED MAN

'That's all very fine,' Major Forest was saying, 'but who sent the telegram? William couldn't have sent it himself. He was at Chalklands. It argues a collaborator in Littlehampton, doesn't it?'

'The aunt or Dr. Wakefield,' suggested Meredith.

'Possibly – but a risk, since we should immediately suspect them. Moreover, they would be known locally and might have been recognized either by the post office officials or anybody in the post office at the time. No, my dear fellow, I suspect somebody unknown in Littlehampton – a down-and-out, perhaps, paid to do the job but with no knowledge of William's criminal intentions. Now what about this skull? Has it turned up yet?'

Meredith shook his head.

Major Forest paused, puffed noisily at his pipe and jerked out: 'You know, Meredith, you've over-jumped the mark. You've assumed that Rother was killed by a blunt instrument. Why not shot or stabbed? You haven't got the skull to prove the type of wound.'

'Not shot, sir,' corrected Meredith. 'There was obviously a violent and prolonged struggle in the car before Rother was rendered unconscious. Shooting at short range like that – you remember there was blood actually on the driving-seat? – would be instantly fatal. Particularly as Rother appears to have been wounded in the head. Stabbing is a possibility – but if so the murderer bungled the job pretty badly. One usually stabs a man in the heart or neck, not in the head. You follow my line of argument, sir?'

'Perfectly. I don't necessarily agree with it. Not that it matters much at this stage how the poor devil was killed. I merely ask because if your "blunt instrument" theory is right there should be a chance of tracing the weapon. You suspect now that William Rother murdered his brother on the way back from Littlehampton. The chances are that he would have used a spanner or a hammer or something of that sort, eh?'

'That's what I imagine.'

'He then places his brother's body in the Morris Cowley – say in the back with a rug thrown over it – drives home to the farm, hides the body somewhere, and later dismembers it and places it

73

piecemeal on the kiln.'

'That's the idea, sir.'

'What about his car – have you examined it? There must have been a tidy mess on the mat and floor-boards. Again – what about William's clothes? Could he have dumped the body in his car without staining his own suit with blood? Remember that he went straight into the house when he got back, had a drink, read the paper, and went to bed. He couldn't have changed his clothes because his wife would have noticed the fact and commented on it. A man doesn't usually change his suit about half an hour before going to bed.'

Meredith looked a trifle dismal.

'You think my theory's a bad egg, sir?'

'A curate's egg, Meredith – good in parts. Look at it this way – according to you William had an hour and a half in which to get from Littlehampton to Chalklands, drive out under Cissbury, murder his brother, place the body in the car, dispose of it in some safe hiding-place near the farmhouse, garage the Morris, remove all traces of blood-stains from the back seat and from his own person. He would have to be a pretty speedy worker to do that, surely? You can't get rid of blood-stains without a great deal of trouble, you realize that?'

'Then it looks–' began Meredith in disgruntled tones.

'As if William Rother is not the murderer,' concluded Major Forest. 'I say, it *looks*. I'm not precluding his name as a possible suspect. I merely suggest that we're in no position to make an arrest at the moment.'

'Then what's your advice now, sir?'

74

'See that aunt. See Wakefield. Check up in Littlehampton. Examine that Morris Cowley. Have a nose-round in all the outhouses at the farm. See if you can find out where the body was cut up. Enough to get on with, eh?'

'Plenty,' laughed Meredith.

Major Forest put a hand on the Superintendent's sleeve.

'And for God's sake don't get disheartened, my dear fellow. We've had cases a hundred per cent more complex than this. To my mind you can only tackle a difficult investigation in one way.'

'And that, sir?'

'Worry it like a terrier worries a rat.'

But for all the Old Man's encouragement Meredith had a tiring and unprofitable day. He left his office about ten o'clock that morning and went direct to Chalklands. As luck would have it William Rother had been driven by a friend into Pulborough on business and his wife had gone to Worthing by bus on a shopping expedition. He was able, therefore, to search the outhouses and examine the Morris Cowley without arousing, any curiosity. But at the end of three hours he had to acknowledge that neither the car nor the outhouses seemed likely to render up a clue. The mat and the flooring at the back of Rother's car were all in order. There was no sign of either the mat or the boards having been scoured of stains, neither did he find anything to arouse his suspicions in the various cow-sheds, stables, granaries and barns in the near locality of the farm.

He then drove to Angmering, had lunch, and went on to Littlehampton, arriving there about

3.30. Dr. Wakefield was in his consulting-room busy with a patient, but the moment he was free he readily gave the Superintendent all the information he wanted. But negative again. He had seen William that evening shortly after eight o'clock. He knew nothing whatsoever about the telegram which, to his mind, was an extremely callous form of practical joking. He attended Miss Emily Rother but he claimed that she was more than normally hale and vigorous for her seventy-odd years. He then gave Meredith the address of her flat and assured him that the old lady never went out in the afternoon.

Miss Emily Rother accepted the Superintendent's arrival with perfect aplomb. Sitting very upright in her tall-backed oak chair before a little tea-table, she waved Meredith into a seat and told the maid to bring in another cup and saucer. She then mounted a most awe-inspiring trumpet to her ear and asked Meredith in a raucous voice what he wanted to know.

'It's about the visit of your nephew to this flat on Saturday, July 20th,' replied Meredith in equally strident tones.

'All right! All right!' contested Miss Emily. 'There's no need to shout. I can hear you perfectly well, thank you, if you'll just speak in your natural voice.'

Meredith hastily apologized.

'What time did he arrive that evening?'

'Eh?'

Meredith repeated the question a little louder.

'All right! Do *please* keep your voice down, my dear man. What time did he arrive? What time

76

did *who* arrive?'

'Your nephew.'

'John?'

'No, William.'

'By the way,' said Miss Emily, 'they tell me that John has had to go abroad for his health. Do you know anything about it?'

'Nothing.'

'Only it seems funny to me – a great, hulking, red-faced man like John. Now, if it had been William–'

'He visited you on Saturday, July 20th, didn't he?'

'How could he when he's gone abroad for his health?'

'No. No,' protested Meredith. 'I mean William.'

'But he *didn't* go abroad. It was John. William came and saw me here only a short time back.'

'On Saturday, July 20th?'

'Was it? Really you policemen seem to know everything. It's wonderful how you find out so much about other people's business.'

'Perhaps your maid might recall the date?'

'But why ask her when you know already? That's very stupid.'

'But I don't, madam. I'm asking you.'

'Well, why didn't you say so at once instead of pretending to be clever. You're a very unintelligent man to be a policeman, aren't you? I thought most of you came from the Universities these days. Are you a B.A.?'

Meredith commented inwardly: 'I feel more like a B.F.' Aloud he went on in wheedling tones: 'Now please, Miss Rother, I must ask you to answer these three questions. Firstly – did your nephew, William Rother, visit you one Saturday evening?'

'Of course he did. I've told you that already.'

'But you're sure it was a Saturday?'

'I'm as sure as you are, young man. Some madman had the audacity to send William a wire to say that I was in hospital. I believe it was that fool Dr. Wakefield. He drinks, you know. He denied it when I tackled him on the front the other day – but when a man drinks you really can't rely on his word, can you? I insist on it – when I die I shall die in my bed and not in a hospital ward.'

'What time did your nephew arrive?'

'At 8.17,' was Miss Emily's prompt and surprising answer.

'You're very certain,' commented Meredith with a smile.

'I can still read the clock, young man. Do you think I'm decrepit? I happen to have just looked at the clock before William came in.'

'And did you look at it when he left?'

'No – I didn't,' crowed Miss Emily. 'But William looked at his watch and said it was time he was going.'

'You've no idea, I suppose–'

'Oh yes, I have!' was Miss Emily's triumphant rejoinder. 'The St. Swithin's clock struck nine just before my nephew left. I'm not such a fool as you take me for, Sergeant. No. No. Don't protest. You're a *nice* man but stupid. I can never understand why foreigners make such a fuss about our British policemen. Another cup of tea?'

Cursing himself for having wasted so much valuable time, Meredith drove back to Lewes in a really bad temper. Miss Emily Rother had certainly fixed the time of her nephew's departure from Littlehampton, but what about the all-vital period between 9 and 10:30? Would anybody familiar with William Rother have recognized him on the road? At Findon, for example, before he turned off to drive along Bindings Lane? He would have reached Findon about 9.20 p.m. and returned through Findon with the body of his brother at any time, say, between 9.45 and 10.15. Coming to a decision he reached out for the 'phone and in a few minutes was in touch with the Findon sergeant.

'Look here, Rodd, I've got some routine work for you. Yes, this confounded Rother case. I want you to find out if anybody in your locality saw William Rother on the night of July 20th pass through Findon or along Bindings Lane at any time between 9.20 and 10.15. What's that? His car? No – a Morris Cowley. Oldish saloon painted dark blue. Got it? Good. Let me have any information as soon as possible, will you?'

Just as Meredith was about to hang up, the sergeant's voice recalled him to the receiver.

'Half a mo' sir. Funnily enough I was just going to get on to you.'

Meredith's interest quickened at the faintly veiled excitement in Rodd's voice.

'What is it? News?'

'Yes.'

'Vital?'

'I think so. Do you know a place called Hound's Oak Farm?'

'Never heard of it.'

79

'Well, it's not far from Bindings Lane. The constable here happened to be talking to the shepherd at Hound's Oak this afternoon. It appears that he'd been over to Bindings for the loan of some wire-netting which he wanted urgently. On his way back to Hound's Oak a chap suddenly dashed out of the wood through which the path runs in those parts, and ran off up the track before he could stop him.'

'When was this?'

'Night of July 20th,' said Rodd importantly.

'Well, go on.'

'Mike Riddle, that's the shepherd chap, thought at first that it was a poacher. He called out for the fellow to stop and got no answer. Just at that point the path leaves the wood and Mike was hoppy enough to catch a glimpse of the man on the open downside. You'll remember that there was a bit of a moon that night?'

'What time was this?'

'About ten o'clock Mike reckons.'

'I see. Well?'

'Well, sir – Mike noticed one or two things about the chap which didn't seem to fit in with the idea of a poacher. For one thing he was carrying an attaché-case, and for the other he wore a cloak and a big-brimmed, soft hat.'

Meredith, for all his interest, guffawed.

'Good heavens, man, it sounds like fancy-dress! Are you sure this Riddle fellow has got it right?'

'He swears to it. It was only because the man was dressed so out-of-the-ordinary that he happened to mention the fact to the constable to-day. Of course Mike didn't connect it up with the Rother case because it was only to-day that the facts of the inquest were published. I mean it was only to-day that he knew John Rother had been murdered.'

'Yes, I see that. Now let's get this straight. This track connects Bindings Farm with Hound's Oak, is that it?'

'That's the idea. It starts out of Bindings Lane just before the farmhouse, runs up through a bit of wood, then on to the open down and ends about a couple of hundred yards higher up the slope at Hound's Oak.'

'And if the chap went on past Hound's Oak – what then?'

'Well, it's all open down for a few miles. Park Brow they call it. After that if he kept a straight course he'd land somewhere down in Steyning or Bramber.'

'Thanks, Rodd,' said Meredith in official tones. 'This may be of some use to us. You might get a signed statement from Riddle and have it sent over here. And don't forget that other business. Good-bye.'

The moment Meredith had replaced the receiver he remained perfectly still, thinking hard. What the devil was this fancy-dress merchant doing on a lonely path at ten o'clock in the night? Yes, and on the night of the murder too, only a short distance from where John Rother had been killed? Why the attaché-case?

A sudden stream of ideas flowed through Meredith's brain. Was this cloaked figure William Rother's partner-in-crime? Had this man actually done the killing before William arrived with his car to take the body to the farm? Was it possible

81

that John Rother had arrived quite early in the evening under the shadow of Cissbury and been attacked at once by the unknown man? Suppose the attaché-case contained a set of surgical instruments and a large rubber sheet – the murderer could have then laid out the sheet in the midst of the gorse bushes and gone about the ghastly operation of dismembering and decapitating his victim before William came on the scene. Confound it! William might have set out for Littlehampton with a metal-lined cabin-trunk in the back of his car ready for the reception of these gruesome relics! Nobody saw him leave in the car for Littlehampton. His wife was up walking on Chanctonbury and Kate Abingworth would scarcely have troubled to accompany her master to the garage. What then? He arrives at the isolated spot along Bindings Lane, the remains are dumped in the metal-lined trunk, and he drives off at once for Chalklands. Why couldn't he have ventured out of the house that night, removed the cabin-trunk from the car and hidden it in his bedroom? Or even placed portions of the body straight on the kiln? To creep out on subsequent nights until the trunk was emptied.

'That would do away with the Old Man's objection to the time-factor,' thought Meredith, growing more and more elated. 'William would easily be able to pick up the remains under Cissbury and reach Chalklands inside the hour and a half.'

Then: 'The clock?' he thought. 'What about the clock?'

It had stopped at 9.55. Was the dial deliberately smashed by the Cloaked Man before he decamped from the scene of his horrible operations? This idea about fitted in with the time he was seen by Mike Riddle on the path to Hound's Oak. He would just about have had time to cover the distance from the car, after smashing the clock, to where Riddle had seen him. Perhaps the whole suggestion of a struggle had been staged by the Cloaked Man to confuse the police in their investigations.

'Theory,' thought Meredith cautiously. 'But a plausible theory.'

According to Rodd, if the man had continued on his route straight over the downs he would have arrived eventually in the Steyning-Bramber district. It would be as well, therefore, to see if the police in that locality had noticed anybody answering this unknown man's description late that night. There and then he put through a call to Steyning and asked the inspector there to question his staff and report back to Lewes.

He then drew a pad on to his blotting-paper and made out the following item, to be inserted in all the Worthing and West Sussex papers.

Will anybody who noticed a man wearing a cloak and a broad-brimmed felt hat and carrying an attaché-case between 6 p.m. and midnight, of Saturday, July 20th, within a five-mile radius of Cissbury Ring, please get in touch with the Sussex County Constabulary at Lewes or the nearest police-station.

This done Meredith put away his car in the police garage and, in a more optimistic mood, returned to his home in Arundel Road. Over the tea-table his seventeen-year-old son, Tony, explained in precise terms exactly how John Rother had been murdered, what clues it would be worth while following up, and could he, please, have the blood-stained cap (if it wasn't wanted) for his new-founded Criminal Museum?

CHAPTER 6

A NEW SLANT ON THE CASE

That same evening there was quite a conclave of 'regulars' in the bar-parlour of the 'Chancton Arms' at Washington. There was only one topic of conversation – the murder of John Rother and the consequent findings of the Coroner at the inquest on the previous day. The morning papers had been quite verbose about the crime, and many of the pictorials included, for some irrelevant reason, a picture of Chanctonbury Ring. From the central theme the talk branched out into all sorts of ramifications; free advice was offered to the police; theories were expounded; heads nodded in agreement over this and that suspicious fact; anecdotes were told of John and William; tankards were lifted to the arrest 'o' the murderer chap, an' may 'ee 'ang, durn it, as all murderer chaps *should* be 'ung'. There seemed to be no doubt in the 'Chancton Arms' as to the efficacy of capital punishment.

'Right an' proper it be that they as takes a life

should lose a life,' observed old Garge Butcher, to the concerted approval of those assembled. 'A h'eye for a h'eye an' a tooth for a tooth as the Book 'as it. A rare nice chap was Mister John, as you'll all agree, an' Oi for one wouldn't be back'ard in upping an' 'itting his ill-doer on the 'ead if 'ee were to walk in at that very door this same second.' And with an outstretched tankard of mild and bitter old Garge indicated the bar-parlour entrance with such dramatic effect that all heads turned towards it, expecting the murderer to enter.

The door, in fact, did at that moment open, and a thin, hatchet-faced youth with lank hair and a receding chin pushed his features inquiringly toward the company. A roar of laughter greeted the appearance of this queer apparition, who was known locally, with all the directness of bucolic nicknames, as 'Crazy' Ned.

'Up an' 'it 'im, Garge!'

'There stands the chap as done in Mister John!'

'T'were better to confess now as that you done it, Ned – constable been looking for 'ee, 'ee 'as.'

As the laughter rose and fell Ned stood eying the crowd with humorous toleration. He was quite used to being the butt and, in his simple way, was proud of the role.

'What be it all about, then?'

'Now don't 'ee say as you haven't 'eard, Ned,' said old Garge. 'You may be simple in the 'ead but not as simple as that.' Garge appealed with a wink to the rest of the bar-parlour. 'Oi reckon 'ee knows 'oo done it, eh? Don't 'ee, Ned?'

'I do, then!' contested Ned, nodding slowly to bolster up his own conviction.

85

''Oo then, Ned?'

''Er,' said Ned with admirable brevity.

'An' 'oo may she be, then?'

'Mister Will's wife.'

Another laugh greeted this opinion, whilst Ned shuffled his feet and glanced defiantly at one to another of the villagers.

'Oi tell 'ee, Oi knows. Oi see'd 'er putting they bits o' body on the kiln. Same night as parson run 'is Whist Drive it was.'

'What did you see then, Ned?'

'Oi see'd Mrs. Will come out o' the gate up at Chalklands with a gurt big parcel under 'er arm.'

Old Garge humoured him. 'And they were the bits o' body, eh, Ned?'

Ned nodded with absolute conviction.

'For what else would she be a-coming out of 'er gate well past midnight if 'tweren't to put they bits o' body on the kiln?'

Tom Golds, the village baker, and considered a clever, well-educated man, broke in: 'Maybe there's something in what Ned says. It certainly do seem a strange thing for a woman to come out of her house well past midnight with a parcel. 'Taint as if she could post it. Are you sure 'twere a parcel, Ned, an' not the cat? That would be more necessitous as 'twere an' explain things like.'

Ned obstinately upheld his opinion.

The baker went on: 'How came it that you were so late 'ome, Ned?'

'Parson asked me to stay an' 'elp clear up the Legion 'All. 'Twere mucky after the Whist Drive with all they chaps a-knocking out their pipes. So Oi stays to sweep up and set the chairs straight.

'Twere after twelve when Oi sets off up the street.'

'An' did she see 'ee, Ned?'

'Nay – Oi 'id in the shadders until she went by to the kilns. Gave me the shudders, it did then, to see 'er with that bit o' body tucked under 'er arm like a brelly.'

'Hey! – wait a bit, Ned! That there Whist Drive were last Thursday week. How did you come to know about they bits o' body when 'twas only set out in the newspapers this marning?' Old Garge looked round with a triumphant air at the exhibition of this piece of cunning. 'Oi got 'ee there, Ned. Ah!'

'Oi *guessed* as they were bits o' body,' answered Ned in a surly voice, upset at having his story crabbed by disbelief.

Tom Golds, however, seemed to take a more serious view of what Ned persisted in saying he had seen. He realized that, whatever the parcel contained, it was a curious thing for Janet Rother to have come out of the Chalklands drive-gate at some time well past midnight.

'I reckon,' he said at length, after a general debate, 'that Ned 'ere may have seen something that wants an explanation. We all know Ned *do* see some quare things at night, but he seems pretty certain about it being Mrs. Will. What's more, he remembered it was on the night of the Whist Drive. I reckon that Ned ought to see the constable.'

'Ay – 'ee 'ad then,' asserted old Garge, now completely won over to the official point of view. 'The law's the law – there's no 'voiding that fact, Ned. You ought to see Constable Pinn.'

Ned shook his head loosely and backed away with an alarmed look in his roving eye.

'Nay – not Oi. Oi don't go making trouble, then! Constable might lock Oi up.'

'I'll see that he won't do that, Ned,' urged Tom Golds. 'You come with me to-night and see if the constable's at home.'

'Oi don't like it,' hedged Ned with great uneasiness.

''Tis a murder case, Ned,' pointed out old Garge. ''Tis as much as 'ee owe to Mister John to see the constable.'

'Oi still don't like it,' protested Ned.

'I'll stand you a pint o' bitter if you do,' said Tom Golds diplomatically.

'Make it two,' put in old Garge.

'Three!' said Charlie Finnet.

'Four!' added Cyril Smith.

'Oi'll go,' said Ned promptly. 'Oi'll do it.'

It seemed that sometimes Ned was far less simple than he appeared to be on the surface of things.

His decision was, in consequence, responsible for Meredith's early appearance at Washington on the following morning. The constable had rung him up late the previous evening and the Superintendent had arranged for Ned to be at the Washington police-station at 9.30. The two officials were now seated in the hot, stuffy little room, with its wooden bench, kitchen clock, official-looking desk, and varnished walls plastered with police notices.

'And how much can one rely on this man's evidence?' Meredith was asking.

'Well,' began Constable Pinn cautiously, ''ee's crazy in one sense and in another 'ee's not. 'Ee's simple over ordinary things like money and politics and farming. 'Ee doesn't understand rightly about any of them things. On the other hand, I don't reckon Ned has brain enough to make up a story like that about Mrs. Rother. 'Ee couldn't have fitted it in so plausible like with the fact of the Whist Drive and the Vicar asking 'im to stay back and help. On the whole, sir, I reckon you can rely on Ned's evidence in a general sense, though perhaps not in detail. But quiet! – 'ere 'ee comes now, sir, so you can question 'im yourself.'

Ned's entry into the police-station was not accomplished without a great deal of pantomime. First he looked up the street, then down, drew out a watch, put it back in his corduroy waistcoat, made as if to retrace his steps, tiptoed to the window, saw the waiting police, touched his forelock, grinned, and once more made off down the hill.

'Hi!' yelled Constable Pinn from the doorway. 'There's a gentleman here wants a word with 'ee, Ned. There's nothing to fear. 'Ee won't bite you.'

Ned, somewhat reassured, came a few paces up the hill and asked in a humble voice: 'Can Oi go as soon as Oi tells 'im about what Oi sees?'

'Of course, Ned.'

'An' 'ee won't lock Oi up?'

The constable laughed.

'Come on! Come on! There's a good lad,' he wheedled, as if trying to entice a dog through the door. 'The gentleman can't wait 'ere all the morning, Ned.'

Finally reassured, Ned came into the little

room, sat down without invitation on the desk-chair, undid his waistcoat buttons, and stuck out his booted legs at a wide angle.

'Now, Ned,' began Meredith with a sort of easy familiarity, 'what's all this I hear about you seeing Mrs. Rother? When was this, eh?'

Ned explained once more about the Whist Drive, whilst Meredith took a few notes in order to impress upon the yokel the importance of his evidence. After sifting a lot of chaff from the few grains of wheat, he finally elicited these fairly reliable facts. On Thursday, July 25th, four days after the tragedy had been discovered, Ned had seen Janet Rother unlatch the drive-gate at Chalklands and make off in the direction of the lime kilns. Under her arm she carried a parcel wrapped in brown paper, about the size of a half-bushel basket. Ned had not followed her, so he could not say for certain that she *had* gone to the kilns. He reckoned the time was about twenty past twelve, a fact which Constable Pinn had already been able to verify before breakfast that morning by a visit to Hope Cottage, where Ned lived with his uncle. Ned's uncle had also been to the Whist Drive, but had gone direct home with his wife, there waiting up for Ned's return. His nephew had arrived home at 12.30, which meant that he had passed Chalklands about ten minutes earlier.

At the conclusion of the interview, which was to Meredith irritatingly prolonged, he left at once for Chalklands. Janet Rother was over at Stor-rington, according to Kate Abingworth, and would not be back until late that evening.

'Who cleans Mrs. Rother's shoes?' asked Meredith.

'Judy.'

'I'd like a word with the young woman,' said Meredith, adding casually: 'By the way, Mrs. Abingworth, you've never seen Mrs. Rother leave the house at night *since* your master disappeared, have you?'

'Never, surr!'

'Who tidies her bedroom?'

'I do, surr.'

'And you've never noticed a peculiar smell in that room?' Kate Abingworth shook her head. 'Or come across any article of attire, a piece of paper, a handkerchief or anything like that which showed any blood-stains?'

'Lord *no,* surr!' was the emphatic denial.

'Right – now let's have a word with Judy.'

'If you'll follow me – she's in the wash-house, surr. But I doubt as you'll get anything out of 'er. She's a stupid gurl.'

Meredith, on the contrary, found the seventeen-year-old Judy an excellent and intelligent witness. She remembered things in clear detail for the simple reason that so little out of the way ever cropped up in her life, and when it did the unusual event was recorded on her mind with all the exactitude of a photographic print. She had particularly noticed that during the week following Mr. John's disappearance her mistress' walking-shoes had been thick each morning with a coating of chalk dust. 'Just as if she had been out helping the diggers,' as Judy put it. She had thought it strange, but made no mention of it as her mistress

91

often walked on the downs, which would have a similar effect on her shoes. On the other hand, her mistress did not walk on the downs *every* day and Judy was certain that her shoes had been covered with chalk 'six days out of the seven'. She was also certain that the shoes were in this condition *only* during the week following her master's disappearance. Since then they hadn't needed more than 'a spit an' polish like'.

Satisfied, yet deeply puzzled by the new trend of his investigations, Meredith went down to where the lime-burners were digging the lime out of the brick arches and loading it on to the waiting wagons. A few brisk questions and answers satisfied him upon another point. Each night a heap of broken chalk and a heap of 'cullum' coal was left ready at the mouth of each kiln for the early-morning replenishment. It was customary for the men to leave the shovel leaning up against the stone wall which edged the upper level of the kilns. A watering-can with a rose was also left on the spot.

'Why?' asked Meredith, interested.

'Because the cullum has to be damped down, see, before it's shovelled on to the chalk.'

'Where do you get the water from?'

'The duck-pond close handy.'

'And this is done every day?'

The man nodded.

Meredith thanked him for his information and, with eager strides, made for the upper level of the kilns. This unexpected piece of lime-burning lore had stimulated a new train of reasoning. If water were poured every day on to the heap of 'cullum' then the ground round about the mouth of the kilns would be pretty moist. Was it too much to hope that among the hobnails, he might find the imprint of a feminine brogue? He went back into the farmhouse, praying that he would not meet William Rother on the way because of explanations, and routed out Judy. No, her mistress was not wearing her walking-shoes that day. She had put on a more fancy pair for the visit to her friends in Storrington. The brogues, in fact, were waiting to be cleaned under the wash-house bench.

Keyed up with the anticipation of a practical clue in a case that was over-packed with theory, Meredith picked up a shoe and hurried back to the kiln-mouth. There he went down on his hands and knees, luckily unobserved, and made a prolonged and careful study of the chalky mud which was blackened with specks of coal-dust. A minute later, exhilarated by the discovery, he found exactly what he had been looking for – a perfect footprint near the edge of the chalk heap into which Janet Rother's brogue exactly fitted!

'Thank heaven,' he thought, 'that it hasn't rained since July 20th! I'd have missed this if it had.'

It was curious that up until that moment he had blamed the drought for a lack of clues in the vicinity of the actual assault. Now, at this point, the powdered chalk, moistened by the surplus water which had trickled from the base of the coal-heap, had since been hardened by the hot sun into the likeness of plaster. Janet Rother's footprint was as clearly defined, therefore, as if a sculptor had made a meticulous cast. But he only discovered, alas, this single imprint.

Having returned the shoe to the wash-house Meredith decided to tramp up to Chanctonbury Ring and back before going on to see Rodd at Findon. He wanted to puzzle and reason and theorize, and he always found the rhythm of a steady walk conducive to mental action. Perhaps he had evolved this habit when he had been stationed in Cumberland, where a long trudge over the fells always had the effect of clarifying his thoughts. He filled his pipe, therefore, blessed the fact that he was in mufti since the day was hot and, skirting the chalk-pit behind the farmhouse, began the ascent through a series of ripening cornfields. Soon he came to a wire fence in which there was a creaky iron gate, beyond which, in a wonderful upsweep, rose the brown-green flank of the down. Gradually, as he mounted, the village of Washington came into view on his left, deep down in its bosky valley. Behind it a windmill stood sentinel over a red sand-pit, whilst the north horizon was fringed with the serrated ridge of a pine forest. It was a magnificent view, expansive yet somehow intimate; the chequered fields, dotted with isolated, red-tiled barns and homesteads, with here and there a tree-edged road winding between the pasturage.

Meredith sighed. He wasn't up there for enjoyment. He must forget the landscape, shut away all sound and scent and colour from his senses and concentrate on the ever-increasing complexities of this accursed Rother case.

Now, more than ever, he was at a loss. From a strong suspicion that William had killed his brother he had now been forced to take up a less

94

certain viewpoint. First there was the strange behaviour of the Cloaked Man to be considered – his part in the mechanism of the crime. Secondly this new, astonishing evidence about Janet Rother. How was she implicated? Was she a third partner in this devilishly conceived murder plot? It was obvious that Ned *had* seen her that Thursday night following the murder, however simple the fellow was in some directions. That she was carrying something under her arm was equally certain. Further, she was making toward the kilns. She had been at some time in the vicinity of the kiln-mouth, a fact to be deduced from that footprint. Finally, her shoes had been more than usually chalk-dusted during the week which directly followed July 20th.

The first bones had come to light on July 31st, and the remainder had been discovered in loads of lime sent out from the Chalklands kilns between July 22nd and July 26th – a fact which Meredith had ascertained from his copy of the order-book. Portions of the body, therefore, had been placed on the kilns during five consecutive nights. It was obvious that this unpleasant task had been prolonged so that only medium-sized portions of the body would have to be concealed beneath the extra layers of chalk and 'cullum' shovelled in at night by one of the partners-in-crime. Further, it was necessary that the residual bones should not appear in the lime in noticeable quantities.

The question remained – had Janet Rother been utilized by the murderer to perform this gruesome task? If William was the murderer it seemed curious that he had not undertaken the job himself. In any case, argued Meredith, if Janet were implicated it was certain that she and her husband must have acted in collaboration. Janet could not possibly have committed the murder and transported the body from Cissbury herself. For one thing she had walked up on to the down that vital evening, and for another there was no car available for her to use in the Rother garage. John's was under Cissbury – William had taken his for that trip to Littlehampton.

Meredith drew up short with a grunted exclamation, clicked his fingers, relit his pipe and started off again up the rise. But during that brief hiatus in his walk a new idea had suddenly flashed into his mind.

Janet Rother and the Cloaked Man? Was that the criminal combination, with William left out of it? Had that telegram been sent from Littlehampton solely to get William out of the way, so that Janet could help smuggle the body back to Chalklands without her movements being checked?

Hastily Meredith tugged his inch-to-a-mile map out of his breast pocket, where providentially he had placed it only that morning. Janet had left the farm ostensibly to climb up to the Ring. What was there to prevent her from making a start in that direction and then working down in a big detour to some point on the Washington-Findon road? There she could have hidden herself until she had noticed William rush by on his way to Littlehampton. At some prearranged spot, a little further up the road, the Cloaked Man could have been waiting with a car. What then? Janet gets in, they drive to Bindings Lane, arriving there shortly after 7.30. John Rother has already been set upon and killed, the body already dissected. In the Cloaked Man's car–

Meredith's thoughts stopped dead and then shot off again at a tangent. How could the Cloaked Man have had a car when he was seen late that night 'legging' it over the downs? If he had a car then he must have got rid of it by then – a difficult and dangerous procedure. Yet a car was essential to his scheme. How the devil, then, had he managed it? Borrowed? Stolen? Hired?

'Good heavens!' exclaimed the Superintendent suddenly. 'Why not Rother's Hillman?'

In a flash he saw the whole thing. John Rother set upon and killed. The dissected body hidden inside a rubber sheet among the gorse bushes. The Hillman driven out to pick up Janet, then back again to Cissbury. The remains, still wrapped in the rubber sheet, dumped on the floor of the Hillman's front seat, where an extra stain or so of blood would cause no comment. Then, with Janet acting as guide, these gruesome remains driven out to Chalklands in William's absence and hidden in some prearranged spot – perhaps a metal-lined cabin-trunk. Whilst Janet kept an eye on Kate Abingworth, the Cloaked Man could have secretly carried Rother's remains to the prearranged hiding-place and stowed them away in the trunk. The Cloaked Man then drives back to Cissbury, leaves the car where it was discovered the next morning, and makes off over the downs towards Steyning. Moreover, thought Meredith, wouldn't this account for the extra petrol used in the Hillman? Rother *had* gone to Cissbury direct, and it was due to the three extra runs after Rother's death that over a gallon of spirit had been burnt. The mileage, Meredith reckoned, would not quite account for the full gallon and a quarter, but the engine might have been left running when stationary – perhaps when the Cloaked Man was waiting for Janet on the Washington-Findon road.

Janet Rother said she had come down off Chanctonbury at a quarter to ten – a time which she realized the housekeeper could verify. The Cloaked Man must have left Chalklands, therefore, shortly after that time. The shepherd, Mike Riddle, had seen the strange figure on the path to Hound's Oak at (about) ten o'clock. Was it possible for the man to have covered the distance in fifteen minutes?

'Confound it,' thought Meredith, disheartened, 'he couldn't. He couldn't have done it under twenty-five minutes at least.'

Had Janet Rother lied about the time of her re-entry into the farmhouse, with the deliberate idea of providing the Cloaked Man with an alibi? Perhaps she had gambled on the fact that Kate Abingworth would not have looked at the clock. It only needed Janet to arrive fifteen minutes earlier for Meredith's theory to hold water. He would have to question the housekeeper now before seeing the Findon sergeant.

For all that Meredith determined to reach the Ring before descending again to Chalklands. He had heard that the view from the huge clump of beeches was unique and never-to-be-forgotten. Passing a dew-pond, at which one or two sheep were drinking, he covered the half-mile of the final hump with a swinging stride. A little later half Sussex seemed to be under his feet, with the chequered weald on one side and a quicksilver glimpse of the sea far away on the other. Sitting at the bole of a great, silver-barked beech, he spread out his map on his knees and began to register the various places of interest – the Devil's Dyke out toward Brighton, the faint blue ridge to the north which was Box Hill in Surrey, Steyning in a near-by valley, Wiston Park under his feet, Washington, and beyond that the distant roofs of Storrington.

At that precise moment, only a couple of miles away, a small girl in a yellow frock was clambering about on Steyning Round Hill in search of wild flowers. She was a solemn child and had high hopes of carrying off the first prize in the 'Wild Nosegay' section at the annual flower show which was to be held in a few days' time. She returned home somewhat earlier than her parents had anticipated, so weirdly garbed that the child's grandfather, who had a kitchen-chair out in the sun, let out a high-pitched bark of astonishment and dropped his clay pipe on the brickwork. On her head the child wore a large, broad-brimmed black hat. From her thin shoulders, entirely con-cealing her gawky legs, hung a voluminous black cloak.

Ten minutes later her father was plodding up the street in search of the Steyning constable. He had noticed rust-coloured stains on the dark material, stains which, as an ex-serviceman, he recognized as dried blood. This fact, combined with the police notice which he had read only the previous day in the local paper, had aroused his suspicions.

99

When Meredith reached Findon after his visit to Mrs. Abingworth, Rodd, whom he had 'phoned early that morning, had already collected this new evidence and handed it to his superior in a brown-paper parcel. He explained where and how it had been discovered.

'Which,' he added with a pleased smirk of self-congratulation, 'corroborates old Mike Riddle's story.'

Meredith agreed. He was in an optimistic frame of mind because in his interview with Kate Abingworth, the housekeeper had stoutly upheld that Mrs. Will had come into the farmhouse 'not later than the strike of half past nine'. Did it mean now that William Rother was out of the running and that Janet Rother plus the Cloaked Man were the perpetrators of the crime?

'Strange,' he thought, 'how suspicion in a case of this sort swings about from one direction to another. I'll end by suspecting myself soon, or the Chief Constable! After all, in these detective yarns it's always the most unlikely person who has committed the murder!'

'By the way,' he added aloud to Rodd, 'have you found anybody who saw William Rother round about Findon on the evening of the twentieth?'

Rodd shook his head.

'Only Clark up at the Filling Station – but you knew about that already.'

'Well I've got a new slant now,' explained Meredith. 'I want you to nose around and find out if anybody saw *John* Rother's Hillman pass through the village at any time between 7 and, say, 9.30. Probably driven by the same chap that Riddle saw up near Hound's Oak.'

'Wearing his hat and cloak?' asked Rodd with a meaning grin.

Meredith laughed.

'A bit too conspicuous, eh, Sergeant? Just as I thought. No – I reckon that hat and cloak act was performed solely for our benefit. He used that disguise simply to take himself from Bindings Lane over the downs to Steyning. By the way, did Steyning say anything about having seen a stranger on the roads late that night – I mean when you collected the cloak this morning?'

'Nothing. I made a point of asking that question myself.'

'Damn!' said Meredith. 'Loose ends everywhere, Rodd, and the murder nearly three weeks old already!'

CHAPTER 7

DEAD END

On his return to Lewes, Meredith found a note on his desk to say that the Chief would like to see him at the earliest possible moment. The Superintendent smothered an oath of irritation, suppressed all thought of an early retirement to his inevitable high-tea, and knocked on Major Forest's door.

'Well,' barked the Chief without preliminary, 'any further?'

Meredith slowly shook his head.

101

'More evidence and less daylight, sir. That's the present situation in a nutshell.'

'Sit down. Take a fill of this. Light your pipe, and post me up to date,' ordered the Major.

With an inward sigh Meredith plunged into a detailed recital of his latest investigations, whilst his superior, every now and then, furiously scribbled a note on his desk-pad. At the conclusion of Meredith's story the Chief studied these notes for about five minutes in a dead silence, rose, snorted, lit a cigar and dumped himself down again with an even louder snort.

'Hopeless, eh? A damned muddle, eh? Complex, what?' Meredith dolefully agreed. 'Yet interesting, Meredith. What about the stains on the cloak? Had them analysed?'

'It's being done now, sir. I've asked them to send the report to you here.'

'Good.' The Chief went on vigorously. 'You seem to be faced with three possible suspects now – William and Janet Rother, this unknown fellow in the cloak and broad-brimmed hat. That so, eh?' Meredith nodded. 'Tell me – what motive would Janet Rother have in helping the murderer of her brother-in-law?'

'Money,' said Meredith. 'She must have known that her husband was the sole heir to John's estate.'

'But damn it, Meredith – she was in love with the chap! Barnet explained that. It's common property in the village.'

'That's not exactly the truth, sir,' corrected Meredith politely. 'Barnet said that John was in love with Mrs. Rother, but as far as *her* feelings were concerned he was uncertain. Don't you see that a faked-up affair with John Rother would provide her with a nice, plausible alibi if she came under suspicion after his death?'

'There is that, of course,' acknowledged the Chief. 'But why should she go to the extent of meeting her brother-in-law at the dead of night with a suit-case in her hand? That couldn't have been done just to produce an illusion that she was in love with him. The girl had no idea that Kate Abingworth or anybody else would witness this escapade, and without a witness it wouldn't have helped along her pretended infatuation. No, Meredith. That meeting was genuine all right. But Lord knows why she took that suit-case. Why did she, eh?'

'Can't say, sir. They both turned up at breakfast the next morning as usual.'

'Precisely. And that argues – what? Not a collaboration between Mrs. Rother and the murderer, but between Mrs. Rother and the man murdered.'

'But confound it, sir!' Meredith felt quite heated on the subject. 'Look at the evidence I've got to the contrary. That footprint by the kiln. Her chalky shoes. Her appearance a few nights after the crime at the Chalklands drive-gate with a parcel under her arm. That curious walk of hers up on to the downs the evening of the murder.'

'Odd, I agree, but not conclusive proof of her guilt. You've got a lot against William. You suspected him strongly, Meredith. Now you *don't*. What about that?'

There was a rap on the door and a constable entered with a chit.

'From Dr. Allington, sir.'

When the constable had retired Major Forest slit open the note and read its contents.

'Human blood-stains all right. Strikes me that cloak was a lucky find, Meredith. I can't help feeling now that this unknown man really did the job, even though William and Janet Rother may have been mixed up in the plot. Unfortunately we know nothing about him and therefore can't lay a finger on the motive.'

'And I have an idea, sir,' went on Meredith, 'that Janet Rother was used as the bait to get John under Cissbury Ring. A note, perhaps, arranging a secret rendezvous. That would be a sure-fire trick to get a romantic chap like John Rother to put in a punctual appearance.'

The Chief agreed. 'By the way, that brings me to another flaw in your latest theory. Rother, if he had gone direct from the farmhouse to Bindings Lane as you now suspect, would have arrived there about 6.30. The Cloaked Man plus Janet Rother arrive there at 7.30 to pick up the dis-membered portions of the body. You know, Meredith, I can't help feeling that it would take more than an hour for your murderer to kill John and perform his gruesome operations. Professor Blenkings' skeleton shows a tremendous number of points where the bones were sawn through. Even if your man was an expert I doubt if he could have done it in the time.'

'Strengthening your theory,' suggested Mere-dith, 'that Janet Rother had nothing to do with the actual murder?'

'Quite. I still think you have more reason to suspect William as the collaborator than his wife.

In any case you'd better ask that young lady a few leading questions. Her answers should give you some idea whether she's got a guilty conscience or not.'

'I intended to go out to Chalklands first thing tomorrow, sir. It's too late now.'

Major Forest laughed.

'Thinking of that high-tea of yours, Meredith? When you're one of the Big Five the newspapers will seize on that high-tea and make it as famous as Baldwin's pipe. Well, I won't keep you from it. I know your wife is a demon for punctuality.'

Meredith joined in the laugh against his very human weakness and cleared out of the building as quickly as he could, making for Arundel Road. His son Tony had now developed an entirely new set of theories to fit the case. He aired them over the tea-table. According to Tony, John Rother had been 'slain' (to use his pet expression) by a member of the Russian Ogpu because he was writing a secret treatise on the Soviet atrocities during the Revolution. It transpired after a time that Tony had just read a sensational article on the subject in a lurid weekly, but Meredith could not help feeling that Tony might have been quite as near to the mark as he was himself. He had evidence of sorts, quite a lot of evidence, but somehow none of it seemed to piece together and make sense. He hoped his interview with Janet Rother would tighten things up a bit.

He found her the next morning lounging in a deck-chair under an ash tree, reading a novel. She accepted his unexpected appearance with perfect calm, offered him a cigarette from her

105

own case, and told him to fetch another chair from the verandah. She seemed to have regained a perfectly normal outlook on life. All the strain had vanished from her features, leaving her ready to deal with Meredith as if he had been a family friend dropping in for a little informal chat.

Meredith jumped his first question on her without preliminary.

'Tell me, Mrs. Rother, what were you doing out on the drive late at night on the Thursday following the murder of your brother-in-law?'

'Late at night?' She smiled as if a little bewildered by the suddenness of this cross-examination.

'Yes – with a parcel under your arm.'

'Oh, that!' She laughed and took a leisured puff at her cigarette. 'I was destroying some incriminating evidence, Mr. Meredith.'

'What on earth do you mean?' snapped Meredith. 'Don't forget that a police investigation is a serious matter to people concerned in it.'

'Quite. That's why I'm going to tell you the truth. I don't know how you found out and I won't be so tactless as to ask. I'll just tell you exactly what I was doing.'

She paused for a moment, looked at the tip of her cigarette, blew off the ash, and went on in measured tones: 'I dare say you've already heard a lot of gossip about poor John and I? Some of it true, some of it gross exaggeration. John was unfortunately one of those men who are quite incapable of hiding the fact when they're in love with a girl. I say unfortunately, Mr. Meredith, because in this case I was the girl. You've heard rumours perhaps?'

Meredith nodded.

'It was very stupid of me. I see that now. But I was rather flattered by John's attentions, although I realized it might cause a lot of trouble where my husband was concerned. During the time that John and I were – well, how shall I put it? – playing this game of make-believe, I kept a diary, an intimate record of all our outings and meetings. It was all part of the game to me, because frankly I can't ever look upon it as more than that. John was serious perhaps. He had that kind of nature. But I was sort of acting the part and then sitting back to enjoy my own performance. You see how I mean? When I learned that poor John had met with some sort of tragedy I was worried about that diary of mine. I didn't know that particular Thursday night that John had been murdered, because the inquest had not been held. I argued rather like this – if by any awful chance John *has* been murdered and if anybody ever came across this diary of mine, they would immediately suspect that my husband had committed the crime through reasons of jealousy.'

'Quite an understandable supposition,' agreed Meredith, who was deeply interested in the girl's explanation. 'Well?'

'Well, late that Thursday night I crept out of the house, went to the kiln, and burnt the diary.'

'But why choose the kiln?'

'Because in the summer the only other alternative was the kitchen-range, and I didn't want to run the risk of interruption from Mrs. Abingworth or Judy.'

'I see. How big was the diary?'

'Oh, the usual pocket size.'

'Then why was the parcel under your arm so very much bulkier than that?' rapped out Meredith. 'I know that it was. You can't deny it.'

'I don't. I decided that as I was going to destroy the diary, I might as well clear my desk of a lot of private correspondence and burn that too. I wrapped the whole lot in a piece of brown paper.'

'You realize now, of course, how dangerous your action was in the light of what the police discovered later?'

'Of course. I was worried to death about it at first. Then later I began to realize that if I told the truth everything would be all right. I know it happens to be an almost unbelievable coincidence, but I've got enough faith in your judgment, Mr. Meredith, to *know* that you will believe me.'

Meredith smiled, but without humour.

'I must, Mrs. Rother – unless I can prove things to be otherwise than you have stated.' He went on after a moment's reflection: 'Was that the only occasion you went to the kiln?'

'Of course.'

'Then how do you account for the fact that on several days running your walking-shoes were coated with chalk-dust?'

Janet laughed and replied in bantering tones: 'Because up here at the farm we are living on a mountain of chalk. You can't walk anywhere without picking up the wretched stuff. You must have noticed this yourself, Mr. Meredith.'

Meredith made no answer to this suggestion, but switched over to another angle of approach.

'On July 20th, Mrs. Rother, you say that you

walked up to Chanctonbury Ring and back after your brother-in-law had left in the Hillman.'

'That's right.'

'Did anybody see you on the hill?'

'Possibly. I don't really remember.'

'Supposing it was vital for you to produce a witness who could swear to have seen you that evening, could you do so?'

Janet hesitated, looked uncomfortable, and then shook her head. 'I'm afraid not.'

Meredith glanced down at his open notebook.

'On July 13th, Mrs. Rother, a week before the tragedy, did you by any chance meet your brother-in-law on this lawn late at night?'

'Meet John late at night! What utter nonsense!' Janet broke into a ripple of unaffected laughter. 'Where on earth did you get that idea from, Mr. Meredith?'

'You deny it?'

'Utterly. It's absolute nonsense. Malicious gossip – that's all. I can't understand how these absurd rumours get about.'

'Thanks,' said Meredith, pushing himself up out of his chair. 'I'm sorry to have bothered you with all this but it's a very necessary part of our routine. Before I go there is just one other matter on which I should like a little information – a personal matter, Mrs. Rother. You're not bound to answer the question, though I assure you that I could find out the answer in the long run from a reliable source.' (A boast which Meredith could have in no way substantiated.) 'At present I understand that your husband is the sole heir to his brother's estate. In the case of your husband's death to whom would the money go? To you, I take it?'

Janet nodded, entirely misled by the Super-intendent's prevarication.

'Unless a codicil has been added to my husband's will without my knowledge – that is the arrangement – yes.'

Satisfied that he could expect nothing more from the interview, Meredith again thanked the girl for her co-operation, bade her good-bye and got into his car, which was parked in front of the verandah.

On the homeward run, turning over all the evidence in his mind, he felt that he was now at a dead end. He had explored every avenue of investigation and in every case been brought up short by a blank wall. If Janet Rother had been telling lies then she was certainly a superlative liar. If not, then suspicion must swing back once more to her husband and the Cloaked Man.

After lunch at Arundel Road, Meredith returned to his desk and spent the afternoon catching up with the arrears of routine work which had accumulated since the opening of the Rother case. Half that night he lay awake trying to disentangle a few certainties from a confused mass of possibilities, parading the details in his mind and examining each one with the eye of an expert engaged in the job of selecting a genuine masterpiece from a collection of fakes. He returned to headquarters next morning tired, disgruntled, ready to jump on his subordinates' slightest faults, sick to death of the whole confounded investigation.

When the 'phone-bell rang on his desk he picked up the receiver with a muttered 'Damn their eyes!' and snapped out 'Yes – what the devil is it now?'

'Toll call just come through for you, sir,' said the level voice of the constable on duty. 'Refuses to give a name. Must speak to you direct. Shall I switch them over?'

'If you must,' growled Meredith, settling himself more comfortably in his chair to take the message.

'Hullo – yes. Meredith speaking. What's that? Who? Yes – I've got that. What's the trouble? What! Good heavens – when?' He was no longer sprawling in his chair, but sitting bolt upright, tense, interested, rapping out his questions with his brain working overtime. 'When did you make the discovery? Yourself. I see. Nothing been touched, I take it? Good. I'll ring through to your local station and get Pinn to come up at once. Yes, I'll be over myself just as soon as I can make it. Terrible shock for you – you had no idea, of course, that anything like this might happen? No – I must confess it's given me a pretty considerable jar too. Totally unexpected. Well, I won't waste time. I'll get through to Pinn at once. Good-bye.'

As Meredith, now alight with a new energy, swung away from the 'phone, Major Forest stamped into the room and took up a dictatorial position by the fire-place.

'Look here, Meredith – I've been chewing things over. Last night, in fact – at it for hours. Got a damned headache now. But here's the result for what it's worth. Taking into consideration all the evidence, it's obvious to me that William Rother was an accessory both before and after the fact.

111

Can't get away from the evidence. You're bound to keep him on your list of suspects. No, don't interrupt, Meredith. You see, if you consider the fact that–What the devil is it? Are you sitting on a tack or what? Come on, man, out with it! What's the matter with you?'

'William Rother, sir.'

'Well – you agree, eh? Under suspicion, eh?'

'Maybe, sir,' said Meredith slowly, 'but we can never make an arrest.'

'What on earth do you mean "Never make an arrest"? Why not?'

'Because,' said Meredith grimly – 'because William Rother was found dead this morning at the foot of the chalk-pit out at the farmhouse. His wife's just rung through.'

CHAPTER 8

CONFESSION

When Meredith arrived at Chalklands, accompanied by the Chief Constable, he found Janet Rother waiting agitatedly for him on the verandah. It was obvious that she had been on tenterhooks for the first sound of the police car. She came forward without any attempt to conceal her emotions and grasped Meredith by the sleeve.

'Oh, thank heaven you've come, Mr. Meredith! It's awful to think of him lying out there without my being able to do anything. It's been a terrible

112

shock. My nerves have been quite enough on edge without this – first John and now my husband. It's seems as if there's a curse on us all up here.'

'Now calm yourself, Mrs. Rother,' said Meredith in a paternal voice. 'We shall need to ask you some questions, so you must keep a clear head. By the way, let me introduce you to Major Forest, our Chief Constable.'

The girl, obviously struggling to repress her feelings, shook hands with the Major and led the two men round the side of the house to where a little wicket-gate in the courtyard gave out on to the stretch of waste land below the pit. As they crossed this to where the constable and one or two farm-hands were grouped, Meredith asked:

'What time did you discover the tragedy, Mrs. Rother?'

'About eight o'clock – about an hour before I rang you. You see I couldn't believe he was dead. I sent one of the men on his bike to fetch Dr. Hendley. After he had made his examination I rang you.'

'Is the doctor here now?'

'No. He said he would return about eleven so that he could have a word with you.'

'Did he say anything as to the cause of death?'

'Only that he thought William must have been walking along the top of the pit, missed his footing, and fallen over.'

By then they had reached the little group standing and conversing in low voices about the recumbent figure on the ground. Meredith turned to Janet Rother.

'I don't think it is necessary for you to go through all this, Mrs. Rother. If I were you I should go back into the house and lie down for a bit. Perhaps later, when you're feeling better, we could have a little talk, eh?'

The girl, who looked terribly white and strained, nodded without speaking, turned on her heel and walked slowly back to the house.

Constable Pinn touched his hat, obviously impressed by the fact that the Chief had thought it necessary to put in an appearance.

'Nothing been touched, sir. I seen to that.'

'Good,' said Meredith. He turned to the little knot of farmhands. 'Rotten affair this, eh, men?'

'You may well say that, surr. First Mr. John and now Mr. Willum,' answered one of them. 'I reckon that's where 'ee come over – up there where the wire be all snapped. See?'

Meredith followed his outstretched arm to where the rusty and dilapidated wire fence which edged the top of the pit hung down in a number of spidery strands.

'Looks like it. Well, I suppose accidents will happen. Now if you fellows don't mind we want to have a bit of private talk about this. Understand?'

'Ay, surr. If there's anything you'll be wanting to know you'll find Luke and Oi down under the kilns. We're loading up, see?'

'Thanks,' said Meredith as the men, nodding and mumbling amongst themselves, trudged off toward the farm. 'Now then, sir, shall we take a look at the body.'

William Rother lay flat on his back, one cheek pressed against the broken chalk which had accumulated at the base of the cliff. One arm was stretched out straight, whilst the other was bent back curiously under the body. His face was streaked with blood, whilst more blood had soaked into the porous chalk pillowing his head. There was a deep and ugly gash in his left temple. He was wearing a sports coat, grey open-necked shirt, and flannel trousers. It was obvious from the way the inert body huddled to the ground that Dr. Hendley had not found it necessary to make more than a cursory examination to realize that Rother was dead. He lay there just as he had fallen.

'Well, sir?'

'Well?'

'Accident, eh?'

'Looks like it. Can't be sure. Looks a sensitive sort of fellow, Meredith. He knew that you were running him pretty hard as a suspect, didn't he?'

Meredith agreed.

'After all, sir, things were black against the poor devil and he must have realized it from the start. What are you suggesting?'

'Suicide, Meredith – suicide through fear of being found out. We'd better comb through his pockets. He may have left a chit for the Coroner. A weakness of suicides, eh, constable?'

Flattered beyond measure at being asked for an opinion by the Chief, Constable Pinn could only manage a noncommittal gurgle well back in his throat and a tug at the collar of his tunic.

'I'm glad you agree,' smiled Major Forest. 'Well, Meredith?'

'Penknife, fountain-pen, wallet, pipe, tobacco-pouch, matches, one or two opened letters, and–'

'What did I say!' crowed the Chief, as Meredith drew a sealed envelope out of Rother's inside breast-pocket. Adding, as he examined the writing on the envelope: 'Here, this is addressed to you, Meredith. Bulky by the feel of it. What d'you suppose it is, a confession?'

'Maybe, sir,' said Meredith as he took the letter and carefully slit it open. He pulled out two or three sheets of closely written type. Appended at the foot of the last sheet was William Rother's signature in ink. Meredith glanced quickly over the contents, looked across suddenly at Major Forest, and let out a whistle of astonishment. 'By Jove, sir, it's more than that! It's not only a confession, but by the look of it a detailed account as to how the crime was committed. I reckon you're right. Our suspicions drove the poor devil to commit suicide.' He stared across the waste land toward the farmhouse. 'Hullo – who's this? We'd better examine this letter later on, eh, sir?'

The new arrival proved to be Dr. Hendley, a short, stout, wheezy man, more like a farmer than a doctor, with his ruddy complexion and muscular physique.

'Well,' he announced, after introductions, 'no doubt how the poor chap met his death, gentlemen. That deep gash in the left temple is nasty enough to have killed him twice over. He must have hit a jagged lump of chalk as he fell – penetrated to the brain. Death must have been instantaneous.'

'An accident?' asked Major Forest. 'Is that your opinion?'

Dr. Hendley laughed.

'That's for *you* to find out, isn't it? I'm only here to suggest the cause of his death. Personally I've always considered that path along the top of the pit a veritable death-trap. You can see for yourselves how near the wire fence and the path are to the lip of the cliff. You see what's happened, of course? They've dug the chalk away from the face of the pit as far as they dared without setting back the fence and making a new path. That's the rural temperament all over. Never do today what you can put off till tomorrow.'

Major Forest smiled.

'I take it that you're a city-man, Dr. Hendley. Otherwise this libel might extend to you. Well, you'll let us have the usual signed statement of your findings? We'll let you know the date of the inquest. And, by the way, you might drop in and have a look at Mrs. Rother. This affair has left her pretty shaken. Thanks. Good-bye.'

The moment Dr. Hendley had retired Meredith, who was down on one knee examining the body, straightened up and said slowly: 'Funny thing about this wound, sir. You'd expect to see chalk particles adhering to the flesh round that gash, wouldn't you? Well, there isn't any sign of chalk. I suppose it must have been washed away by the flow of blood.'

The Chief nodded, without paying much attention to the observation, and suggested that two of the men be fetched from the kiln to carry the body into the house. Whilst Pinn went to collect the farm-hands, he and Meredith climbed a steep little track which made a detour round the shelving end of the pit and came out on the path which edged the forty-foot drop. Dr. Hendley was right – in some places the path no longer existed, for large portions of undermined subsoil and turf had collapsed, leaving a gap in the rough track. At these points the wire fence, no longer supported, stretched flimsily in mid-air from one side of the gap to the other.

'Curious,' said Meredith. 'You'd have thought that Rother would have chosen one of these gaps instead of a point where the wire had to be broken through.'

The Chief disagreed.

'He wanted to make sure, Meredith. And to do that he needed a clear leap into space. If he had dropped behind the fence into one of the gaps, he might have just bounded down the face of the cliff and only injured himself.'

Meredith saw that point at once and gingerly leaning forward he caught hold of one of the severed strands of wire and drew it in toward him.

'Cut,' he announced. 'Pair of pliers or wirecutters, I imagine. They must be lying around somewhere, sir.'

A few seconds' search rewarded them. A stout pair of pliers lay almost at their feet, partly hidden by a big clump of thistle.

As Meredith slipped them into his pocket he nodded toward a near-by cluster of beech trees.

'What about sitting over there in the shade, sir, and having a run through the letter.'

Once seated with their backs against a giant bole, pipes drawing, Meredith slipped out the typewritten sheets and began to read. The letter bore no date or heading. In the left-hand top corner Rother had typed: *To Superintendent Meredith, Sussex County Constabulary.*

In cases of this sort it is customary, I realize, for the Coroner to bring in a verdict of Suicide Whilst of Unsound Mind. I want to dispel this polite illusion at once. I am setting about this business with a logicality that must preclude any suggestion of insanity. The whole thing had been too much for me so I am putting an end to it. As the 'means' by which I do this lies within your province, I will save you the trouble of a lengthy investigation before the inquest by describing exactly how I intend to end my life. To-night when everybody is asleep I shall walk up on to the top of the chalk-pit to a point I have already selected. Once there I shall sever the wires of the fence with a pair of pliers, walk few steps back and then jump outward so that my body will clear the face of the cliff. You see how simply and logically the job has been thought out?

Now I come to a more vital point – the reason for my actions. To a certain extent I know you have already formed a very strong suspicion about other actions of mine. You have cross-questioned me on the matter. I have been hounded by an accusing conscience, gradually increasing in intensity, ever since that terrible night of July 20th. I have had scarcely any sleep. My thoughts have been centred on one subject. The last few weeks have existed for me as a waking nightmare, made more awful by the thought that it was a nightmare which had no end for me. So I have decided to kill myself. And the reason?

I killed my brother at the spot where you found his car abandoned under Cissbury Ring!

My motive for this calculated murder was jealousy. I realized that John was gradually alienating the affection of my wife, a state of affairs which was slowly driving me to desperation. My brother hated me, has always hated me, with that sort of hatred which has its roots in no definite cause. The ultimate manifestation of this was his devilish delight in forcing his attentions upon my wife and, bit by bit, seeing her won over to his side.

Now I come to the technical side of the murder, the side which must naturally interest you most.

Meredith stopped reading for a moment, tilted back his hat, and mopped his brow.

'Hot?' inquired the Chief.

'It's the sheer cold-bloodedness of the thing that gets me, sir,' said Meredith, scarcely able to repress a shudder. 'I've dealt with a good few cases and met a good few murderers – but this customer's up a street of his own. Fancy any chap being able to sit down in front of a typewriter and tap out a confession like this. Inhuman – that's what it is!'

'On the other hand,' added Major Forest, 'obliging. This reconstruction of the crime is going to save you a hell of a lot of thinking, Meredith. Don't forget that. Well, go on. Go on. It reads like a speech from the last act of a Lyceum melodrama.'

'Strikes me,' concluded Meredith with an unaccustomed turn of philosophy, 'that life's a bit nearer melodrama than drawing-room comedy anyway.' He returned with increasing eagerness to the letter.

I will place the various events before you, as far as I am able, in their proper sequence. On July 10th my brother first spoke of his intention of going to Harlech for a holiday. He was going alone, and spoke of starting on July 20th after he had attended an afternoon meeting of the Church Restoration Committee of which he was chairman. From this I anticipated that he would be leaving the house shortly after tea. On July 12th I purchased a metal-lined cabin-trunk and a surgical saw in London, returning in my car with the trunk covered by a rug in case of awkward questions. I hid the trunk in my bedroom cupboard, a roomy affair, until it was needed. On July 17th, three days before the murder, I slipped off unnoticed by anybody to Littlehampton where I picked up a likely-looking street-lounger. I handed him a copy of the telegram which you now have in your possession with precise instructions as to when and from where he was to dispatch it. I gave him five pounds then and promised him a further five pounds if he would meet me outside the Littlehampton General Hospital at eight o'clock on the night of the 20th. I knew, you must understand, that if the man did not fail me I was bound to visit the hospital at that particular time. I felt, too, that the promise of this extra money would ensure the telegram being sent off.

On July 29th I typed a short note purporting to come from my wife to my brother. It ran: 'Meet me without fail at 9.15 p.m. tomorrow. Something vitally important to discuss. Go along Bindings Lane at Findon as far as the iron gate which leads on to Cissbury Hill. Park the car where it will not be seen from the road in the gorse bushes. Impossible to discuss things at length here. William already suspicious.' I did not sign this note, and reckoned that my brother would think that Janet had typed it because she was

121

frightened of using her own handwriting. I added a PS. 'Destroy this and make no verbal or written mention of this request.'

On the evening of the 19th I slipped this note under the clothes of my brother's bed, and later carried the cabin-trunk out to my car and concealed it, as before, under a rug. The rest of the facts you have more or less at your fingertips.

'I like that "more or less" put in the Chief with a smile. 'Rather less than more, eh, Meredith? Well, go on!'

The faked telegram duly arrived [continued Meredith], *and I left for Littlehampton just before 7.30, arriving there just as it was striking eight. To make my alibi convincing I visited the hospital where I paid out the second five pounds and afterwards called on Dr Wakefield and my aunt. I left her flat about 9 o'clock and drove all out to Findon. I put on black sunglasses, removed my hat, and slipped on a mackintosh golf-jacket over my ordinary coat. In this manner I hoped to avoid recognition in the locality of Findon, which would be dangerous to my plans. I had previously called at Clark's garage for petrol and mentioned that I was making for Littlehampton. If by any chance he should be about as I passed the garage on my return journey he would naturally expect to see me dressed as before.*

I reached Bindings Lane about 9.20 and got out of my car some distance from the iron gate. Then cutting through the gorse bushes I came to the spot where my brother was sitting in the parked car. I had armed myself with a heavy spanner. As he made to step out of the car, obviously amazed at seeing me, I struck

122

him two or three times in quick succession on the head. He fell back on to the driving-seat without a sound. I rushed back, started up my car and drove it through the iron gate to a point just beside my brother's Hillman. In the cabin-trunk I had placed a tarpaulin used for covering over loads of lime in wet weather. This I spread out behind the Morris Cowley, and taking care to get no blood on my person I placed the body on it. I had had some experience of surgical work in France, when I was attached to a Red Cross unit, and steeling myself to the job I decapitated and dismembered the body. I fetched the trunk and stuffed the remains into it, closing and locking the lid, after folding the tarpaulin and placing it over the body. The saw and the spanner were also in the trunk. I then dragged the trunk to my own car and managed to get it into the back seat, where I covered it with a rug. Returning to the Hillman I splintered the windscreen and smashed the dashboard dials to give the appearance of a struggle. The clock stood at five minutes to ten. From Bindings Lane I drove as fast as I could back to Chalklands where I garaged my Morris.

As soon as the house was quiet that night I crept out again to the garage, which is set well back from the sleeping quarters, opened the trunk, took out the tarpaulin and the saw and began the unpleasant task of dissecting the body into smaller pieces. This done I pushed back my car and slid aside the iron manhole-lid which covered the inspection-pit. One of the diggers had constructed this pit as I had always been keen on doing my own repairs. Into this I lowered the trunk, still containing the tarpaulin and the remains. The lid of the pit fitted so tightly that it would be impossible to detect any odour in the garage. I wheeled

123

back the car, washed the blood-stained spanner under a tap and returned to the house. During the next few days I managed to get rid of the remains on the kiln, all save the skull. This I buried in a near-by wood as I realized that its discovery in the lime, unlike the other bones, would be certain and immediate. My brother's clothes I also burnt on the kiln so that I was left solely with the cabin-trunk, the blood-stained tarpaulin, and the surgical saw. Finally I decided to drive out to a lonely spot near Heath Common, where I managed to bury the trunk with the other evidence inside it.

My plans had gone without a hitch save for one unforeseen event. On the night of Thursday July 25th, as I was moving toward the kiln from the garage I saw a figure in front of me, outlined against the sky, which I recognized as that of my wife. There was a faint moon, and from the shadow of some bushes I saw my wife throw something on to the kiln, wait for a few minutes watching the flames, and then return via the drive-gate to the house. I rushed forward at once to see what she had been destroying, but by the time I reached the kiln there were only a few charred remnants of what looked like paper glowing on the red-hot chalk.

And that I think completes this confession in full detail. I had not anticipated, perhaps, the harrowing investigations which followed, nor the gradually increasing fear on my part that I was under suspicion. I knew that it was only a matter of time before I went to pieces and gave myself away. Rather than face the drawn-out ordeal of a trial I decided on this alternative course of action.

I hope that with my death the whole terrible affair will soon be forgotten in the locality, and that my wife, *with the help of a capable manager, will be able to carry on at Chalklands.*

William Rother

CHAPTER 9

TYPESCRIPT

'And that's that!' exclaimed Meredith as he carefully replaced the folded sheets in the envelope. 'About as conclusive a collection of evidence as one could wish for. I never thought of that inspection-pit when I was searching the outbuildings. Not that it matters a damn either way now, eh, sir?'

'Don't be too hasty,' warned Major Forest. 'You've got to check up. You've got to see if this confession fits in with every one of the known facts. It rings true. Personally, I think now that there's no doubt William Rother killed his brother. But you can't just bring forward that letter, Meredith, and write "Finis" to the case. We ought to corroborate some of his statements with facts. That skull, for instance – the burial of the cabin-trunk. Know where Heath Common is?'

Meredith pulled out his inch-to-a-mile map.

'Soon find out, sir. Yes – here we are, to the north of the village. A pretty extensive stretch of woodland by the look of it.'

'We'll get out a squad to comb through, anyway. Pity he was so vague about that skull.

Curious, too, since he has been so exact in all the other details. "A near-by wood" – that's how he put it, wasn't it? Might be anywhere. The whole damn' locality is full of woods. Do our best, Meredith. Can't do more.'

Meredith nodded and jerked out suddenly: 'By the way, sir, there's another curious point.'

'Eh?'

'Why didn't anybody detect the odour of burning flesh?'

'You mean from the kiln?'

'Yes – at night.'

'What was the prevalent direction of the wind the week following July 20th?'

'Can't say off-hand, sir. Kate Abingworth may be able to help us there with old newspapers.' Meredith called down to the advancing figure of Constable Pinn, who was returning from the house after seeing the body stretched out on a sofa in a lower room. 'Hi! Pinn! Cut in and ask the housekeeper if she keeps the old newspapers. We want all those from July 22nd to July 28th. Understand?'

'Ay, sir.'

The Chief refilled his pipe and threw his pouch across to Meredith.

'Now – what about the time factor?'

'Fits in,' said Meredith promptly. 'If you remember, when I tried to reconstruct the crime with William as the central figure I worked out his movements exactly as he has set them down in his letter.'

'Smart reasoning.'

'Thanks.' Meredith grinned and went on more

seriously: 'Fact is, sir, apart from a few extra details I seem to have anticipated most of this confession. Luck, I dare say – but important because it makes Rother's statement seem more genuine. Further – Janet Rother can now more or less be wiped off the slate. I mean her husband's evidence about what happened on the night of the 25th tallies exactly with her own story. She said she was burning paper on the kiln and William states that he saw the charred remnants of paper. That's conclusive, isn't it? Mrs. Rother has told us the truth?'

There was a silence punctuated by the scratch of a match as Meredith lit his pipe and handed the pouch back to Major Forest.

'You're conveniently forgetting something, Meredith.'

'How do you mean, sir?'

'Why did you suddenly abandon the theory that William was the guilty party? At one time you were ready to put your shirt on him as the murderer.'

Meredith let out a violent oath and snapped his fingers.

'The Cloaked Man? You're right, sir. Clean forgot about *him*. Where does he enter into the case? Just a matter of coincidence, perhaps, that he was near the scene of the crime that night?'

'Possibly. But a powerful coincidence. Remember that his cloak and hat were found by that kid at Steyning. The cloak subsequently proved to have human blood-stains on it.'

'But Rother has made no provision for him in his statement.'

'Precisely.'

127

'Which means?'

'As I said before – that this confession needs a lot of careful checking up.' Major Forest looked up as the solid stump of boots approached along the path. 'Ah, here's Pinn. Got them, Constable? Good. Now then Meredith, take a look and let's have the verdict?'

'What wind there was – due east, sir,' said Meredith after he had carefully gone through the weather-reports.

The Chief tackled the constable.

'Now then, Pinn – if you were standing at the mouth of the kilns and the wind were due east, in which direction would the smoke be blowing?'

'To the west, sir.'

'I know that, you idiot – I mean to which part of the landscape.'

'T'ward Highden Hill, sir. Out over the valley.'

Meredith suddenly recalled the unexpected expanse of countryside which had greeted him when he had first visited the kilns.

'Of course, sir. I remember now. There's nothing but space to the west of the kilns. Just a deep valley which rises up to the downs on the far side of the main road. I reckon there wouldn't be a house of any sort for miles in that direction.'

'Hence the fact that the odour was not noticed?' concluded Major Forest glumly.

'By the way,' he added, as the three of them moved down toward the farmhouse, 'I'm sending a few of our men out from headquarters this afternoon, Pinn. I want you to meet them at the local station here and take them out to Heath Common?' He turned to Meredith. 'What about Mrs.

128

Rother? Will you see her? She doesn't realize yet that it's suicide.'

'All right, sir. I'll have a word with her and meet you at the car. She'll take it badly, I'm afraid, coming on top of the other upset.'

But Janet Rother seemed to have reached that point where shock so dulls the senses that the mind seems incapable of taking in the full import of events. She accepted the fact of her husband's suicide, if not without emotion, at least without any unnecessary outward display of feeling. She just sat there nodding, and at the conclusion of the interview thanked Meredith in a quiet voice for his sympathy and showed him out on to the verandah.

Back once more in Lewes the Chief hurried off to a lunch appointment, whilst Meredith slipped into his office before going on to Arundel Road. A memorandum-slip lay on his desk. It was from Rodd at Findon.

Re Rother case. John Rother's Hillman seen on Findon-Worthing road evening of July 20th. Witness – Harold Bunt, Wisden House, Findon. Knows the Rothers personally. Witness states that at 9.5 p.m. the Hillman passed him about half a mile out of Findon going in direction of village. Car driven by John Rother himself. Emphasize this point as in our last interview you anticipated car might have been driven by man in cloak. Available on 'phone till one o'clock today.

Rodd.

Meredith glanced at his watch. Ten to. He picked up the receiver, stated his number, and was put through to Findon by the internal exchange.

'That you, Rodd? Meredith speaking. Just read your 'phone message. No doubt about this matter, I suppose? Your witness is certain that it was John Rother?'

'Dead certain. He says Rother acknowledged him as he went by. Since then I've had corroborative evidence from Wilkins the postman here. He was just clearing the box on the main road when he saw Rother go by in the Hillman. He happens to know Rother well because they're both on the Washington Flower Show committee. Wilkins lives just inside the parish boundary there.'

'And the time?'

'Just after nine.'

'Excellent.' Meredith was unable to keep the satisfaction out of his voice.

'Yet – but I thought–'

'I know you did, Rodd. But I've progressed a bit since then. Thanks. Good-bye.'

So John Rother, coming from the direction of Worthing, had passed through Findon just after nine o'clock. What time had William arranged for that faked rendezvous with his wife? 9.15, wasn't it? So one would *expect* John to be passing through the village at the time he was seen.

'One more bit of evidence,' thought Meredith, 'to prove the validity of that confession.'

With certain reservations, Meredith could not help feeling that the end of the case was now in sight. It was only necessary to check up on that confession and the investigation could be dropped. The one inexplicable point now seemed to be the furtive behaviour of the strange man in the cloak. Why hadn't he stopped when the shepherd called out to him? And why had his cloak been found with blood on it? William obviously had no place for him in his meticulously thought-out scheme of things. No confederate was necessary. Yet somehow Meredith found it impossible to dissociate the man's actions from the murder. Was William Rother holding something back?

Leaving this question in mid-air Meredith returned to his Saturday lunch, determined to put his feet up over the weekend and take a well-deserved rest. Before leaving headquarters, however, he passed on the Chief's order for the squad to be sent out to Heath Common that afternoon. He also got in touch with the Coroner, and the inquest was arranged for the following Tuesday. At the Coroner's suggestion it was to be held at the farmhouse, and the usual routine was set in motion for the various witnesses to be subpoenaed and for the calling of a jury.

But Meredith's luck was ill-starred where that restful weekend was concerned. In the cool of the evening as he was watering the rectangle of lawn in his back garden, his wife came out in a fluster through the french windows and announced that a gentleman had called to see him. With a rare concern she hustled Meredith into his coat, told him to run a comb through his hair, straightened his tie, and preceded him back to the drawing-room. Seated in one of the big plush arm-chairs was Aldous Barnet, the Washington writer of crime stories. He rose, shook hands, and apologized for intruding on the Superintendent's leisure. Meredith grinned.

'As the author of detective yarns you ought to know that we poor devils don't have any leisure, sir. We're like the members of the medical profession – always on tap. Well, Mr. Barnet, what is it? Something important, I reckon, to bring you over here for a personal interview.'

'It is important,' agreed Barnet in a grave voice. 'Vital, in fact. It's to do with the death of William Rother. I only got back to Lychpole at tea-time and found a note from Mrs. Rother. Suicide, eh? What makes you think that?'

Meredith ran briefly through their reasons for this assumption. At the conclusion of his story Barnet pulled a letter out of his pocket and slapped it down on Meredith's knee.

'If, as you believe, William committed suicide because he felt he was under suspicion, how do you account for that? It arrived by post yesterday morning. Read it.'

Meredith slipped the single typewritten sheet out of the torn envelope.

Dear Barnet [he read],

I am in an awful predicament and don't know which way to turn for help. As I value your judgment on matters I have decided to take you into my confidence and ask your advice. It concerns the murder of my brother. Terrible as the indictment may sound, I have strong reason to believe that my wife is in some way mixed up with this horrible affair. I was, in fact, the unseen witness of certain of her actions on the night of July 25th – actions which in the light of what came out at the inquest, appear to me both damning and incriminating.

132

Tell me, Barnet, what am I to do? I am faced with the awful duty of going to the police with this information about my wife. I have wrestled with my conscience, turned things over and over and over in my mind, and still am incapable of coming to a decision. My wife knows nothing of what I saw that night. On you must rest the onerous task of deciding for me. I will accept your advice without reservation, but I feel I must have this second opinion.

I will make no move until I have heard from you.

Ever yours,
William Rother.

'Well, I'll be–' began Meredith as he looked up from this extraordinary epistle. 'What are we to make of that? What the devil does it mean?'

'It's hardly the letter of a man who is contemplating suicide, is it?' asked Barnet. 'I mean, why let me into this incriminating secret if he intended to kill himself a few hours later? The secret would have died with him. Death would have done away with the necessity of making a decision.'

'Quite.' He decided that it was imperative to take Barnet into his confidence over that confession. As luck would have it, Meredith had brought the document from his office, intending to re-examine it over the week-end. 'Before we talk this over, perhaps you will read this, sir.' Meredith held up the confession by one corner. 'Do you mind nodding, sir, when you want me to turn over. I've got to be careful of extraneous finger-prints.'

There was a long silence. Eventually Barnet looked up.

'Incredible! I can't make head or tail of William's

133

state of mind. In this confession he actually draws attention to what he obviously wished to hide. Was he mad? Did he do it? Had the murder unhinged his mind?'

'*Did* he murder John Rother?' demanded Meredith forcibly. 'That's what we're up against now. These two letters aren't consistent.'

Almost unconsciously he spread them out side by side on a near-by table and stood gazing at them. Suddenly he let out a sharp exclamation, caught Barnet by the arm and dragged him over to the table.

'Here, take a close look! Do you notice anything? Anything peculiar?'

Barnet after a careful examination shook his head.

'Both the letters look in order to me.'

'Sure?'

'Well, the two signatures look identical anyway.'

'The signatures – yes. That's possible even if one of them happens to be a careful fake. It's the type that interests me.' Meredith went on with the enthusiasm of an expert. 'I've made a study of typewriting – trained myself to notice little discrepancies in work from the same machine. These letters, for example – I should say that they're both written by a portable Remington. The Remington, I take it, which I noticed in the farmhouse kitchen. But the "touch" is different. Take the capitals. In one case they're struck boldly with the full force of the keys. In the other they're quite faint. In one letter – the confession – the full-stop almost punctures the paper. In the other it's normal. Notice how in the letter to you the small *a* is always weak and the small *e* strongly defined. This doesn't happen in the confession. Yet in each particular letter these eccentricities are consistent. They occur with the regularity of clockwork. You see what I'm getting at, Mr. Barnet?'

'That the letters were—'

'You've got it!' cut in Meredith. 'Written by two entirely different people. Which tells us something at once. Something vitally connected with William Rother's death. In short, one of these letters is faked!'

Aldous Barnet, now caught up in the same excitement, broke in emphatically.

'But which, man? Which? Don't you see the crucial fact which must accrue from this answer?'

'Of course I do,' snapped Meredith. 'That's what I've been leading up to. If William's note to you is genuine then it's pretty well certain that he didn't commit suicide. He couldn't have written that confession.'

'And if the confession is genuine?'

'Then what, in the name of thunder, was that letter sent to you for, eh? It's pointless. Ridiculous.'

'What are you going to do?' asked Barnet, obviously delighted at being able to follow the workings of an official mind at first hand. 'How are you going to find out which is the real letter?'

'Easy,' smiled Meredith. 'Get a sample of William Rother's typewriting from the same machine and compare it. Have you got a car here?'

'A car!' Barnet laughed. 'I've got something better than that. A super-charged Alvis sports with a cruising speed of eighty. Any good?'

'I'll risk it,' grinned Meredith.

Five minutes later the long, lean automobile was roaring toward the parish of Washington, impatient of 30 limits, pedestrians, and subordinate policemen. Barnet glanced at Meredith's mufti.

'I wish the devil you were in uniform. I'll have a whole string of summonses served on me for this.'

'All you need worry about, sir, if you *don't* mind, is keeping both eyes on the road and both hands on the wheel. I've got a wife and child to think of *and* a murder case!'

In an incredibly short time, it seemed to Meredith, the car swung off the main road and shot up the rutted incline to Chalklands.

'We'll park the car in the lane and sneak in the back way, if you don't mind, Mr. Barnet. I don't want to upset Mrs. Rother any more. Kate Abingworth will be able to give us what we want.'

As the two men entered the kitchen the housekeeper looked up from her solitary supper.

'Oh Lor, sir, you did give me a turn. Don't you be telling me that more trouble's come to pass. My old 'eart couldn't stand another shock an' that's a fact!'

Meredith reassured her and explained the reason for his visit.

'Well, that should be aisy enough, sir. There's enough letters on poor Mr. Willum's desk there to paper a 'ouse with. Dare say you'll find what you want among 'em. Would I call Mrs. Rother?'

'Better not disturb her,' said Meredith. 'In fact I should keep quiet about this visit of ours altogether. Understand, Mrs. Abingworth?'

'Ay, sir.'

Striding over to the large table which served as the farmhouse office, Meredith went carefully through one or two files until he found what he was looking for. Curiously enough it was a signed letter, dated the day before, written by William Rother accepting an invitation to attend a special meeting of the Flower Show Committee in place of his brother. The meeting was arranged for the following Tuesday.

'Another point,' whispered Meredith to Barnet, who was reading the letter over his shoulder, 'which suggests that William was not contemplating suicide.' Aloud he added: 'Well, Mrs. Abingworth, I've found what I was after, thanks. I should just like to borrow this typewriter at the same time if I may. Return it in a few days.'

Once seated in the car, stirred by a growing interest and excitement, the three letters were compared.

'Well?' demanded Barnet with impatience, waiting on the expert's verdict. 'Which is the faked document?'

'Which do you think?'

'The letter to me,' said Barnet promptly.

'You're wrong,' growled Meredith. 'We're all wrong. The whole case is wrong. I've got to start all over again. *The confession's false!* Though how the devil all those corroborative details were collected and served up like that beats me. Who wrote that confession? Some of the details are proved facts in the case. How did the writer know that? What's his big idea?'

'Sure you're right?'

'Dead sure. Look at William's capitals and full-stops. Look at his *l's* and *o's*. See how this letter to the Flower Show Committee matches up with that note to you. Point now is, did that confession come off the same machine? It came off a Remington all right, but was it the same Remington?'

'Can you find that out?'

'Yes – under a microscope.'

'In the meantime,' suggested Barnet, 'what about coming along to my place for a drink before I drive you back?'

Seated in the long, beamed sitting-room at Lychpole over a couple of whiskies, Barnet inquired: 'What exactly can you deduce from these new facts, Mr. Meredith?'

The Superintendent hesitated a moment before answering. The implications were so unexpected and inexplicable that he wondered if it would be politic to discuss them with a mere layman in crime. He had seen in a flash what that faked confession indicated. Other facts hinted. It only needed further facts to prove up to the hilt. But should he tell Barnet? Then, with the realization that in a few days the whole affair would be public knowledge, he asked: 'Are you prepared for a shock, Mr. Barnet?'

'Why?'

'Because I can only deduce one terrible thing from these new clues.'

'And that?'

'*Your friend, William Rother, was murdered!*'

'Murdered? Impossible!'

'Not a bit of it, sir. I wish it were impossible. But just listen here for a moment. We have two good reasons to suppose that William did not do away

138

with himself. First that letter to you, and secondly that letter we found just now up at the farm. A man contemplating suicide would hardly trouble to accept an invitation to a meeting which he knew he wouldn't attend. Your own letter we discussed before. Apart from that faked confession there seems to be no proved reason why William should *want* to commit suicide. As we were driving down here in the car I was hard at it approaching his death from a new angle. I remembered, for instance, that the gash in the man's temple had no chalk-scratches around it, although, according to Dr. Hendley, it was this wound which had caused his death. Now the impact of his head against a chalk boulder, softened as it would be by weather, seemed in my mind incompatible with this fact. Other parts of his person were thick with chalk-dust and scratches. Moreover, the body had not been moved. Why, therefore, should the wounded temple be uppermost? As the body struck the boulder with such terrific force Rother must have been rendered unconscious instantly. How had he managed to turn over? That's another point in my non-suicide theory. Accident then? But I knew I could rule that theory out at once. The strands of wire were cut, not broken, and we found the pliers with which the job was done.

'Secondly, the body in the case of accident would have half-slid down the cliff and come to rest at the foot of it. Actually the body lay some six feet away from the base of the cliff. So you see, Mr. Barnet, that I'm bound to suspect the other alternative – murder. The confession was faked, the wires were cut, and the pliers left on the ground to suggest that it was suicide. That's my opinion for what it's worth. What d'you think of it?'

Aldous Barnet did not quite know what to think. The very suggestion that William had been murdered had shocked him beyond measure. He could follow the Superintendent's reasoning quite clearly, but somehow, at the back of his mind, he entertained a hope that this reasoning was wrong. Who could have murdered William? And why had he been murdered? He put these questions to Meredith, but the official was not going to air any more of his theories in front of the amateur. After a full discussion of the Rother family, during which Meredith learnt many interesting facts concerning both past and present Rothers, he tactfully suggested that it was time he got back to Lewes. The ins and outs of William's death were analysed no further. Meredith had dropped the iron shutter of officialdom.

Driving the Superintendent back to Lewes through the moonlit countryside, Barnet asked: 'As a police official and a reader of detective fiction, what exactly is your idea about that type of story? You know, I should value your opinion.'

'Well,' said Meredith, flattered to be asked, 'I think every yarn should be based on a sense of reality. I mean, let the characters, situations, and the detection have a lifelike ring about 'em. Intuition is all very well, but the average detective relies more on common sense and the routine of police organizations for results. Take this case, for example. The clues have led me all over the place, and quite honestly I'm very little further after a month's intensive investigation than I was a couple of days after the crime was discovered. That's normal. Half the work of a detective is not to find out what is but what isn't! You might remember that fact in your next yarn, sir. As for the crime itself, choose something neat but not gaudy. The gaudy type of murder is more easily found out. The neat, premeditated crime is by far the most difficult to solve and will provide your readers with a load of neat detection. This crime, for instance. There's a story to be written round the death of John Rother if you only approach it from the right angle. At least that's my humble opinion.

'I reckon, Mr. Barnet, that you should let your readers know just as much as the police know. That's only fair. And one up to the reader who can outstrip the police and make an early arrest. Not guess-work, mark you, but a certainty based on proven facts. That's only fair to us because we can't arrest a chap just because we *think* he's guilty. Of course a thriller's a different type of story. But when it comes to a proper detective yarn give me something that's possible, plausible, and not crammed with a lot of nice little coincidences and "flashes of intuition". Things don't work that way in real life. We don't work that way. At least, sir, that's how it seems to me anyway.'

CHAPTER 10

INQUEST

On Sunday Meredith took a well-earned rest. He did not feel easy in his mind about putting his feet up with the new problem of William Rother's death confronting him, but he realized that detection is like sport – play the game too hard and you get stale. So Mrs. Meredith packed up a sandwich lunch and the family took a bus into Brighton, where Tony insisted on taking out a boat. That lazy day in the sun (for Meredith let Tony do all the rowing) was stimulating to both mind and body. He returned to his office on Monday morning, humming a little tune, full of new energy, in a mood not far removed from optimism. He went at once to the Chief Constable.

'Ah, Meredith! Just the man. What about this suicide? Any further details? What?'

Meredith grinned. He liked exploding bomb-shells in the Chief's office.

'A whole lot, sir. An unexpected twist. I'm inclined now to think that it isn't suicide but murder.'

'Have you got a touch of the sun? You look red round the neck, Meredith. All right, eh?'

'Perfectly, sir. Just listen here for a moment.'

And for five minutes the Superintendent's voice droned on in the close atmosphere of Major

142

Forest's office. As the new facts were set out the Chief became more and more fidgety. It was obvious that he was having the greatest difficulty in controlling his desire to interrupt. At length he could stand it no longer.

'But damn it, man, who the devil wanted to kill William? How was he killed? Where was he killed? Who killed him?'

'Which question do you want me to answer first, sir?' asked Meredith with overdone politeness.

The Chief guffawed.

'All right. You win. Unjustifiable excitement. Inexcusable, Meredith. But confound it, you can't expect me to sit here like a monument. How was he killed? Let's tackle that problem first. Any idea?'

'None, sir.'

'Very well. Why was he killed?'

'I *have* got an idea about that, sir,' said Meredith tentatively. 'Just a suggestion. We know that the letter to Aldous Barnet was genuine. William knew something incriminating about his wife. Don't you think it was possible he was murdered to prevent that incriminating fact coming to our notice?'

'Good heavens! By Janet Rother? That's a bit thick.'

'Not necessarily, sir. She may not have actually committed the crime, but William was murdered to save her from suspicion with regard to John Rother's death.'

'The brown-paper parcel evidence, eh?'

'That's about it, sir. Do you think we can fix the murder on the Cloaked Man?'

143

'Oh, rather!' replied the Chief sarcastically. 'Or Kate Abingworth, or Judy, the maid, or that old blunderbuss Dr. Hendley. As much cause to suspect one as the other. Where do you think he was killed?'

'On the path above the pit, I reckon. I thought of going out this morning and having another look round.'

'Far the best. Can't come myself. Busy. But you know the case better than I do. By the way,' added the Chief, 'those chaps I sent out to comb through Heath Wood yesterday – they've drawn a blank. No sign of the cabin-trunk.'

'That's just about what we should suspect,' concluded Meredith as he rose from the chair in front of the Chief's desk. 'Since that confession appears to be a faked job I expect some of the evidence in it is faked too.'

'Quite. Well, see me later today, Meredith, if you're any further.'

Before leaving for Chalklands Meredith went through to another office in a remote corner of the building where a studious-looking young fellow was examining some printed sheets under a microscope.

'Hullo, Bill. Have I looked in too early?'

'Can you waste a couple of minutes, sir?'

'Right,' said Meredith as he hitched himself up on to the edge of a table and watched the young man at work. He had three sheets. One was a page taken from the faked confession. The second was the letter to Barnet. The third a copy of an old statement which had been specially typed by a constable on the Remington from the farmhouse.

'I'm concentrating on the *t's* and *h's* and *g's*' explained the young man. 'They showed the strongest characteristics in the special copy. The *t* is weak in the cross-bar and strong in the upright. The *h* has a very defined upright but the looped bit is very faint. I've followed this up in the Barnet letter, sir. There's no doubt that it was written on this machine.' As he was talking he was at the same time sliding a line of type here and there under the lens of the microscope. 'I'm just checking up on the third sheet now.'

'Well?'

'The *h's* correspond, sir. So do the *t's*. But I'd just like to make sure by having a final squint at the *g's*.' A minute later he looked up and added: 'It's O.K., sir. The three sheets have come from the same machine. Care to have a look?'

'Not at the moment, Bill. I'm rushed this morning. Thanks for finding out so promptly. Cheerio.'

Outside the police-station Hawkins was waiting with the car. Meredith hopped in, warned his chauffeur to hold his tongue during the journey to Chalklands, and settled himself down to a nice bit of comfortable thinking.

The foremost point in his mind was the fact that Janet Rother was in some way incriminated in the crimes. For all her glib answers to his questions about that parcel, for all the clever suggestions in that faked confession, Meredith now had no doubt that the parcel contained, not a diary and a pile of old correspondence, but a sawn-off portion of John Rother's body. William must have realized this horrible and gruesome fact, hence his letter to Barnet. And Janet must have known that her

145

husband knew, hence his murder on the cliff-top. So far so good. But surely Janet had not murdered her husband? As an accessory she might be useful, but, however prejudiced her feelings, Meredith could not and would not envisage her as a murderer. Women don't usually murder a man by hitting him on the head with a blunt instrument. They, as the weaker sex, rely on methods less crude. Their instruments are the automatic and arsenic. They kill, as it were, from a safe distance for fear that their efforts may be foiled by the man's superior strength. And William had been neither poisoned nor shot. His head had been staved in because it was necessary for the murderer to suggest that he had been killed by a fall from the top of the pit. The question was–

Meredith's mental processes stopped with a jerk and shot off in another direction at breakneck speed. The confession. Who wrote it? The author of that confession *was the man who murdered John Rother*. Must have been. There were too many proved facts incorporated in that false document for it to be otherwise. What the police *did* know about the time factor this fellow must have known equally well. He knew that the dashboard clock had stopped at 9.55. He knew all about that telegram and William's journey to Littlehampton. He knew about the inspection-pit in the Chalklands garage. He knew the whole locality inside out. Of course some of this knowledge, the details about Chalklands for example, he could have learnt from Janet Rother. More and more Meredith was inclined to think that she was inseparable from the two crimes. A dreadful indictment, but unavoidable in the light of actual evidence. And surely it was pretty safe to assume that both John and William Rother had been murdered by the same man?

'Here, not so fast,' Meredith suddenly cautioned himself. 'I'm running beyond the known and proven facts. It's not certain yet that William Rother *was* murdered. I've no direct and indisputable evidence.'

Out on the sun-baked cliff-top, however, he set about his new investigation with this assumption in mind. Accompanied by Hawkins, he was determined to make a series of new tests which might prove profitable.

On their way up to the chalk-pit Meredith had borrowed a large sack and a spade from the men working down under the kilns. From the farmhouse kitchen he had obtained one of those weighing-machines fitted with a hook, which one hangs up so that the object to be weighed is clear of the ground. This particular machine was capable of weighing objects up to 14 stone. Fastening the instrument over the stout limb of a beech-tree, Meredith began to fill the sack, which Hawkins held open, with earth and chalk rubble from the top of the cliff. Every now and then he hooked it on to the machine and weighed it. When the pointer indicated 10½ stone he instructed Hawkins to drag the sack along the cliff-path to the point where the wire-fence had been severed. Meredith then made a detour down to the foot of the pit and took up his position a few feet away from where the blackened blood-stains marked the spot where the body had been found. He

147

looked up at Hawkins, who was peering nervously over the edge of the forty-foot drop.

'Ready, m'lad?'

'O.K., sir.'

'Then one, two, three, and swing her out!' called Meredith. 'Only for God's sake don't forget to leave go!'

The uniformed figure vanished for a moment, there was a brief pause, and suddenly the loaded sack came hurtling over the rim of the cliff to hit the ground with a sickening crunch a few feet from where the Superintendent was standing.

Meredith moved forward.

'O.K.,' he called up. 'Just as I expected. Did you have any difficulty?'

'Once I'd got the swing it was all right, sir. She cleared the lip easily, didn't she?'

'Yeah. There's an overhang just there. Stay there; I'm coming up.'

Once more on the higher level the Superintendent went down on his hands and knees and began to examine every inch of the ground in the vicinity of the severed wire fence. Hawkins helped him. For ten minutes they worked in silence, cursing inwardly as the sun struck like fire on the back of their necks, wishing there were a bit of shade to shield them from its fierceness.

Suddenly Hawkins called out:

'Come here, sir. Quick! I've hit on something, I think.'

Meredith got to his feet in an instant and joined his subordinate.

'Well?'

'There.'

The Superintendent let out a low whistle.

'Blood, eh? Dried blood.'

'Looks like it, sir. Of course it's soaked in a bit, but it's got that sort of sticky look that dried blood's got.'

'Don't be foul, Hawkins. Sticky. Pah! Here, empty that sack and fetch me the spade, will you? We've got to dig out about a foot square of that earth and have it analysed. No good suspecting it's dried blood. We want the certainty of a laboratory test. Careful does it. Hold that sack open.'

Although Meredith was adverse to displaying his excitement in front of a subordinate, underneath he was thrilled and immensely satisfied. In a flash he had seen the import of that discovery. Blood at the base of the chalk-pit was one thing. Blood on the top of the pit was another. Blood below – accident or suicide. Blood above – murder! No other interpretation. William Rother had received that fatal gash in the left temple before his body had gone over the drop. His dead body had been hurled over by the murderer after he had killed his man with some blunt instrument. The 10½-stone sack, roughly equivalent to the weight of the dead man, had fallen plumb on the spot where William had lain. Once *prove* that the specimen earth contained human blood and the verdict of the Coroner's jury was a foregone conclusion.

The blunt instrument? What had the murderer fancied? A spanner? No, something which would render a more jagged wound than that. Almost instinctively Meredith glanced around. Flints. Why not? The ground was strewn with great jagged flints peculiar to that locality. Surely a flint

149

would answer the murderer's purpose better than anything? No wonder the wound was innocent of chalk-dust!

Sending Hawkins to the car with the earth-filled sack, Meredith returned to the farmhouse with the weighing-machine. He had other inquiries to make there.

Kate Abingworth, a less lively matron than on the day when Meredith had first met her, was turning the handle of the milk-separator. She seemed lifeless and doddery and little inclined to chatter.

'Can I have a word?' asked Meredith politely.

'Oh dear! Oh dear, surr. I'm all behind 'and as 'tis. But if you must you must I suppose. There's no gainsaying the pleece. What would you be wanting to know?'

'You remember that typewriter I borrowed? Who used it?'

'Mister John and Mister Willum. Business and so forth they used it for, surr. Mostly Mister Willum.'

'You've never seen anybody else use it?'

'Never!'

'Mrs. Rother, for example?'

'Never, surr.'

'And as far as you know the typewriter has never been taken off that table during the last few months?'

'It has not,' averred Kate Abingworth with conviction. 'Seeing as I make a point to flick my duster over it every morning, I ought to know.'

'Did you notice if Mr. William had used it at all during the last few days?'

150

Mrs. Abingworth heaved a sigh, somewhat constrained by her corsets.

'Day afore he met his death, surr. He was a-sitting there as large as life tapping away as if 'ee 'adn't a care in the world. Poor man. Little did 'ee know, eh? Little did 'ee know.' And Kate Abingworth shook her greying hairs as if censuring all the pain and wickedness which walks the world. 'A letter all about the Flower Show it was. "Kate," he ses, "I'm going a-Tuesday to sit on that there Flower Show Committee in place of poor Mister John. Now, what's your 'umble opinion," he ses, "about the cockernut-shy? Shall we or shall we not?" You see, surr, 'ee knew as there was a lot of strong feeling down in the village about the shy. The young folk reckoned as we should move with the times an' have a shooting-alley instead. They reckoned a cockernut-shy was only fit for childers an' such. O' course I don't go for to say myself–'

But at this point Meredith, realizing that the housekeeper's verbal restraint was only skin-deep, hastened to change the subject. He knew all he wanted to on that point.

'Mrs. Rother laying down?'

'Gone to Lunnon, sir, to see 'er solicitor.'

'I see. Thanks.'

As he went round to where Hawkins was waiting with the car he thought: 'Mrs. Rother *must* have written that confession. She's the only one, besides Mrs. Abingworth, who has had access to the machine.'

After the inquest he would have to have another talk with that particular young lady. It was obvious now that she was by no means as innocent as

151

she appeared. It was not a principle of his to be led astray by a pretty face and a charming manner. Many a girl like that was just a– Now, what the devil was that bit from Shakespeare? About the apple. Ah – 'a goodly apple rotten at the core'. Well, Janet Rother might quite easily be rotten at the core. Quite a number of pretty girls were criminals, though actually the type Meredith had come across were usually brazen and cunning with it. In the meantime the really blank page in his chapter of evidence was that dealing with the Cloaked Man.

Meredith grinned absent-mindedly to himself as he got into the car and muttered: 'Lychpole – down in the village.' The Cloaked Man. His grin broadened. Quite a Sexton Blake touch about that! On the other hand that's all they knew about this particular man – that he wore a cloak and a broad-brimmed hat on the night of July 20th. Thin data at the best of times when it came to unearthing the fellow's identity. Perhaps Barnet might know of somebody with a grudge against the whole Rother family. Perhaps in the past the Rothers had done this man or his family some injustice. It was worth making an inquiry now that it was practically certain that the second brother had been murdered.

But Barnet was not particularly helpful. He knew very little about the Rothers' private lives. He had already primed Meredith with their local doings and explained the part their ancestors had played in the formation and upkeep of the parish when they were virtually Lords of the Manor; but over the Rothers' more recent relationships he was hazy. He had an idea that John had friends in Brighton and that it had been his habit to run over there for week-ends. During the last eighteen months he had more often than not spent his week-ends away from Chalklands. But he was reticent over his private affairs. Barnet doubted if either Janet or William had the slightest inkling where he had stayed on these occasions.

Meredith automatically noted these facts, but he placed little value on them as a means of tracing the identity of the Cloaked Man. He concluded his interview with the crime writer by airing his grave doubts as to the possibility of William having committed suicide, and left Barnet in a puzzled and unhappy frame of mind.

The following morning at eleven o'clock the Coroner's inquest on the body of William Rother was held in the spacious kitchen of the farmhouse. Chairs had been ranged round the well-scoured deal table – a massive wheelback presiding in the place of honour at the head. In this, punctual to the minute, the Coroner took his seat and cast a look round at the solemn faces of the jury. Five minutes earlier they had clumped over the flag-stones of the courtyard, dressed in their Sabbath clothes, murmuring in lowered voices, investing the commonplace proceedings with an ecclesiastic air. To Mr. Oyler, the Coroner, this was merely another inquest. To the jury, recruited from the village, it was an occasion for reverence and a ritualistic correctness in the carrying out of their duties. In the background, snuffling quietly into an apron, sat Kate Abingworth, and beside her pale, restrained, yet unflinching in the face of the ordeal

153

which awaited her, Janet Rother awaited her call as witness.

The proceedings unwound with clocklike precision. In a low, even voice Janet Rother gave formal evidence of identity and went on to describe how she had discovered the body of her husband at the foot of the chalk-pit. The Coroner asked her a few brief questions. Had her husband ever mentioned suicide? She shook her head.

'When you discovered the body, Mrs. Rother, how far was it from the base of the cliff?'

Janet hesitated, appeared to be considering the matter for a moment and then announced: 'Six feet, perhaps. I really can't say for sure.'

'Quite. In what attitude had your husband fallen, Mrs. Rother?'

'On his side.'

'Which side?'

'His right side.'

'So his left side was uppermost?'

'Yes.'

'Was there any serious wound visible on his person?'

'Yes – in his left temple.'

'In your opinion, Mrs. Rother, did it look as if your husband lay exactly as he had fallen?'

Again the girl hesitated. It seemed to Meredith, who was watching her closely, as if she were hastily trying to weigh up the import of the question in order to answer it in what she considered to be the most advantageous manner.

'Yes,' she said at length. 'I think it looked like that.'

Dr. Hendley was the next witness. Bluff and

blustering, he brought to his evidence all the ponderous weight of his own learning. He was out, quite obviously, to impress on the Coroner the fact that a village doctor was not necessarily slow-witted or a reactionary. Although the majority of country-folk were fools he was the golden exception. Death, he explained, had been due to loss of blood from the wound in the temple and, in his opinion, instantaneous. There was no doubt that some jagged object, probably a chalk boulder or a flint, had actually penetrated the brain. Questioned by the Coroner, he was emphatic in his denial that the deceased could have turned over once he had struck the ground. No, he could not say that he had noticed any chalk particles adhering to the dried blood about the wound.

'And the body was in the position as described by Mrs. Rother?' demanded the Coroner with an insistence which rather puzzled the jury. 'Please consider this point carefully.'

'It was,' boomed Dr. Hendley, with a defiant glare at the expressionless faces of the jury, as if daring them to contradict him.

'Thank you, Dr. Hendley. You can stand down,' said the Coroner with a faint smile. 'Superintendent Meredith.'

Meredith gave a half-salute and jumped to his feet amid the excited murmurs of the villagers. Even respect for the dead could not curb their natural curiosity in a man whose job it was to bring thieves and murderers to justice. The glamour of the professional detective still had the power to draw forth their rustic respect and admiration. Meredith was a novelty, like the annual fair, and they were determined to enjoy him as much as the solemnity of the occasion allowed.

With the clarity and ease of a man who is used to giving evidence, Meredith described how he had examined the body and noted the absence of chalk dust around the wound. Deceased, he explained, had been lying on his right side about five feet from the base of the pit. There had been considerable loss of blood, judged by the stains which had soaked into the chalk rubble about the dead man's head. The wire fence on the edge of the pit had been cut and a pair of pliers were found a few feet from the path. A confession had been found in the pocket of the dead man, purporting to have been typewritten by him, but since proved by the police to have been faked. The confession referred to the death of the deceased's brother. It was the opinion of the police that the document had been placed in the dead man's pocket in order to mislead them as to the manner in which William Rother had met his death.

At this point the Coroner broke in to ask with a suave smile: 'Have the police any further evidence with which to substantiate the claim that this document was not typed by the deceased?' Mr. Oyler knew the answer, as it happened, but he had to put these more-or-less rehearsed queries in order to guide the jury.

'Yes, sir, they have. Last night, in the ordinary course of my investigations, I tested the envelope and typewritten sheets for finger-prints.'

'With what result?'

'I found two sets present.'

'And those?'

'The Chief Constable's and my own, sir.' At this a faint titter, due to the tension of the cross-examination, flickered round the table. The Coroner rapped with his knuckles, requesting silence.

'I take it,' he continued, 'that the Chief Constable and you were the only people who had handled that document since it was taken from the deceased's pocket?'

'Correct, sir.'

'Were there any other finger-prints, Mr. Meredith?'

'None, sir.'

'None!'

The rest of the assembly silently echoed the Coroner's obvious astonishment. How could the confession have got into the dead man's pocket without showing finger-prints? How had the sheets of paper been placed in the envelope and the envelope sealed without them picking up the tell-tale imprints? The jury was puzzled.

'What exactly did this extraordinary fact suggest to you?' asked the Coroner when the little murmur had faded.

'Well, sir, to my way of thinking it looked as though the person who placed that document in Mr. Rother's pocket was anxious to hide his identity. We imagine that he must have worn gloves on every occasion that he handled the document.'

'I see. Well?'

'Well, sir, my suspicions having already been aroused, I examined the ground round about where the wire fence had been cut on the top of the pit. I found blood-stains.'

'Blood-stains!'

157

Again that little shiver of excitement and interest ran round the table.

'Yes, sir. I took a specimen of the stained earth and had it analysed. The presence of human blood was definitely proved by Dr. White.'

'Did this suggest anything further to you?'

"Well, sir, it seemed a peculiar factor in the case, because I could not for the life of me see why there should have been blood on the top of the pit when to all apparent purposes deceased had met his death by a fall. I was forced to adopt a strong doubt as to whether deceased was not dead *before* his drop over the pit.'

'Thank you. That's all.'

At the conclusion of the Superintendent's evidence the jury was roused to a frenzied twitter of conjecture and argument. They had come to the inquest quite certain in their own minds that 'Mister Willum' had committed suicide. Dr. Hendley had aired this opinion in the village and seemed to have no doubts about it. From what they had already gleaned for themselves *they* had had no doubts about it. They had all trooped up to the farmhouse that August morning ready to bring in that unpleasant but unavoidable verdict. Now they felt at sixes and sevens. From what they had heard of the police evidence it was beginning to look as if their duty was going to force them to a far more unpleasant and unanticipated decision. Dark hints were in the air. The room seemed suddenly airless and over-hot, the Coroner invested with all the menace and majesty of the inexorable law behind him. Their discomfort increased when Dr. White spoke of the tests he had carried out on the bloodstained earth.

At length the Coroner was summing up – his voice droning on, dry as dust, in the close atmosphere of the overcrowded kitchen. Three things to consider. Whether it was accident? Whether it was suicide? Whether it was murder? In his opinion the fact that the wire fence had been cut precluded the idea of accident. Deceased was familiar with the dangers of the cliff-path. There was that curious document found in his pocket. Suicide then? At first glance it appeared that deceased had deliberately taken his own life. On looking closer into the evidence, however, there seemed to be some reasonable doubt that this might not be the case. He lay on his right side. The fatal wound in the left temple was uppermost. How, if the wound had been caused by the fall, had he managed to turn over? Secondly, according to police witness, no chalk scratches were evident round the fatal gash, although the whole of the ground at the foot of the pit was strewn with chalk boulders. Did this suggest that the wound had been sustained at some time *previous* to the fall? Perhaps on the cliff-top, where blood-stains had been discovered in the vicinity of the severed wire?

There was that curious document to consider. A document which had been placed in the dead man's pocket without sustaining a single fingerprint. Was the whole terrible affair staged by some unknown person to look like suicide, when in reality it was something quite different? This brought them to the third alternative. Murder. Had deceased been set upon on the cliff-path, killed by a violent blow on the left temple, and *then* thrown over the pit? There seemed to be evidence which might substantiate this supposition. It was for the jury, however, to examine all the evidence at length, without prejudice, and to find accordingly. If in its opinion it was a case of wilful murder, then it might, on evidence given, name the murderer or murderers. In his, the Coroner's, opinion, there was no such evidence.

At the conclusion of his speech, much as Mr. Oyler had anticipated, the jury elected to retire. With a clumping of hobnailed boots, therefore, they filed out in the wake of Kate Abingworth and shut themselves up in the Chalklands dining-room.

Twenty minutes later they all clumped in again and solemnly took up their positions around the kitchen table. Then, to Meredith's surprise, having anticipated an open verdict, they brought in 'Murder by Person or Persons Unknown'. It seemed that the police evidence was more impressive than he had thought!

CHAPTER 11

THE THIRD PROBLEM

Cedric Clark, proprietor of Clark's Filling Station at Findon, had a business friend coming to see him that morning. He was hoping to sell John Rother's Hillman. Since Meredith had last examined the car, the windscreen and dashboard had been repaired, the blood-stains carefully erased, and the bodywork entirely repainted. Clark had followed the report of the inquest in the evening paper of the day before and, in keeping with the rest of the locality, had been shocked by the findings of the jury. William's death, moreover, had placed him in a quandary with regard to the sale of the car. He would now have to make a visit to Chalklands and get Mrs. Rother's authority to go ahead with the sale. Thornton was coming over to see him at eleven, so Clark hopped on to his motor-cycle and ran out to Chalklands directly after breakfast. He did not actually see Janet Rother – the housekeeper explained that she was still in bed resting – so he sent a message and in return received permission to go ahead with the sale of the car.

At eleven o'clock Tim Thornton rattled up in his weather-beaten service-car and stopped with a plaintive screech of brakes just beyond the petrol-pumps.

'That's a blooming good advert for you – that car is, and no mistake,' said Clark. 'Economizing on oil, eh?'

Thornton, a big-boned, lazy-looking fellow with sandy hair and a ginger moustache, climbed slowly out of his car and stood staring at the premises known as Clark's Filling Station.

'Excuse me. Can you tell me if there is a garage anywhere near here? I understood that a damn' fool called Clark was running a place in this one-horse village.'

'You *need* a garage,' retorted Clark pointedly,

161

nodding at the relic and slapping Thornton on the back. 'Come inside, m'lad, and we'll see what we can do for you. We've a wreckage van at your disposal. Care to borrow it?'

'Grrrr!' growled Thornton as he followed his friend into the poky hole which went by the grandiloquent title of office. 'Well, how's business?'

'Oh, so-so. Can't complain. How are you doing out your way?'

'Not too bad. Had a bit of bother in this district, haven't you?' he went on after lighting a cigarette. 'See from last night's paper that they brought in a verdict of murder on that Rother chap.'

'Yeah,' agreed Clark. 'Funny business that. First this spot of bother under Cissbury – now it seems that William Rother has copped it in the neck too. Sort of family curse, eh?'

'That Hillman handy?'

'Round the back, Tim. Want to see it now?'

'Well, I've got to be back by twelve to interview a customer.'

'Then we'd better snap into it, ole man. You'll need all the time you can get if you're going back on that barrel-organ outside. I bet the thirty limit has never worried *her*, eh?'

'We do at least keep our pumps painted,' countered Thornton as he followed the proprietor through a maze of cars to where the Hillman was parked in a far corner of the main garage. 'Hullo – is this the little wonder?'

'That's her. Good as new – only done six thousand – freshly painted – new windscreen – good tyres and–'

'–licensed up to the end of the quarter,' went

162

on Thornton with a mocking grin. 'Go on. You can cut the cackle. That sort of snappy sales-talk won't get any change out of me. You lift the bonnet and I'll soon tell you if she's the car for my customer. I promised him a snip and *I've* got a reputation to uphold. Not like some chaps.'

'There you are then,' said Clark, raising the bonnet and holding an inspection-lamp over the engine. 'Take a squint at that. Nothing wrong with her guts, ole man.'

Just as Thornton was about to bend over the engine, however, he suddenly let out an exclamation of surprise and stepped back, the better to examine the car.

'Here – half a mo' – I've seen this car before. Light green, wasn't she, before you painted her this filthy colour?'

'That's it. How'd' you recognize it?'

'See those two brass-headed nuts on the battery clamps? Fixed 'em myself when the owner garaged with me one week-end.'

'When was this?'

'Can't say for sure. About a couple of months back, I dare say. But the chap's been garaging regularly with me over week-ends for the past eighteen months or more. Funny, eh?'

'What was he like to look at?'

'Stocky, well-built sort of chap. Red-faced. Loud-voiced. Typical farmer, I reckon. Name of Reed, he said.'

'Reed?' Clark's voice was quite shrill with excitement. 'That wasn't Reed. That was Rother. Betcher life it was! That was John Rother – the chap that was murdered under Cissbury here.

163

Haven't you ever seen his photo in the news-papers?'

'No time to read 'em, m'lad. I get all my news over the wireless. So that was John Rother, was it? Well, I be blowed. Never struck me that I'd ever met the chap when they broadcast an S O S about him. Funny 'im giving a false name like that, eh?'

'Fishy – if you ask me,' agreed Clark. 'Darn' fishy. I reckon Superintendent Meredith ought to know about this. Straight I do. He'd do well to come over and see you, Tim.'

Thornton laughed.

'Bit of third degree, what? Though I don't see that I can help him much. He's the fellow investi-gating these murders, isn't he?'

'You never know,' said Clark meaningly. 'These police chaps pick up all sorts of odd bits of evi-dence, then they piece 'em together, and before you know where you are some poor bastard's booked for the long drop. Anyway, what about the car?'

'Just turn her over,' said Thornton. 'I guess she'll suit all right. She was running sweet enough when I last saw her.'

Ten minutes later the deal had been concluded, and after a 'quick one' in the pub up the street Thornton mounted his thunderous barouche and rattled off through the village.

Clark returned to his office and took up the 'phone. In a few minutes he was through to Meredith.

'Just caught me in time, Mr. Clark. I'm coming over to Chalklands this morning. What's the trouble?'

Clark explained about his talk with Thornton. Meredith was interested at once.

'Look here, I'll drop in on my way. Then you can give me details.'

Although Meredith did not expect to get much from this new data he was in no position to ignore even the flimsiest of clues. In an investigation one thing led to another, and quite often, in the long run, to the wanted man. He was still perplexed with regard to the part that the Cloaked Man had played in the crimes, though he was now inclined to think that his was the major rôle. These weekends which Rother had spent, according to Barnet, at Brighton may have first brought him in contact with the man who was destined to murder him. Yes, most decidedly, this new thread of evidence would have to be followed up.

Clark was standing by the petrol-pumps, having a smoke, when the police car drew up. The two men at once retired to the little office. There Clark handed on all the information he had received from Thornton, embellishing the bare details with ornamental theories and opinions of his own. Meredith, however, soon sorted the wheat from the chaff.

'Where is this place of Thornton's?'

'You know the Arundel-Brighton road which runs through Sompting and Lancing?' Meredith nodded. 'Well, just beyond the toll-bridge which crosses the River Adur there's a crossroads.'

'I know the spot. Near there, is it?'

'About a couple of hundred yards on the Brighton side of the cross-roads – yes. Newish place – a bit flashy in its decoration to my mind. But old

Thornton's like that. He likes to make a splash.'

'I see – thanks. I'll run out there and have a word with your friend as soon as I can. Decent of you to ring me up.'

'Oh, that's O.K. I know how you chaps work. Nothing more you want to know?'

Meredith shook his head and, anxious to get on his way to the farmhouse, jumped into the car and told Hawkins to step on it. The little blue-black police car shot off up the road like a bullet from a rifle. Inside ten minutes it was parked in front of the long white verandah.

Kate Abingworth answered the Superintendent's ring, and on asking for Janet Rother he was shown into the drawing-room.

'Mrs. Rother said that she didn't want to be disturbed like, but I'm sure she'll see you, surr. She's lying down in her room.'

Whilst the housekeeper was absent Meredith mentally rehearsed his method of attack. He realized now that a good old-fashioned dose of third degree was absolutely necessary if he were to drag the truth from the girl. All along she had been keeping something back. There seemed little doubt now that she *had* placed the portions of John Rother's body on the kiln. It looked, too, as if she must have written that faked confession. If the Cloaked Man were implicated in the crimes, then Janet Rother was the one person who could give him a line on his identity. She must be made to speak. He would have to put the fear of the devil into her and frighten her into a true statement of the facts.

Kate Abingworth came in. Meredith looked up.

166

She was alone.

'Mrs. Rother not dressed?' he rapped out.

'Oh dear, surr,' agitated the housekeeper, 'I can't get no answer. I knocked and knocked but couldn't get no reply. Her door's locked, moreover. I called out for her to open it but she–'

'When did you last go up to Mrs. Rother?'

'About nine, surr, when the garridge chap called. I spoke to her through the door.'

'You didn't see her?'

'No, surr.'

'Take up her breakfast?'

'She didn't have no breakfast, surr. She told me last night particular not to disturb her this marning, though when the garridge chap come–'

'I see.' Meredith felt suddenly keyed-up. 'Take me up to her room, will you?'

He followed the housekeeper along the corridor, up a broad, winding staircase to a second, narrower corridor on the second story. At the first white door on the left Mrs. Abingworth stopped.

'This it?' The housekeeper nodded. Meredith rapped sharply on the door and called out to ask if Mrs. Rother were inside. He listened. No answer. He banged hard with his fist and called out a second time. Still no answer.

'Oh dear, surr! Oh dear me, surr!' fluttered Mrs. Abingworth, already on the verge of tears. 'What can it mean? I hope as nothing–'

'We must break in the door,' cut in Meredith. 'Stand back a moment, and for heaven's sake don't get flustered.'

Exerting all his strength, Meredith put his shoulder to one of the upper panels. He was unable to

167

move it.

'Got a coal-hammer downstairs? You have? Then trot down and fetch it. I'll get my man from the car.'

Returning with Hawkins, just as Kate Abingworth came breathlessly up the stairs portering a large coal-hammer, Meredith snatched it from her, swung it back and brought it down with a crash on the panel above the lock. There was a rending of splintered woodwork and half the panel caved in, leaving a large gap through which the whole of the room was visible. Wasting no time on conjecture Meredith stuck in his head and took a quick look round. The room was empty!

'Maybe she's hung herself in that cupboard, sir!' exclaimed Hawkins. 'Like that old gal we found out at—'

'Shut up, you fool!' snapped Meredith with a warning glance in Kate Abingworth's direction. 'If you want to help, act, not think.'

He followed up this sensible piece of advice with a practical example, stretching down his hand inside the door to turn the key in the lock. Then he received a shock. There was no key!

'Good God!' Meredith ejaculated. 'This door's been locked on the outside. She's taken the key with her. Here, take this hammer and break the lock. I want to get into that room and quick!'

But once inside the room Meredith's belief that the girl had flitted received substantiating evidence. The bed and floor were littered with odd garments, shoes, tissue paper, and discarded coathangers. It was obvious, at a glance, that only a few hours before Janet Rother had been up in that room feverishly packing. And the reason for that? Meredith smiled to himself. Here was undeniable evidence of that clever young lady's guilt.

As he and Hawkins were making a thorough search of the room, Meredith was thinking: 'Well – what the devil am I to do now? I don't reckon we've got enough evidence against that young woman to demand a warrant for her arrest. Dead sure the Chief would be against it. No – it looks as if we've got to trace her whereabouts and then keep her in sight until we *do* know enough to arrest her.'

Already his mind was busy at the job of working out a plan of campaign. General inquiries in the vicinity to find out if anybody had seen her leaving that morning. A 'phone-call to the Yard for them to interview those London solicitors. A description of the missing girl to be included in *Police Orders*. A watch on the ports to see if she left the country.

He could not for the life of him bring himself to believe that she had just slipped off to visit friends. One doesn't pack in secret and leave the house without a word of farewell or any indication of one's destination, unless one is desirous of doing a vanishing act. No – Janet Rother hadn't just left for a week's stay with the Littlehampton aunt!

'Anything of interest, Hawkins?'

'Nothing, sir.'

Meredith turned to Kate Abingworth who, for the last five minutes, had been 'Oh dear-ing' all over the room and generally putting herself on the one spot where she was not wanted.

'I'd like you to keep quiet about this for the

moment. Understand? I'll let Mr. Barnet know what has happened and put him in charge of the arrangements up here. Mind you,' he added reassuringly, 'there's probably a perfectly simple explanation for Mrs. Rother's departure. Don't forget that she was overwrought after all she'd been through during these last few days. So, for heaven's sake, don't upset yourself, Mrs. Abingworth. Ten to one we'll have your mistress back in this house, safe and sound, within twelve hours. Unless, of course, she's just slipped off on a visit.'

But Kate Abingworth refused to be comforted.

'It's no good, surr. You can't fool an old woman such as I. I *knows* that we shall never see Mrs. Rother again. There's a Hand on this family. You mark what I'm saying – a Hand of Evil. Its shadow has fallen athwart this house as sure as my name's Kate Abingworth. First Mister John, then Mister Willum, and now–'

'Look here,' broke in Meredith with a filial smile, 'suppose you pop downstairs and make us a cup of tea, eh? You could do that, couldn't you? And mind,' he added, 'no more worrying or I'll take you off to the station. Get that?'

A little less tearful and prophetic, the house-keeper went down into the kitchen, where a little later the two men joined her in a cup of tea. When they left the farmhouse for Lychpole, the good-hearted old dame had already regained some of her natural liveliness. The shadow of the Hand seemed to have receded a little.

Aldous Barnet was sitting out in his thatched summerhouse, engaged on his latest novel, when Meredith came out to him across the lawn. He

170

was obviously disturbed by the news which Meredith brought, at a complete loss as to why Janet Rother had gone, and quite unable to suggest her destination. He gave Meredith one or two addresses, including that of her solicitors, but he was inclined to agree with the Superintendent that there was something more behind her disappearance than a simple desire for a change of air. He promised to deal with matters up at Chalklands should Janet fail to materialize. Save for the Littlehampton aunt he knew of no relatives, either of the Rothers' or Janet's, who could be called upon to help. He suggested that Mrs. Abingworth should be sent to her married sister at Arundel, and the house, for the time being, shut up. Meredith concluded their talk by promising to keep in touch with him as the new investigations proceeded.

Back in Lewes, Meredith spent the rest of the day putting in motion the vast machinery of police routine, a tiring and uninteresting occupation, but an essential one if Janet Rother's whereabouts were to be discovered. By nightfall only one stimulating piece of information had come in. The Yard officials had interviewed the Rothers' solicitors and, though they had been reticent over Janet's affairs, the police had elucidated the following facts: (1) William Rother had left everything unconditionally to his wife; (2) This legacy now included all monies and estates left to William by his brother; (3) Mrs. Rother had instructed them to realize all money invested by her brother-in-law in industrials. This, the solicitors affirmed, could not be done in a moment as there was quite a lot of legal work to be undertaken before Mrs. Rother could benefit by her husband's will. Her signature would be required for several of the documents and instructions had been left that all correspondence dealing with this matter was to be forwarded, poste restante, to a post office in Kensington High Street. The Yard were taking the precaution of having the post office watched for the next few days in case Janet Rother should turn up. They were not sanguine of results, however, as it would be a simple matter for the girl to send somebody else to collect her letters. They might be able to shadow a confederate to an address – on the other hand they might not. It was not easy in Town.

'About that money she's withdrawing from the industrials,' asked Meredith over the 'phone, 'any idea how her solicitors are handing it over to her?'

'Yes – in pound treasury notes.'

'How much?'

'About ten thousand pounds.'

'What!'

The voice at the other end of the wire burst into laughter. 'Yes – I know. Struck us as rummy, too. Sounds a bit cumbersome, doesn't it? But it's suggestive.'

'You think so?'

'Yes. It looks as if your lady friend is anxious to clear out of the country, and pound notes are more difficult to trace than those of larger denominations. She's got her head screwed on the right way, hasn't she?'

'Somebody behind her, I reckon,' said Meredith. 'She's only the tool. It's the brains of the partnership we're anxious to lay our hands on. You find the girl for us and we ought to be half-way to finding the man.'

'Do our best.'

'Thanks. That all? Cheerio!'

And the problem of Janet Rother's whereabouts occupied the whole of the Superintendent's time for the next week. He was here, there, and every-where, making inquiries, taking down statements which led nowhere, instigating spurts of local police routine, checking reports, 'phoning, writ-ing, cursing. But of no avail. At the end of the week he had learnt precisely nothing. Janet Rother, like Prospero's spirit actors, had melted into air, into thin air. He felt depressed, worried, and ready to kick himself.

Evidence, he thought. He had shoals of evi-dence. Bags of it. Too much evidence. Yet some-how the key-word to the puzzle was still missing. It looked now as if in the long course of his investigations he had failed to register the vital clue. Just one small oversight, perhaps, and the three cases were at a standstill. He was ready to believe now that once the mystery of John Rother's murder was solved, the second murder and Janet's disappearance would, *ipso facto*, be solved as well. The three cases were so closely knit together and the common denominator was – surely? – the Cloaked Man. It was imperative, Meredith de-cided, to turn back the clock for a couple of months and begin a new phase of his investigation by finding out something about John Rother's week-ends away from home. He must pay a visit to Tim Thornton.

Was it possible that this slender clue, brought to light by a chance conversation, was the equivalent to the key-word in the cipher? In any case it seemed to be his one remaining hope. If this line of inquiry failed then he might as well get ready to write 'Unfinished Case' as a footnote to all his laborious investigations.

CHAPTER 12

THE MAN WITH THE PSYCHIC EYE

Tim Thornton, the proprietor of the Riverside Service Station, was what is commonly called 'a character'. He had personality, a naturally funny face, 'the gift of the gab', and plenty of time to air his original views on things and people. It was a habit of his to assert that he was rushed off his feet and then stay talking to an acquaintance for the best part of an hour. The older inhabitants of the scattered cottages and bungalows round about the toll-bridge looked upon the Service Station as a kind of debating club. With time to kill they drifted up the road to the garage, sat about on oil drums, lit their little blackened pipes under large notices which prohibited smoking, spat to left and to right, and gossiped with Tim Thornton. In this manner Thornton knew pretty well everything which was said, thought, and done in the locality.

The rumour that John Rother had been in the habit of garaging his car at Thornton's drew the old men like a magnet. The proprietor was hard put to it, enlarging and decorating on his contacts with the murdered man, for he had an inborn sense of the dramatic and sensational.

'You take it from me, Ned, the moment I set eyes on the chap I said to myself, "There walks a man with death in his pocket." A doomed look he had – a terrible fear in his glance. Fair gave me the jim-jams when I talked with him. Mark you – he looked 'ealthy. To an ordinary chap like you, Ned, he would have seemed just like Tom, Dick, or 'Arry. But I've got what they call a psychic eye. Fact, Ned – when I looks hard at a thing – same as I might look at you now – I see right into it. It's just a natural gift. Nothing to boast about. Like a natural capacity for drinking beer.

'Well, when this poor fellow stepped out of his car the first time I saw him, something in me went click. My cylinders missed a couple of strokes as you might say. You see, my psychic eye had got going with a jerk and I knew that I was face to face with a chap 'oo's number was already chalked up on the celestial slate. Course, being a man of tack, I didn't let 'im see that I *knew*. "Garridge for the week-end, sir?" I ses. "That's O.K. with me. Just shove 'er" – meaning his Hillman – "over in that corner." But as he turned and walked away from the garridge I said to myself, "That chap's got a stick of dynamite tucked in his trousis – his bucket's been placed ready for 'im to kick." But just an ordinary-looking chap like you, Ned – not the sort of cove you'd look at twice – that is, unless, like me, you've got a psychic eye.'

It was natural that after a week of this sort of

thing other people should have recognized John Rother wandering about the district. Everybody discussed him. Old newspapers were dragged out of coal-sheds and the case re-examined from a more personal angle. The good folk who lived about the toll-bridge began to adopt a proprietary air toward the murdered man. Tim Thornton's stock soared to unimaginable heights.

It was into this highly charged atmosphere that Meredith descended one Monday morning toward the end of August. Although himself in mufti, Hawkins was in uniform, and the sight of the little shining police car drawn up by the Riverside petrol-pumps caused a major sensation. And when Meredith retired with Tim Thornton into the latter's adjacent bungalow, Jake Ferris, who had been passing the time of the day at the garage, tip-tapped up the road and spread the news abroad. By midday the whole hamlet knew that the police were investigating in the district. Small boys and girls, released from school, stole twenty minutes from their luncheon hour to congregate outside Tim's bungalow and stare with hungry eyes at Hawkins in the police car.

Inside the bungalow Meredith was wrestling with a witness who knew, not too little, but too much. Tim Thornton recognized that his chance had come at last and he was prepared to spread himself. This conversation might in time pass into the annals of criminal history.

'There are two points on which I want you to be dead sure,' Meredith was saying. 'First that it was John Rother and second that the car was Rother's Hillman. If you're hazy on either of these points, then quite honestly, Mr. Thornton, you can't be of any help to us. Well?'

'Well.' Tim Thornton took a big, big breath. 'Well, you see, it was like this – one Saturday afternoon just as I was going to grease a back axle of the butcher's van, a shortish, red-faced–'

'What date was this?'

Thornton tailed off, stared at Meredith in surprise and made ready to continue his interrupted narrative. He was unused to interruption.

'Well, as I was saying a shortish, red-faced–'

'But I must have some idea of the date,' persisted Meredith. 'Was it last year, last month, yesterday, or when?'

Thornton eyed the Superintendent with a sly grin.

'It couldn't have been yesterday now, could it? He's been dead over a month.' Thornton winked. 'You police chaps and your tricks. Trying to catch me out like that.'

'All I want is some idea of the date when you first saw this man,' demanded Meredith impatiently.

'About eighteen months ago, I reckon. Let's see now, I had the 'flu that February and this would be about a month later. Toward the end of that March it would be when I first saw 'im.'

'Good. Well?'

'Well – now where the jimmy was I? All these interruptions put me off my stroke. Oh, I reckerlect – in comes a shortish, red-faced man in a Hillman car. And the moment I set eyes on 'im something inside me went click. You wouldn't believe what it was, so I'll tell you, Sergeant. It was my psychic eye sort of getting into its stride. I ought to have explained at the starting-post that I *'av* a psychic eye. I can sort of see through things same as an X-ray sees through flesh and–'

'Now suppose, before we go any further, you give me a more concise idea of this man's appearance. How old was he, for example?'

'No chicken.'

'Quite, but that means he might be anything from forty to a hundred. You must try and be more precise, Mr. Thornton.'

'O.K., Sergeant. I should say he was about forty, then.'

'Shortish, you say, and red-faced. Any other peculiarity?'

'Yes–'is eyes. He had a terrible look of fear in 'is eyes. "Tim Thornton," I ses to myself, "this here chap carries a stick of dynamite in 'is trousis." Meaning, of course–'

'Look here,' rapped out Meredith sharply, though inwardly tickled by the man's flow of speech, 'you must keep to the plain facts. How was he usually dressed?'

'Plus fives, as I called 'em, on account of their extra bagginess round the knees. Sort of sporting outfit – brownish usually. Though once or twice I seem to remember he wore flannel trousis.'

'That's the kind of information I'm after,' beamed Meredith with approval. 'How did he speak?'

'Nice enough. None of this haw-haw stuff, but he was a gentleman right enough, if that's what you mean.'

Meredith pulled a packet of photographs out of

178

his pocket and spread them out on the hearthrug at his feet.

'Do you recognize the chap among those?'

Thornton quizzed the collection for a moment and then selected one of the photos.

'That's 'im,' he announced triumphantly. 'You can see what I mean about his eyes. A sort of doomed look as if he already 'eard the 'arps tuning up for his reception. Course my psychic eye took that in as quick as–'

'Well, that's John Rother right enough,' broke in Meredith. 'That's the first point settled. Now you told Mr. Clark that you recognized the car by two brass-headed nuts. How are you so sure that it was the same Hillman?'

'Because I put those nuts on myself one week-end. The battery-clamps on that particular make are usually secured with black nuts, see? I didn't happen to have any handy – so I fixed him up with a couple of makeshifts. His own had worked loose and one of 'em had dropped off.'

'I see. How often did Mr. Rother garage his car here?'

'Pretty near every week-end during the summer months. In the winter not so regular. Sometimes he didn't turn up for a month or more.'

'When was the last time you saw him?'

'Shall I ever forget it, Sergeant! I tell you the psychic flux – that's a technical expression which you wouldn't properly understand – the psychic flux was strong on me that afternoon. It wrung my withers to see the poor chap so cheerful and innocent of the doom which 'ung over his head. I could see death staring out of his eyes. It was all I

179

could do to preserve my usual tack and hold back from tipping him the wink. You see, when a chap's ticketed like no amount of warning can turn aside what's coming to 'im. Terrible thought, isn't it? How would you feel, for instance, if I saw death in your eyes and prophesied that, soon or late, you'd be stretched out in a car-smash? Ghastly, eh?'

'I should take to a bicycle,' laughed Meredith.

'Maybe – but you can't cheat fate. I tell you it isn't all beer and skittles having a psychic eye. I felt sorry for that chap. I did straight, Sergeant.'

'Which brings us back,' said Meredith firmly, 'to the question I asked. When did you last see John Rother?'

'Let's see now – it was about a fortnight after I'd had a touch of asthma. That would make it early July. I reckon the last time he garridged his car here was the second week-end in July.'

'Was he always alone?'

'Always. Never had a bird with 'im. He didn't look that sort anyhow.'

'When he left the garage where did he go?'

'Now that's a funny point,' began Thornton, taking another big, big breath. 'I used to wonder that myself. You see, he used to take a little suit-case out of the car and walk off up the road in the direction of the toll-bridge. There I lost sight of him, because he used to turn to the right along the river-bank and make off up the Steyning road. Now, a lot of the old chaps round here, having nothing to do, come up to the garridge and stand about gossiping. Makes a chap wild when he's rushed off his feet as I am. But I learnt a thing or two from these old wind-bags. "This here John

Rother," I ses a couple of days ago to Jake Ferris, "where do you think he stayed over the weekends? Major Codd's?" "Not on your life," ses Jake, "I seen him come regular by my cottage a Saturday afternoon and I live beyond the Major's gate," ses Jake. Well, what with talking to one and another, it seemed that Rother walked a tidy way up the Steyning road and then disappeared. Just seemed to melt away. Funny, eh? Sort of sunk into the ground like a drop of water on a hot day.'

For the first time since the interview had opened Meredith was really interested. He felt that little glow of increasing satisfaction which normally accompanied the garnering in of unanticipated clues. Here was something definitely unusual and, therefore, of importance.

'You're sure he hadn't just slipped into one of the cottages?'

'Dead sure. Jake's is the last cottage up that road until you come to the outlyings of Bramber.'

'Bramber?'

'Little village this side of Steyning,' explained Thornton. 'Got a bit of a castle there and a museum of natural freaks – ducks with three legs, lambs with two tails, a calf with a couple of heads and so on. Oddities.'

'Ah – I recall the place now. Perhaps Rother just walked on until he came to the village. When you say he disappeared – what do you mean exactly?'

'Well, there's a bus service plying atween Brighton and Steyning. Most of us fellows here know the chaps what work the route, see? So Jake asks out of curiosity, "Ever see a chap with a suit-case walking to Bramber 'bout three o'clock most

Saturday afternoons?" Bill ses, "No, not as I re-members, and I've a pretty good memory too for what I see on the road." He was certain that he never picked up a fare answering to Rother's description. I tell you, Sergeant, he just sort of evaporated.'

'Could he have taken a boat up the river?'

'Impossible. There's not so much as a ship's dinghy moored on that stretch of the Adur. You can take my word for that.'

'Look here,' said Meredith pleasantly, 'I sup-pose you wouldn't care to come along in my car and show me a few of the landmarks?'

'Sure I will,' boomed Thornton heartily. 'I'm up to my eyes in work, but it won't run away if I leave it. I'll just get my 'at and tell the lad that I'm popping up the street for a spell. Join you out by the pumps.'

A couple of minutes later Hawkins had swung the car round in the road and started for the toll-bridge. There he turned sharp right as directed and droned along a fairly wide road which ran parallel to the left bank of the river. [A railway has been omitted here in order to simplify this part of Meredith's investigation – J.B]. At first there were a few cottages bordering the right of the road, with an occasional larger house set back in its own grounds and approached by a drive. Half a mile ahead, however, the last habitation had been left behind and the road pursued its lonely course along the foot of gently rising downland.

Thornton jerked a thumb at the highest of the grassy hummocks.

'Thundersbarrow 'Ill,' he announced.

Meredith nodded and ordered Hawkins to draw in to the side of the road. They were then about a quarter of a mile from Jake Ferris' cottage.

'According to you, Mr. Thornton, he must have performed his disappearing trick somewhere about here, eh?'

'You've said it, Sergeant. You can just see the roof of Jake's cottage back there round the bend.'

Meredith stepped out of the car and made a long and careful survey of the locale. On his right, bare as a bone, the downs offered not the slightest suggestion of cover. There were one or two scattered farmhouses and barns higher up, but a man approaching them would have been conspicuous for miles. On his left a steep, wooded embankment sloped to the river, which Meredith could see gleaming through the over-hanging branches of willow and alder. Thick undergrowth rioted beneath the taller bushes and trees, forming a perfect retreat for anybody who did not wish to be seen from the road. It seemed pretty obvious to Meredith that if Rother had suddenly vanished then he must have vanished in this particular direction. But what was the point? Even if this brambly undergrowth lined the river-bank as far as Bramber, it would have taken Rother hours to have covered the distance, the more so since he was portering a suitcase. Quite apart from the fact that anybody could have noticed him from the road if they had heard the sound of his advance through the dry branches and twigs underfoot.

On the other hand, it was equally certain that he had not spent his week-ends sitting under the bushes by the river. Why had he come to that remote spot? How had he disappeared? Were these strange week-ends connected with the motive for his subsequent murder? Had some blackmailer got his talons into him? Had he been murdered because, driven to desperation, his blackmailer had threatened exposure?

'I should like to meet this chap Ferris and anybody else that you think could give me any information,' Meredith said to Thornton. 'Will you show me around?'

'Sure,' said Thornton.

But Jake Ferris and the other cottage dwellers along the roadside could do little to solve the mystery. Ferris upheld that he had often noticed Rother passing his windows on a Saturday afternoon. He had also seen him returning about nine o'clock on a Sunday night on his way to Thornton's garage. Thornton declared that Rother usually called in for his car between nine and ten on Sunday evening. Yes – he always carried that suitcase. On one occasion Ferris had watched him walking up the road toward Bramber. The man had turned once or twice and looked back over his shoulder, as if suspicious of the fact that he was being watched. Ferris had eventually lost sight of him round a bend in the road. Other cottagers corroborated Jake's evidence. But that was all. Meredith was disappointed.

'What's the name of the bus service which covers this route?' he asked Thornton as they drove back to the garage.

'South Downland,' replied Thornton.

'Headquarters?'

'Station Road, Brighton.'

'Thanks, Mr. Thornton. Very kind of you to waste so much of your valuable time. I'm hoping your information may lead us somewhere.'

'Justice,' orated Tim Thornton. 'That's all I want. An eye for an eye and a tooth for a tooth. They're my sentiments in a nutshell. You can't go against fate, but you can level things up with, what might be called, Fate's Travelling Representative. The moment I saw that poor devil come into my garage something inside me went click. To an ordinary chap it's difficult to explain – but, as I said before, I've got a psychic–'

But Meredith was already waving an arm of farewell from a hundred yards up the road.

'Left at the toll-bridge,' he ordered Hawkins. 'I want to go to Brighton.'

CHAPTER 13

THE MAN IN THE SUN-GLASSES

Pending the discovery of Janet Rother, Meredith was decidedly interested in this new phase of his investigations. He was now approaching the first murder, not from the viewpoint of what had happened after John Rother's death, but from the more hazy viewpoint of what had happened before. He was trying, in fact, to forge a link between John and the Cloaked Man. That these strange week-ends might have something to do with his

185

subsequent death was already a strong possibility. Here was a man disappearing, it seemed, for nearly two days out of the seven, with nobody so far able to suggest where he had been. Barnet had been led to believe that John visited friends at Brighton, but surely that idea was now discredited? Instead of continuing along the road which eventually ran into that popular resort, Rother had parked his car in a garage and set off on foot in the direction of Steyning. Why? Another woman, other than his brother's wife? But surely Rother could have arranged a less conspicuous way of approaching her?

A second explanation was that of blackmail. Perhaps Rother was being forced to make weekly contacts with some scoundrel who had him under his thumb, in order to pay the various instalments of his 'silence' money. But again it seemed a very thoughtless method of approach when his one idea would be to keep the thing hushed up.

Whatever the explanation for his actions, thought Meredith, it was dead certain that Rother was up to some sort of secret business. For one thing he had deliberately misled Barnet and the others up at Chalklands by suggesting that these week-ends were spent in Brighton. It seemed pretty obvious now that they were not – at least not wholly.

Again, according to the evidence of all the cottagers along the river-side road, Rother had been last seen walking on the way to Bramber or Steyning. Now, Meredith knew from a study of his road-map that there was a far more direct route from Washington to those particular villages. It ran along round the broad base of Chanctonbury Ring and was a mere matter of four miles or so. Instead of taking this obvious route Rother had elected to make a detour through Findon, Sompting, and Lancing, a journey covering at least fifteen miles. Now, if Rother wanted to reach either Bramber or Steyning without people knowing, it was certain that he wouldn't have taken the shorter route because of the danger of being recognized by persons who lived in the locality. Again, since he had hinted at Brighton, it was up to him to preserve the illusion by starting off along the Brighton road. But it still remained for Meredith to put forward a likely reason for these week-ends over which Rother was so mysteriously reserved.

One point struck Meredith at once. Important, as he saw it. Perhaps a vital clue in his hoped-for solution of the crimes. The blood-stained cloak and the broad-brimmed hat had been found by that child at a spot on the downs above Steyning itself. In other words, after John Rother had been battered to death, the unknown man had made straight tracks in the Bramber-Steyning direction. This fact, coupled with Rother's strange appearance over week-ends in that same district, surely was suggestive of two further important facts. One – that the Cloaked Man probably lived in one of the villages named. Two – that Rother had visited him there in secret. These two facts were in a way interdependent on each other. Prove the validity of one fact and the other was proved valid as a matter of course. Meredith decided that it might be profitable to pursue a few inquiries in

Bramber and Steyning, to see if Rother had been recognized there any Saturday or Sunday.

In the meanwhile he had better follow up Thornton's evidence by cross-questioning the men who worked the Brighton-Steyning bus route.

Meredith had little difficulty in finding the headquarters of the South Downland Omnibus Co. Their premises occupied an imposing frontage in Station Road at Brighton and the interior of the vast garage was crowded with the familiar blue-and-cream buses.

After a short wait Meredith got in touch with the manager, explained the reason for his visit, and asked for a word with the men on that particular route.

The manager glanced up at the garage clock.

'Well, they're not due in for another ten minutes, but if you care to wait–'

'Thanks. I will. How many men are employed on that run?'

'Only two,' explained the manager. 'It's a shuttle-service. One bus. Brown's the name of the driver and Gill's his mate. We don't find it necessary to run a shift as the service is not particularly frequent. The men get plenty of time for rest and meals in between their journeys.'

'And you make no change over the week-ends?'

'Not as a rule. Only when the men's annual holiday makes it necessary.'

'I see. Thanks. Now don't you worry about me. I'll potter around until the bus comes in.'

In less than ten minutes the single-decker swung in through the gigantic sliding-doors and came to a standstill. The two men were just climbing down when Meredith crossed over and intercepted them. He stated his business with his usual conciseness and began his cross-examination.

'Now what about your Saturday afternoon runs? Are you anywhere near the toll-bridge round about three o'clock?'

Brown, the driver, nodded.

'Yes – we're scheduled to reach the cross-roads there at 3.25.'

'Arriving at Bramber?'

'Three-forty-three to be exact.'

'Now from the description I gave you just now can either of you swear to having seen this man Rother on the road at any point between the toll-bridge and Bramber between the times you mentioned?'

'No,' said Brown after a moment's thought. 'I for one can't say I have.'

'And you?'

Gill, the conductor, shook his head.

'Nor me. Chaps out that way have been talking, too, so I've had plenty of time to think the matter over. I reckon, too, that if that fellow Rother *was* on the road at that time I should have noticed him. Particular if he was carrying a suitcase. 'Tisn't often you get a chap in plus-fours walking along a lonely road with a suit-case, is it? See my point?'

'Exactly,' agreed Meredith with a nod of approval. 'Now, since you're an observant chap, tell me this, have you ever picked up a regular fare at any point along that stretch of road on a Saturday afternoon?'

Gill pondered the question carefully and then said tentatively: 'Well, there's that queer old josser

189

who often gets on outside the Cement Works, eh, Jim?'

Brown enlarged: 'Yes – there is 'im, of course. Though I don't see that he'd be of any interest to the Superintendent here. Mild little fellow. Wouldn't 'urt a fly.'

Meredith, always on the alert for even the remotest clue, pricked up his ears.

'Don't you worry – *any* bit of evidence, however slight it may seem to you, may be of use to us. I'd like to hear more about this old fellow. Well?'

'Well,' began Gill glibly, 'we've often picked this chap up as I say on a Saturday. I noticed him particular because he was unlike the ordinary run of folk that we get on that route. Learned sort of bloke, I should say. He always wears one of them old-fashioned Norfolk jackets what I used to wear as a kid. Tight sort of breeches, too, such as you don't often see these days. More often than not he'd be carrying a couple of musty-looking books under his arm, which he'd read in the bus. But his eyes must have been weak because he'd hold the print only a couple of inches or so from his nose. Wore a pair of them tinted sun-glasses, too. Not a talkative gent by any manner of means. Just an exchange about the weather, that's all I'd get out of him. Sometimes he had a butterfly-net with him and a sort of little case slung on a strap over his shoulder. Naturalist we reckoned he was, didn't we, Jim?'

As Gill's description evolved Meredith's interest had quickened to a rare excitement. The very queerness of the character which Gill had so accurately pictured was enough to arouse his suspicions. The old-fashioned garments, the books, the butterfly-net, the tinted glasses, the old chap's obvious dislike of conversation – these facts cried aloud to a man who had spent half his life in dealing with crime. The implication was obvious.

He rapped out: 'These Cement Works – where are they exactly?'

'About a mile and a half outside Bramber.'

'Any houses near?'

'None.'

'Then where do you reckon the old chap came from?'

'Ah,' said Brown, 'that's just it. I asked Fred here the same question, but when we saw the butterfly-net we thought he must have walked down off the hills.'

'Where did he get out?'

'Bramber.'

'Ever pick him up during the winter?'

'Once or twice – yes.'

Meredith laughed. 'He must have found it pretty nippy up on the downs round about Christmas, eh?'

'By George – that *is* a point!' exclaimed Gill. 'Where did he come from in the winter? Never thought of that.'

'Ever take him back about eight or nine on a Sunday night?' asked Meredith, hammering out his questions now as fast as he could think.

The two men looked at each other and nodded.

'You did?' snapped Meredith, barely able to control his immense elation. 'Pick him up again in Bramber?'

'Yes.'

191

'And dropped him?'

'As before – at the Cement Works.'

'Excellent!' exclaimed Meredith, unable to keep the broad grin off his face. 'I don't mind telling you men that you've handed out the biggest chunk of useful information which has come my way since I started this darned investigation. You've given me a whole heap to think about. There's just one other point – I suppose you never noticed if this old chap was ever met by anybody when he got off the bus in Bramber?'

'Never,' said Gill. 'Certain of it.'

'Well,' said Meredith briskly, 'I won't take up any more of your lunch-hour. I'd just like to jot down a full description of this man in my notebook while it's fresh in my memory and I'd like to have your private addresses for future reference. Now let's see if I've got it right? Norfolk jacket,' he wrote. 'Tight old-fashioned breeches. Stockings, I suppose? Yes. Hat? Panama in summer. Thanks. Soft tweed hat in winter. Good. Tinted sunglasses. Any beard or moustache? Grey droopy moustaches. Excellent. Shortish with a slight stoop. Broad-shouldered. Well, I think that's fairly – here, half a moment though. Did you happen to notice if the colour of his hair matched his moustaches? I see. You didn't because his hat covered the whole of his head. Well, that's just what I wanted. You've helped a lot.' Meredith held out his hand. 'Lucky for us that some people don't go about the world with their eyes closed. Good-day.'

Meredith strode quickly to where Hawkins was waiting with the car and vaulted lightly into the seat.

'Lunch! And step on it, Hawkins. There's a good place down on the front. We're going to celebrate.'

'Good news, sir?'

'Headline stuff, m'lad.'

'Somebody going to swing for it, sir?'

'Don't be so blasted morbid, Hawkins – you'll spoil my appetite. No – we're not as far as that yet, but, by Jove, we're on the way – we're well on the way!'

So that was why John Rother had disappeared? Simple, of course. Obvious now that it was the only really plausible explanation, but like a good number of plausible explanations obvious only because certain facts had been thrust under his nose. Half a mile from the toll-bridge John Rother vanishes. A mile and a half from Bramber a broad-shouldered, shortish naturalist with tinted sun-glasses suddenly appears on the road. And if that wasn't suggestive then Meredith didn't know the meaning of the word. Gill's precise description shrieked aloud of disguise. It was curious how people were inclined to overdress when called upon to play the false part in a dual-role. Those dark glasses, for example, the musty books. Yes, thought Meredith, poor old Rother had rather underlined his mild but untalkative bug-hunter. He had been artful but not quite artful enough. Unlike a true artist, he had not learnt what to leave out.

'It may interest you to know, Hawkins,' said Meredith over their excellent lunch, 'that Rother seems to have been acting a double rôle before he met that packet of trouble under Cissbury.'

'John or William, sir?'

'John. It appears he had a rendezvous of some sort with an unknown person in the village of Bramber. He used to visit the place during weekends disguised as a naturalist. Question is – why did he find it necessary to take such a precaution? What sort of shady business was he mixed up in?'

'Counterfeiting. Illicit distilling. Blackmail. Women,' recited Hawkins with the glibness of one familiar with all and every sort of crime. 'Probably women, sir.'

'Bit near home for that kind of thing, surely?' argued Meredith. 'I reckon somebody must have had a hold over our friend Rother, otherwise he wouldn't have risked walking about in disguise only five miles or so from Chalklands. I still uphold that he was being blackmailed by the man in the cloak. Question is – why was he being blackmailed?'

'Women,' said Hawkins promptly.

Meredith laughed.

'You've got a one-track mind, my boy. Not that I disagree with you. How about this for a theory? X – that is the man in the cloak – knew something pretty intimate about his relationship with Janet Rother. He threatened to tell his brother, William. John gets the wind up and, like so many of his kidney, starts putting his hand in his pocket. X suggests that John shall make contact with him at Bramber, as he naturally refuses to divulge his own address or receive anything incriminating through the post. John, fearing to be recognized in the village and frightened of gossip, decides to adopt this somewhat obvious disguise. He may have rented a cottage in Bramber so that X can visit him without causing comment. That we can find out, of course. Eventually fed up with paying out, John threatens to expose X to the police. X arranges a final meeting under Cissbury, perhaps with the promise of handing over some material evidence such as a letter or photograph, and there murders him. How's that, Hawkins?'

'Sounds plausible, sir. How do you reckon he managed to change his clothes after garaging his car at Thornton's?'

'Remember that stretch of road we visited this morning? Well, there was that thick belt of trees lining the riverbank. John had his disguise in that suit-case, of course. All he had to do was to wait until the road was clear, slip into the under-growth, change his things, add the sun-glasses and the moustache, and emerge as a full-blown bug-hunter. His own clothes he packed into the suit-case, which he hid somewhere safe in the undergrowth. He then caught the bus outside the Cement Works, probably working his way through the bushes so that he could reappear some dis-tance from the point where he entered the belt of trees. In this way I expect he thought to prevent the locals from suspecting that the Gentleman in Plus Fours was in any way connected with the Naturalist in the Norfolk Jacket. Successfully, it seems.'

'And where do we go now, sir?'

'Lewes,' said Meredith with a twinkle in his eye. 'We may as well end our celebrations by taking a half-day off. Any objections?'

Hawkins grinned.

'Yes, sir – my young lady has her day off on

Thursday. You couldn't put off celebrating until then, I suppose.'

'Much as I should like to – I cannot! Waiter – the bill, please.'

CHAPTER 14

BROOK COTTAGE

The little village of Bramber, although it boasts a castle, a railway station, a river, and a museum, is not exactly a lively place. A certain amount of traffic passes down its main street, but the inhabitants themselves, untouched by the contact of 'furriners', continue to live inside that limited circle which transcribes all real village life. Miss Kingston, at the post-office, would have considered herself cheated if she had not been able to discuss everybody's business as well as her own. Her shop (the post-office only occupied one corner of it) was the accepted clearing-house of local gossip. Over the purchase of a three-halfpenny stamp Miss Kingston got to know a great deal about George Putt's lumbago, Mr. Sullington's infidelities, and Mrs. Aldwick's latest confinement. People not only went to the post-office to impart knowledge; they also went there to learn. And on Tuesday, August 17th, Superintendent Meredith, in search of just that kind of information which the post-mistress purveyed, found himself in close conference with this voluble spinster.

He was still puzzled by the new facts which had come to light, but, so far, he had seen no reason to advance any other theory than that which he had put before Hawkins the day before. And if, as he suspected, John Rother was being blackmailed, then his immediate job was to find out if the locals knew anything about the naturalist or his mysterious visitor. It seemed fairly certain that in so small a parish the presence of two strangers over the week-ends would have been noted. It was possible, of course, that the Cloaked Man actually lived in Bramber – perhaps, to all outward appearances, a perfectly respectable and respected member of the little community. If this were the case, then it might prove more difficult to extract information about him for the simple reason that his movements and actions would not be commented on as those of a complete stranger. He decided, therefore, to tackle the post-mistress first about this studious Mr. Reed, who arrived most Saturday afternoons by the 3.43 bus from Brighton.

Meredith hung about looking at a postcard stand until he and Miss Kingston had the shop to themselves. The moment they were alone he began briskly: 'Excuse me, Miss–?'

'Kingston,' beamed the post-mistress through her pince-nez.

'Ah, yes, Miss Kingston. I've come along to see you because I want to ask you a few questions. I'm a police officer – no, nothing to do with you personally – just a little information about a week-end visitor which you may be able to supply. Ever heard of a Mr. Reed?'

From Miss Kingston's sudden change of expression Meredith guessed that Mr. Reed was the one person that she knew all about. A kind of rapacious glint appeared in her watery eyes – the look of an inveterate gossip about to give of her best. Nor was Meredith disappointed. Miss Kingston, in her pseudo-cultured voice which she adopted in the presence of strangers, lowered herself on to the high stool behind the counter to ease her varicose veins, and announced confidentially:

'Oh dear, yes, I know quate a lot about Mr. Jeremy Reed – quate a lot. Not that I have ever set eyes on the gentleman myself – from all accounts he lakes to keep himself to himself – a recluse as I always say. But one can't help hearing things – I mean even the nacest people talk, don't they? He stays here quate often over the week-ends in Brook Cottage, which I understand he has bought. An elderly gentleman, so they say, with weak eyes. I believe he is wrating a book on British moths and butterflies and that he lakes to come here because of the quiet. But he never talks to people if he can avoid it and – really this does seem a little strange – he's never bought anything in any of the shops here. How he does for edibles I can't imagine. I suppose he has things sent down from London.

'Of course, between you and I, I don't think he is quate rate in the head – not quate rate, if you understand what I mean? He's eccentric. Wears the queerest attire and shuts himself away in his cottage and won't see anybody! Young Mr. Trigg, our Vicar, called on him I understand, and Mr. Reed just took one look at him and slammed the door in his face. Our melkman called, too, to see if he should leave any melk over the week-ends,

but Mr. Reed treated him in the same rude men-
ner. Of course, he mate have been in the middle
of wrating his book, but it does rather look as if
he is not quate rate in the head, doesn't it? I
mean our Vicar is such a nace, unassuming man.'

'Quate,' murmured Meredith absent-mindedly.
'So, apart from these unfortunate visitors, nobody has really seen Mr. Reed at close quarters
or spoken to him?'

'Except getting on and off the bus – no.'

'Perhaps he has people staying with him sometimes – strangers, eh?'

'Never as far as I know,' protested Miss Kingston in the tone of one ready to defend a slight on
her own knowledge. 'I think I should have heard
if he had. Besides, how could he entertain when
he has nobody to cook for him?'

'Yes, there is that,' mused Meredith. 'And
where is this cottage of his?'

'You go up the street past the castle, take the
first to the rate, and his cottage lies about two
hundred yards up Wate's Lane.'

'Waits Lane,' repeated Meredith with a nod of
thanks.

'No. No. Wate's – W-h-i-t-e-s Lane.'

'Oh, sorry. I see – thanks. And has he been
down lately, Miss Kingston?'

'Oh dear, no. Not for weeks now. Not since early
July. I understand there's a sale-board up in the
garden. We think he must have given up coming
any more.'

'And when did he buy the cottage?'

'About eighteen months ago?'

'Any letters ever come for him during his stay?'

199

'None. Very peculiar, I thought.'

'Very,' answered Meredith dryly. 'Well, you've told me quite a lot about Mr. Jeremy Reed. It's been kind of you to give me your time like this.'

'Oh, not at all. Not at all. I always lake to be of service if I can. Good morning. Good morning.'

Outside, where the police car was drawn up, the local constable was chatting with Hawkins. As Meredith came out he touched his peaked hat.

'Well, sir,' he grinned, 'any use to you?'

'Confirms more or less what you've already told me, Fletcher. She's certain he's had no visitors. Maybe the contacts were made at night.'

'Possible, sir, though I reckon I should have noticed a strange bird flitting around any time after midnight. The village is not exactly crowded in the small hours.'

'She said there was a sale notice up – do you know who the agents are?'

'Forgot to mention it, sir – she's quite right. London firm by the name of Stark and West if I recall aright.'

Meredith nodded.

'I know 'em. Big concern with their main offices in Victoria Street. Believe they have a branch office in Brighton.'

'What are your plans for the moment?' asked Fletcher deferentially. 'Want to see the Vicar, sir?'

'No, I'll leave you to take his statement and that of your local milkman. They won't be able to do more than confirm the description we've already got. In the meantime ... we're going to do a bit of house-breaking.'

'House-breaking? Where, sir?'

'Up at Brook Cottage.'

The cottage, so named because of the stream which formed the end boundary to the garden, stood well back off the road, screened by a tall hedge of quickset. It had a thatched roof with a half-brick, half-weather-board frontage, and a brick path which led up to the porch of the front door. Climbing roses rioted over the lower windows, whilst a ragged vine of clematis dripped from the right wall, beneath which another, narrow path ran round to the back of the house. The garden was unkempt with masses of overgrown grass and foliage so that it was difficult to say where the lawn ended and the flower-borders began. There was, in fact, a general air of untidiness and dilapidation about the place, which suggested that little or no work had been done about the cottage since it had been owned by Mr. Jeremy Reed. Stark & West's sale-board projected over the front hedge.

The three men filed round to the back-yard and ran their eyes over the doors and windows. Hawkins upheld that, if the others gave him a shove up, he could easily get at the latch of one of the upper windows with the longest blade of his pen-knife. The others thereupon hoisted him up so that his head and shoulders were level with the sill. In a short time he called down to say that the catch was free. After one or two attempts Hawkins managed to swing open the window and, after a further series of heave-hos, his wildly kicking legs disappeared through the very limited aperture.

'Cut down to the back door,' ordered Meredith.

'The chances are that it's only bolted on the inside. That'll save us any more acrobatic displays.'

Meredith's expectations were realized, and the next minute the three men stood inside the minute kitchen. Here again there was evidence of neglect, a suggestion that the naturalist had paid only a fleeting interest in his culinary arrangements. A heap of empty tins labelled Fortnum & Mason had been thrown into a corner; the sink was black with dirt; the draining-board littered with an array of unwashed crockery; dust and webs filmed the little window which looked out on to the weedy yard. Proceeding to the two other rooms on the ground floor Meredith noted the same air of muddle and dirtiness. Every article of furniture was thick with a rime of dust, whilst the open fire-place was littered with pipe dottles and cigarette-ends. Books and newspapers had been thrown about on tables and chairs, so that, save for the big leather arm-chair drawn up at the hearth, there was no other available seating accommodation in the tiny sitting-room.

'Strikes me,' observed Meredith dryly, 'that our Mr. Reed didn't worry overmuch about his personal comforts during his week-ends. Never seen such a mess. Just as he left it, I imagine. If ever a place suggested a hide-out ... well...'

Leaving the others to nose about downstairs Meredith climbed the rickety stairway and examined the two bedrooms. In the first was an unmade bed and a further consignment of cigarette-ends. In the second, virtually unfurnished, stood a large oak chest and an iron wash-hand-stand. Glancing from the windows Meredith saw at once that the cottage was quite isolated and was not overlooked from any neighbouring point. There was no hope, therefore, of any other cottager in the vicinity being able to give information about the possible visits of the Cloaked Man. Rother had certainly chosen a fool-proof rendezvous – it rather looked if this slender thread of investigation was going to be snapped off short like so many others in this perplexing and annoying case.

Faced with the actual apparatus of Rother's hide-out, the furniture, the crocks, the empty tins, the cottage itself, Meredith suddenly doubted if his interpretation of Rother's reason for these week-ends was the right one. Wasn't it a trifle elaborate when all he wanted to do was to make contact for a few minutes with his blackmailer? A dark lane, a deserted street in Brighton, the corner of a saloon-bar – surely these seemed more feasible meeting-places on the face of things? What about Hawkins' suggestion – a woman in the case? Meredith shook his head. A woman would never have allowed the cottage to have become so untidy – the kitchen, at any rate, would have reflected the touch of a feminine hand. Then, in heaven's name, what? What the devil had driven Rother to the expediency of adopting a disguise and taking the cottage in a backwater like Bramber? Was there no answer to this problem in the appointments and litter in the place itself? Some clue which might prove the key-word to the cipher?

He went down into the sitting-room again where Hawkins and the constable had been rooting through drawers, turning over the litter, poking their noses into ornaments, and examining

203

every little detail of the parlour.

'Any luck?'

The men shook their heads.

'Nothing so far, sir,' said Fletcher. 'Whatever he was up to here, he seems to have covered his tracks pretty thoroughly.'

Meredith agreed, still wrapped up in his own thoughts, and moved as if by instinct to the fireplace. The remains of a burnt-out fire still littered the hearth. With an absent-minded gesture Meredith began to poke about among the ashes. Suddenly he went down on one knee and let out an involuntary exclamation.

'Huh! What's this?'

The others craned forward over his shoulder.

'Looks like a half-burnt book, sir,' said Hawkins.

Gingerly Meredith withdrew the charred remains from the ashes and turned it over carefully in his hand. Some of the print still being decipherable; he began to read. Then, fired with a sudden increasing interest, he went on reading. For a full minute he crouched there in silence, absorbing the broken sentences of those printed pages. A tiny spark of light flashed in his brain. The light grew brighter.

'But why the devil should this be here in the cottage?' he asked himself. 'It strikes me that Rother wasn't the only one to use this as a hide-out.' He looked up at the others, who were craning over trying to fathom the source of their superior's interest. 'Know what this is, eh?'

'Looks like a sort of price-list,' ventured the Bramber constable.

'You're right, Fletcher – that's exactly what it is.

204

It's a price-list of surgical instruments. As far as I can decipher it's issued by Dawson and Constable of 143 Wigmore Street. Strange finding it here, eh?'

'Has it any bearing on the case, sir?' asked Hawkins.

Meredith smiled.

'Use your brains, m'lad. I've posted you pretty well up to date with all the details of my work, haven't I? Do you remember that remark of old Professor Blenkings about the bones?'

'Good Lord – yes!' exclaimed Hawkins, snapping his finger and thumb. 'Of course. He reckoned that the bones had been sawn through by means of a surgical saw.'

'Exactly. And it looks as if our man ordered his instruments from Dawson and Constable's, doesn't it?'

'But why should it be found in the cottage of the chap that was murdered?' asked Hawkins.

'How the deuce should I know?' retorted Meredith. 'It rather suggests that John Rother did come here to meet the Cloaked Man. Strikes me my blackmail theory is going to hold water after all.' Meredith rose; snatched up a piece of newspaper and carefully wrapped up the flimsy exhibit. 'Well, I don't think we can do much good by hanging on here any longer. You'd better get those statements from the Vicar and the milkman, Fletcher, just to make sure that the various descriptions of Mr. Jeremy Reed tally up. We're going back to headquarters, Hawkins.'

The Superintendent walked down to the car and left the others to lock the place up again. A

205

minute or so later Hawkins, who had bolted the scullery door on the inside and got out through the upper window, climbed into the driving-seat and headed the car for Lewes.

Meredith was deeply puzzled. It seemed certain now that John Rother, alias Jeremy Reed, had been visited at Brook Cottage by the man who was destined to murder him. It was unfortunate, of course, that nobody had caught a glimpse of this sinister visitor. But if he only put in an appearance at night that was perfectly understandable. What really perplexed Meredith was the fact that a little bit of incriminating evidence had been partially destroyed in the very last place that one would expect to find it. Why had the Cloaked Man – assuming that it was he who had visited Rother – chosen to burn the catalogue at Brook Cottage? Did it mean that the murderer had visited the place *after* John Rother's death?

At first Meredith was inclined to dismiss this possibility as being too risky. Then suddenly he remembered something – something he knew about the movements of the Cloaked Man. According to the Hound's Oak shepherd, the stranger had been making for the open down in the direction of Steyning. The little girl had discovered the blood-stained cloak and the broad-brimmed hat on the hills above Steyning. Steyning and Bramber were adjacent villages. Didn't it rather look as if the murderer had made straight tracks for Brook Cottage as soon as it was dark? After all, could there have been a more perfect hide-out? He knew he was safe from interruption there because Rother was already dead. He knew by associating with

206

Rother that the villagers had given up any attempts to visit the cottage. What more God-sent haven could a fugitive have asked for?

And wait a minute! – what about this? Meredith's inward excitement grew as his thoughts flowed faster. Why shouldn't the Cloaked Man have adopted Jeremy Reed's disguise and used the cottage as a hide-out until he could make his arrangements for getting away – probably the night after the second murder had been committed? He could easily have purchased a facsimile outfit, breeches, Norfolk jacket, dark glasses, and everything, and hidden these things previously on the hill-side where he had discarded his cloak. When he had visited John Rother he would have had plenty of opportunity to record every detail of his make-up as Jeremy Reed. Then, if by any unlucky chance anybody had noticed him passing through the village on the night of the first murder, they would merely think it was the eccentric naturalist having a midnight prowl after moths.

This new idea was reassuring. There was a more than plausible ring about it. It meant, of course, the adoption of an earlier theory, that Janet and the Cloaked Man were working hand in hand. It meant that Rother's body had been dissected on a rubber sheet among the gorse bushes. The Hillman driven out to meet Janet on the Findon-Washington road, Janet acting as guide to the Cloaked Man, and the remains being hidden in a metal-lined cabin-trunk somewhere at Chalklands (probably the car inspection-pit) during William's absence on his wild-goose chase to Littlehampton. The Hillman driven back to the spot under

Cissbury, and then the Cloaked Man's flit over the downs to enter Brook Cottage as Jeremy Reed the naturalist. And the motive for the double murder – money? Two people stood between Janet and the Rother fortunes – John and her husband. For some reason Janet was intimately connected with the Cloaked Man and between them they had hatched a terrible plot for the sake of the money. Hence Janet's flit to London and her strange request that the ten thousand pounds should be handed over to her in treasury notes. She had probably joined the Cloaked Man there as soon as possible after the inquest on William – the Cloaked Man himself having gone to London directly after the second murder.

A little more than theory this time, thought Meredith. The facts were beginning to fit in. The case was beginning to take shape. He was on the move again!

CHAPTER 15

THE MYSTERIOUS TENANT

Back in Lewes, Meredith at once inquired whether the Chief Constable could see him. On receiving an affirmative reply he went along the corridor from his own office, rapped on Major Forest's door and went in. The Chief was standing at the window, staring out with his hands clasped behind his back. It was a typical attitude of his when worried or in a black mood.

'Well?' he snapped, without turning round.

'Meredith, sir – I want to have a word with you about the Rother cases.'

'All right. Take a cigarette and sit down. I've wanted to see you. Not satisfied, you know. Things don't seem to be moving. Half a mind to get in the Yard, Meredith. Sorry, but there it is.'

Meredith suddenly felt angry and depressed. Why, dammit, he was doing all that a man could to hasten along results! It was unfair of the Old Man to drag in the Yard to polish off a case that he himself had slaved on for nearly six weeks. But that was often the case – a County chap did all the spade-work and then, just when a glimmer of daylight appeared, the Yard came in and reaped the benefit.

Swallowing down his annoyance, Meredith said politely:

'Sorry you think that's necessary, sir. Particularly as my investigation's on the move again.'

'But is it, Meredith? Is it? That car was found on July 21st. It's now August 27th. It's certainly time something moved. That Horsham case didn't do us any good, you know. You weren't in on that – granted. But this is a newspaper affair. I've got to have results. If you can't get 'em for me, then I've got to turn to the Yard – see?'

'I quite understand, sir. But with this new evidence–'

'Well, let's hear it,' barked the Chief, plumping himself down into his desk-chair. 'I may be able to stave off the evil moment – come on.'

With a careful choice of words Meredith set out,

209

point by point, his final theory about the doings of the Cloaked Man. He stressed the importance of the evidence discovered in Brook Cottage and showed how plausible was the idea that the Cloaked Man, in the disguise of Jeremy Reed, had used the cottage as a hide-out until he had committed the second murder. As he proceeded the worried look on Major Forest's features gradually relaxed, until finally he began to nod and throw in little exclamations of agreement and approval.

'Quite... Quite so... I see that... Yes, of course... Let's see now – how long was it between the two murders?'

'Just on three weeks, sir. William Rother was discovered dead on August 10th.'

'And you suggest that this unknown man hid away in Brook Cottage for three weeks without being discovered. What about food?'

'Well, Rother apparently had an arrangement with Fortnum and Mason's about that. I presume that their deliveries were continued.'

'A point to find out, Meredith.'

'Yes, sir.'

'There's another thing – what about that sale notice?'

'How do you mean?'

'If there was a board up somebody must have got in touch with the agents about the sale of the cottage. Couldn't have been Rother. He was dead. See what I mean?'

'By Jove, sir! I hadn't thought of that. This chap must have visited the agents.'

'Yes – or left the job to Janet Rother.'

'A bit difficult for them to convince the agents

210

that they had the proper authority, surely, sir?'

'Same point went through my mind. It's up to you to find out how they did it.'

'Quite.'

'Pretty obvious, too, that the agents were not approached until somewhere near August 10th.'

'I don't quite–'

'Simple. Our man wouldn't be such a fool as to run the risk of prospective clients wanting to see over the place while he was using it as a hide-out. I reckon he must have got in touch with the agents on the 9th or thereabouts.'

'I'll follow that up as well, sir.'

'Right. I suggest your line of inquiry should be to find out if anybody noticed whether Brook Cottage was occupied during those three weeks. Interview those agents. Find out about the food deliveries. It depends on what sort of report you put in, Meredith, whether I'm justified in keeping out the Yard. Up to you. Understand?'

'Quite, sir. You agree that this is an advance?'

'Certainly – provided it's in the right direction. You know as well as I do that it's only too easy to advance down a sidetrack. We want main-road progress. I don't want to dishearten you, Meredith – but it's only fair to let you know what's in my mind.'

Still feeling a little sore, though somewhat relieved by the Chief's promise to hold off from any immediate action, Meredith went back to Arundel Road for lunch. He had warned Hawkins to have the car ready for him at two o'clock.

Over lunch Tony observed to his father:

'See that bird over at Storrington got a lagging

211

for whizzing those sparklers out of old Rushington's peter, Dad.'

Meredith eyed his son with obvious distaste.

'Good heavens – where did you pick that up?'

'Just read a book, Dad – jolly good yarn – it had all the thieves' lingo in it. To whizz means to steal, you know.'

'Really?' said Meredith dryly, with a lift of his eyebrows.

'Yes – and a peter's a safe.'

'So what you're really trying to tell me,' said Meredith, admirably controlling his inward amusement, 'is that Slippery Sid has got a stretch of penal servitude for stealing Lord Rushington's diamonds from the safe – is that it?'

Tony nodded.

'It was all in today's edition of the *Courier*. Care to see it, Dad?'

Meredith chuckled and shook his head.

'George Hanson cleared up that job, Tony, and since he's done it we've heard nothing else *but* that case up at headquarters. So you can darn' well spare me the newspaper report, see?'

It was Tony's turn to grin and look wise.

'You haven't arrested the chap that murdered William Rother yet, have you, Dad?'

'You know I haven't,' growled Meredith. 'I wish you wouldn't talk shop at meal-times. Eat up your greens!'

'Well, I only *asked*,' was Tony's plaintive explanation. 'You see, Slippery Sid did his job on August the tenth'

'And what of that?'

'That was the night that William Rother was

212

murdered, wasn't it?'

'During the early hours of the tenth – yes,' admitted Meredith.

'Well, you see, Dad, Sid lived in Worthing, so the newspapers said, and he worked that stunt over at Storrington with a bicycle. Chances were that he went through Washington – he couldn't really go any other way, could he? Chances are he may have seen or heard something. Might be able to give you a clue, Dad.'

Meredith looked at Tony sternly and slowly shook his head as if censuring his consuming interest in crime.

'If you knew as much about your job as you do about mine you'd be a first-class Bond Street photographer in a couple of years.'

'Perhaps,' agreed Tony. 'But it *was* a darn good idea of mine, wasn't it?'

'That's just the trouble, m'lad – it's a first-class idea. Worthy of your father in fact. And what's more, Tony, I'm going to follow it up. Sid may be just the witness I was looking for. And now he's jugged he'll speak all right. Probably hope to get a bit off his sentence. Quite smart of you, Tony.'

'Thanks. Oh, by the way, Dad. Green's have got a new five-valve, super-het wireless on display. I wondered if you'd like to–'

'Yes,' said Meredith as he got up and filled his pipe. 'And you can go on wondering.' He glanced at the clock. 'Good heavens, look at the time! I must be off!'

Hastily kissing his wife he walked briskly to the station where Hawkins was already waiting with the car.

'Bramber first and then on to Brighton.'

Back once more in Bramber, for the second time that day, Meredith's run of good luck continued. Accompanied by the local constable, Fletcher, he interviewed all sorts of diverse, unprofitable Bramberites, until finally they ran up against Tom Biggins, the portly landlord of the 'Loaded Wain'. Tom was as round as a barrel, as talkative as a parrot, and as pessimistic as an astronomer in a thick fog. But, as Meredith soon learnt, he had good cause for his pessimism. Tom was a chronic sufferer from insomnia. He had tried everything from counting sheep to a hop-pillow, but all of no avail. Finally in despair he had taken to walking around the countryside during the small hours in the hope of getting a little sleep before it was time to get up and breakfast. And Tom, when questioned by the Superintendent, had noticed more than one odd thing about Brook Cottage.

'Yes – 'bout the end o' July it would be – I was walking up White's Lane making a bit of a round of it – see? And jigger me if I didn't see smoke coming out o' the cottage chimney. Struck me queer like seeing as it was as stuffy a night as we've had this' year. But o' course I knew the ole chap was a bit off his rocker so I didn't think much more to it. Any idea as what 'ee was up to, Sooper?'

Meredith grinned.

'Burning something, I expect – where there's smoke there's fire, you know.' He was thinking of that charred catalogue and wondering. 'Can you fix the date a trifle more closely, Mr. Biggins?'

'Easy. I marked that particular night down in

my diary as being the hottest so far this year. Half a jiffy – I'll fetch it outa my other suit.'

In a short time Tom Biggins returned with the open diary in his podgy hand.

'Yes – here we are. Last night o'July. Thought I'd made a note of it. Can't sleep a wink on them stuffy nights. 'Orrible.'

'Ever noticed a light in the place?' demanded Meredith, delighted with the new facts he was garnering in.

Tom rubbed his chin and said slowly: 'Well, I have and then again I haven't. Not what you might call a proper light, I haven't. Just a glimmer in an upper room once or twice – same as if a chap was trying to shield a bit o' candle from the road. Blinds down too. But once or twice I saw just a crack of candlelight round the edge o' the blind – see?'

'Any idea of the dates?'

'Luck's out, Sooper. Couldn't say at all for sure.'

'But recently?'

'No – not so recent neither. There hasn't been a sign o' life in the place since about the first week o' August. I reckon I noticed the light somewheres around the end o' last month and the beginning of this.'

'Excellent,' beamed Meredith. 'That's just what I was after. The exact dates don't really matter. Tell me – did you ever see another chap visiting old Jeremy Reed's place in the small hours any time before the middle of July?'

'Can't say I did. You see, Sooper, I didn't start this walking out o' nights until the middle o' last month. Doctor chap told me it might do me

215

good. But it don't. Not a bit. Makes me feel more tired – that's all.'

'Ever seen parcels or crates taken into the cottage at any time during the day?'

'Never that way then,' said Tom curtly. 'Business.'

'Nothing else you've noticed, Mr. Biggins, that might be of interest to me?'

Again Tom rubbed his multitudinous chins.

'Yes – I have,' he wheezed, lowering his voice as he considered appropriate for the delivery of unusual and surprising news. 'One night about the end o' the first week in August I saw a chap wheel a bicycle out o' the cottage gate, mount it and make off in the direction o' Steyning.'

'A bicycle!' exclaimed Meredith eagerly. 'Don't tell me you've forgotten the date, Mr. Biggins. I'll wring your neck if you have! You *must* fix it. It's vitally important. Strikes me you've got just the sort of evidence that I've been praying for. Well?'

'It was the ninth,' said Tom slowly. 'A Friday, I remember. Day of Jerry Hancock's sale up at Beech Farm. Or more rightly,' he hastened to correct himself, 'the tenth. Church clock had struck midnight, you see, just before this chap walks out.'

'Did he see you?'

'Not him. It was a darkish night and I was standing back under the hedge just going to light my pipe.'

'Did you see him? That's more important.'

'Well, as luck would have it – I did. You see, when the chap gets out in the road 'ee gives a quick look round, strikes a match and lights his oil-lamp. Then the darn' thing smokes and 'ee

216

leans down in the rays to have a look-see. Course the lamp was pointing away from me so I got a good look at him.'

'Well?' rapped out Meredith, on tenterhooks.

'Shortish, middle-aged chap with a scrub of a blackish beard. Dressed like a commercial he was – dark coat and starched collar with a black tie, if you take me? Wore a hard hat, which struck me as funny seeing as he was riding a bike. Ar – and there was another thing as I noticed – his left wrist was kind o' bandaged up and looked stiff like. He didn't get up into the saddle none too easy neither.'

'Wasn't wearing dark glasses by any chance, was he?'

'What, in the middle o' the night – not likely!' And Tom Biggins allowed his usually drawn and doleful countenance the comfort of a broad wink.

'You say he made off in the direction of Steyning?'

'Yes – I saw him pedal down to the end o' White's Lane and turn left up the village street.'

'You've never seen the man about before – in the bar here or up the village?'

'Never – a complete stranger to these parts I swear.'

Meredith glanced up at the clock which hung in the bar.

'Look here, Mr. Biggins – we're just going to shut our eyes to the law. Although it's out of hours you're going to have a drink on me and I'm going to join you. What do you say, Fletcher?'

'Mild and bitter, sir,' was the constable's prompt reply.

217

Over their illicit drinks Meredith put his final question to Tom Biggins.

'On the night of July 20th – a Saturday, Mr. Biggins – we rather suspect that a man came down off the downs near Steyning and made for Brook Cottage. We have an idea that he might have been disguised as Jeremy Reed. You didn't by any chance see this man yourself or know anybody who did?'

Tom Biggins set down his tankard and wiped his mouth on the back of his sleeve. For a few seconds he pondered the question.

'No,' he said at length, 'I never set eyes on the chap myself, neither that night nor at any other time. But come to think of it – there's been gossip in the bar about that ole josser. Lot o' speculation as to 'oo he really might be and so on. 'Mongst other things I recall Bert Wimble, our carrier here, saying as he saw the ole chap walking up the village street in the middle o' the night. Couldn't rightly say when this was – you'd better see Bert yourself, Sooper, and get him to tell you.'

'I will,' said Meredith promptly. 'He sounds promising. Can you let me have his address?'

Biggins gave the address, and the three officials left the 'Loaded Wain' more than satisfied with the result of the cross-questioning. Meredith was in a particularly optimistic mood, for at every point he was seeing his latest theory substantiated by solid evidence. There was no doubt in his mind that the fellow on the bike was the Cloaked Man, or that he was setting off on that particular evening for a little job of work which was to be done on the top of the Chalklands pit. Biggins

218

had given, moreover, the first real description of the Cloaked Man as he actually was. The beard, of course, might have been specially grown during his three weeks' concealment in the cottage, and the clothes meant nothing when the man had plenty of opportunity for changing his attire a dozen times over. But his height and age were useful and so was that bandaged wrist. He was hoping that Bert Wimble might have noticed this same singular feature about the man he had seen that night in the village street.

The carrier, as luck would have it, was just stabling his horse after his usual Friday journey into Worthing. He was an elderly man with long grey moustaches, intensely blue eyes, and a thin, aquiline nose which lent his kindly features an aristocratic air. His voice, too, was quiet and well modulated. Meredith saw at a glance that he had in Bert Wimble a reliable, level-headed, and intelligent witness.

Yes, explained Wimble, he had noticed that queer old fellow from Brook Cottage late one night about the middle of July. He was walking up the main Bramber Street coming from the direction of Steyning. He was wearing knee-breeches and a Norfolk jacket. The thing which struck him most, however, was the fact that the old man was wearing dark glasses. It seemed a curious thing to do in the dark. The time must have been just after midnight, as Wimble had had a removing job which had taken him over to Ashington after his usual carrier's round. He had not stabled his horse, at any rate, until just on one o'clock. The date? Well, he could easily fix that by a reference to his books. The removal job would certainly have been entered up by his wife. Wimble thereupon consulted a well-thumbed memorandum book and announced, to Meredith's delight, that the date was July 20th.

'Tell me, Mr. Wimble, did you notice anything in this man's appearance which might have suggested an injury of some sort?'

'Ay, surr – I did. His left wrist was a-bandaged up. As I came up ahind him in my van the lights picked out that white bandage as clear as could be. What's more the old chap was a-carrying a suit-case. Queer, I thought, to be arriving for a week-end after midnight like that. Made me ponder where he had come from.'

'A suit-case?' Meredith felt the old familiar thrill course through his veins which was always his when unsolicited clues tumbled into his lap. 'You're sure about that?'

'I be sartin about it,' upheld Wimble stoutly.

'A suit-case,' thought Meredith. 'Just what I ought to have anticipated. He had to take his Jeremy Reed disguise up on to that hill and he needed something to put his own clothes in when he changed after committing the murder. By Jove, if I'm not on the right track this time – what the Old Man called the main road – I'll eat my hat!'

Meredith went on with his cross-examination of the carrier, but nothing further came to light. If large crates or parcels had arrived from London for Brook Cottage then Wimble knew nothing about them. The railway people had their own delivery van. They might be able to help.

Five minutes later they were able to help. On

several occasions they had carted large crates to Brook Cottage. The goods had been sent out by Fortnum & Mason. No, they had not made contact with the owner of the cottage, though they had heard he was a bit of a queer card. Deliveries had been made during the week, when Mr. Reed was absent, and instructions had been sent that the crates were to be left in the back-yard. All goods had been sent from the London firm carriage paid. The letter? Unfortunately it had been destroyed. It had been typed, bore the address of Brook Cottage and was signed J. Reed. On searching through their books the railway clerk assured Meredith that the last delivery had been made on July 18th. On this occasion two large crates had been sent by Fortnum & Mason.

'So much for the food problem,' thought Meredith. 'Now for the house agents.'

On inquiry in Brighton Meredith learnt that Stark & West had offices in High Street. He found them without trouble, an imposing modern frontage of concrete, plate-glass, and metal frames painted a pea-green. The interior was luxurious with thick carpets, easy chairs, and deferential, sleek young men who moved soundlessly about their employers' flourishing business. One of these elegant acolytes approached Meredith and began to drawl at him. Meredith bristled. He loathed drawlers when the drawl was obviously not the outcome of a good education.

'You can cut your sales-talk and all the rest of the soft-soap, understand? I'm a police officer and my time's limited. I want some information about a place called Brook Cottage in Bramber.'

The young man's hauteur became suddenly deflated. 'Would you care to see the manager, sir?'

'No – you'll do for the moment. I want to know two things. First, when and by whom the cottage was bought. Second, when it was put up for sale again. Can you get that information from your records?'

The young man felt certain that he could, and hastened off to lose himself behind a tall ground-glass screen. He was away for the best part of twenty minutes, and when he returned he was not alone.

'I've brought Mr. Harris, our manager, to see you, sir.'

'Well, Mr. Harris?'

'I think you've come to the wrong agents, officer. We've no record of a cottage by that name in Bramber. We certainly have property in that district, as we have in most districts around here, but that particular place has never been through *our* hands.'

'But good heavens, your board is up outside the place. How do you account for that?'

The manager goggled at him through his horn-rims.

'Our board? Impossible! If it's being shown then it's quite without our authority.'

Meredith was perplexed. He hadn't expected this surprising set-back. He had rather imagined that Rother had bought the place through Stark & West, and that the Cloaked Man, realizing this, had somehow managed to wangle the re-sale through the same firm. Possibly with the help of Janet Rother.

'Any other property for sale in Bramber – I mean on your books?'

The manager retired to consult the records again.

'Yes – a twelve-roomed, detached house near the Vicarage,' he informed Meredith on returning. 'But that's all.'

'Have you had any inquiries here with regard to Brook Cottage?'

'How could we – seeing that we're not handling the property?'

'All the same,' said Meredith quietly, 'I'd like you to find out from your various assistants, Mr. Harris.'

This took another twenty minutes as one or two of the staff were engaged with clients.

'Extraordinary!' exclaimed the astonished Mr. Harris. 'But no less than three inquiries were made during the last month. Our clerks were naturally forced to point out that a mistake had been made and that we weren't dealing with the place. I should have been informed, of course. How on earth do you account for it?'

'I don't,' smiled Meredith. 'Not yet. But I have an idea. I'll let you know if my suspicions are correct after another visit to Bramber. Can I have your 'phone number? Thanks.'

'We'll get to know this route soon, sir,' observed Hawkins as the car sped back to the village.

'You keep your sarcastic remarks to yourself, m'lad,' grinned Meredith, who was now in a happy and expansive state of mind. 'The most we can do is to thank our lucky stars that we don't have to foot our own petrol bills!'

223

Back in Bramber Meredith had no difficulty in finding the house near the Vicarage which was up for sale. No less than five agents' boards proclaimed the fact over the top of a well-groomed holly hedge. But Stark & West's board was not among them!

'Hit it first time,' thought Meredith triumphantly. 'Just as I imagined. Our man's got a headpiece on him all right. He wanted to suggest that Brook Cottage was unoccupied, so he did the obvious thing – pulled down the blinds, locked the doors, closed the windows, and shoved up a board to say the place was for sale.'

With his usual thoroughness, however, Meredith took the trouble to enter the grounds of the house and find the exact spot from where the Cloaked Man had uprooted the board. He had no difficulty in finding what he was looking for, and it was in a jubilant mood that he ordered Hawkins to drive him back to Lewes, where he intended to ring up Harris to let him know what had transpired.

A good day's work. Progress. Main-road progress. The Old Man ought to be pleased that things were working out so well. He had got the movements of the Cloaked Man, after the first murder and before the second, more or less taped. It now remained to follow up Tony's sensible suggestion and interview Slippery Sid, who was now being detained at the King's expense behind the walls of Lewes gaol. A long shot perhaps, but if luck continued to sit at his elbow Slippery Sid might prove a valuable witness!

CHAPTER 16

REVIEW OF THE EVIDENCE

Directly Meredith reached his office on the following morning he learnt that Scotland Yard wanted him on the 'phone. The sergeant on duty understood it was to do with the Rother cases. Meredith, therefore, got through at once to Detective-Inspector Legge, who was watching the case in the metropolis. Legge had disturbing news.

'Yes – it's to do with the Rother case. Our man down at Dover reports that somebody answering to the description of Janet Rother crossed to Calais on the night boat last evening. Of course as there's no warrant out for her arrest he couldn't do anything. Thought you'd like to know.'

'Yes – that's awkward,' grunted Meredith, immediately irritated by this set-back. 'Damned awkward Legge. I'm hoping to close in on this case during the next few days, and that young lady would have been an essential witness. Still is for that matter. Possibly an accessory both before and after the fact. But there it is – you know as well as I do that one can't get hold of a warrant these days without serving up a whole lot of fool-proof reasons. Trouble is, I've got some evidence against her but not enough. Any idea where she'd be making for?'

'My dear fellow!' Legge's ringing laugh nearly

split Meredith's ear-drums. 'Warsaw, Jerusalem, Tokio, or Timbuctoo! Nothing to prevent her from changing course when she pleases and as often as she pleases. If her passport's in order – and she's had plenty of time to arrange that – there's nothing except money to prevent her from legging it anywhere.'

'Which reminds me – what about your watch on that Kensington post office? Her solicitors pointed out, you remember, that they'd have to get in touch with her before she benefited from that will. Anything doing?'

'Nowt,' said Legge shortly. 'Nary a bite. We reckon up here that that poste restante business was a blind. Nothing to prevent her, was there, from ringing up the next day and altering the address at which she wanted to pick up her correspondence? And you needn't think that her solicitors would blab. Not them! You know the kidney. Clams and oysters, the lot of 'em.'

'Nobody with her when she boarded the boat?'

'Nothing about it in the Dover report.'

'Well, here's news,' announced Meredith, not without a glow of satisfaction. 'I'm going to push for a warrant of arrest. Unknown chap at the moment but answering to the following description: Shortish, middle-aged, stubble of dark beard, bandage round the left wrist. When last seen – about a fortnight ago – wearing dark coat and trousers and bowler-hat. Looks like a commercial traveller. I'll get that into *Police Orders* – see? We'll have all the ports under observation and get all the usual routine under way.'

'Right. Think the chap might have made a bolt

for it already?'

'That's my pet nightmare at the moment,' said Meredith bitterly. 'He's had nearly a fortnight in which to make himself scarce. On the other hand, I reckon he was essential to Janet Rother. He wouldn't leave the country until she was well under way. So the chances are he's still at large. I have an idea that he might have collected that correspondence and acted as go-between where the solicitors and Mrs. Rother were concerned. Wish the devil we could worm a bit more information out of those damned solicitor chaps. Any chance?'

'You wangle that warrant and leave the rest to me,' said Legge cheerily.

'O.K. I'll let you know what luck I have. In the meantime make a note of that description and tell your regular fellows to keep their eyes skinned... Thanks. Cheerio.'

Meredith then got through to Harris at the house-agents and explained what had happened to their sale-board. Harris was so dumbfounded that he could only gurgle out what sounded like a collection of first-class oaths.

So Janet Rother had got away? If they could trace her and the evidence against her was serious enough they might get an extradition order. Better get in touch with the Paris Sûreté if the Old Man agreed. They probably wouldn't be able to do much but it was a necessary action. In the meantime, it was more than ever essential to concentrate on the doings and present whereabouts of the Cloaked Man. Meredith decided to visit Slippery Sid.

He walked, therefore, through the drizzling rain

227

of the Lewes streets to the imposing but forbidding entrance of the gaol. At his ring the outer gate was opened and locked behind him, while he stated his business to the janitor. A warder was then summoned to conduct him to Slippery Sid's cell. The inner gates were then opened to admit the Superintendent into a bleak, rain-wet courtyard across which he was hastily piloted by the warder. They passed into a tall stone building, studded with barred windows, and proceeded along a stone corridor which smelt of soap and carbolic. On each side of the corridor were numbered iron doors with small square grilles in them. At one of these the warder stopped, drew out a bunch of keys and opened up.

'Friend to see you, Sid,' was his cheery announcement. 'Wants to have a nice little chat I reckon.' He grinned at his own pleasantry. 'I'll just lock the door and leave you with 'im, shall I, sir? I'll be outside. Just give me a call when you've finished.'

'Right,' said Meredith as the iron door clanged to behind him and left the place in semi-darkness.

Slippery Sid was squatting on the side of his bunk reading (of all things) a Bible. On the Superintendent's entry he carefully closed the book and marked the place by turning down the corner of a page.

'Improving the shining hour, eh, Sid?' asked Meredith in friendly tones. 'Didn't know you were much of a chap for religion!'

'On an' orf,' explained Sid with a non-committal gesture. 'On an' orf. Don't do a beggar no 'arm in 'ere to do a bit o' sky-piloting on 'is own account.' He quizzed Meredith with deep interest across the confined area of his cell. 'Seen you afore somewheres, ain't I, sir? You ain't a busy, are yer? Flattie o' some sort, I reckon, eh?'

'Remember that little job which was done up at Colonel Harding's house back in '27, Sid?'

'Blimey – I gotcher nah. You're the sooper what got me 'arf a stretch, all a 'cos I 'ad a gold 'unter left me by my ole dad. You reckoned that was a fanny [tall story], didn't yer?'

'And I still do,' observed Meredith with a grin. 'Feel like a little chat, Sid?'

'Wot abaht?'

'Night of August 9th or early hours of the tenth.'

Sid considered the dates for a moment then, suddenly realizing, flared up.

''Ere, wot's the gime, sir? I bin up the steps for that, ain't I? You ain't got no right ter–'

'Oh, it's nothing to do with your little job,' put in Meredith soothingly. 'I want some information – that's all.'

'Want me to turn snout, eh?'

'That's about it, Sid. Might do you good, you know. I make no promises, but if you can be of any use to me I'll do my best to see that the proper people get to hear about it. Well?'

'Orlrite,' said Sid in a surly voice, after a long pause. 'But there weren't nobody in wiv me on that Rushington's job if that's wot you're 'ooking for. Solo – that was.'

'Used a bike, didn't you, Sid?'

'Yers.'

'Took the Worthing-Horsham road perhaps – passed through Washington, didn't you?'

229

'Yers.'

'About midnight?'

'Arpas one,' corrected Sid.

'Know the cross-roads in Washington by the "Chancton Arms"?'

'Yers – turnin' to Steyning almos' opposite the boozer.'

'That's it. Know the Bostal?'

'Yers – big 'ill just afore you come into Washington.'

'Right. Now think carefully, Sid – did you notice anybody on the stretch of road between the Bostal and that turning to Steyning – either before or after your little job at Storrington?'

'Might 'av.'

'In other words you did?'

'Yers – mail van going toward Worthing.'

'On the outward journey, eh?'

'Yers.'

'Nobody else?'

'Yers – chap on a bike.'

'Chap on a–!' Meredith felt a quick thrill of excitement. 'Where was this exactly?'

'Bottom of the Bostal. Know a little lane wot runs up orf the main-road, doncher?' Meredith nodded. He knew it right enough! He recognized it as the rutty track which ran up past the lime-kilns to Chalklands. 'Well, 'ee turned orf up there.'

'Could you describe the man?'

'Bowler 'at,' said Sid shortly.

'Anything else?'

'Yers – face-fungi.'

'A beard, eh? What was he dressed in?'

'Couldn't rightly say – too muckin' dark to see much.'

'Notice anything about him which suggested he might have been injured, Sid?'

'Nah.'

'Sure?'

'Yers.'

'And the time you reckon was–?'

'Arpas one,' put in Sid glibly. He was a practised hand in answering questions in cross-examination.

'Would you be ready to sign a statement about this if it were necessary later on?'

'If you think it might 'elp I would.'

'Good.' Meredith rose and glanced round the cell. 'Comfortable in here, Sid?'

'I've known worse.'

'Quite – well, that's all. Thanks.'

'Luck. Luck. Luck,' reiterated an inward voice as Meredith made his way back to the station. The first real bit of luck which had come his way since the case had opened. That those two men should have passed one another on that short stretch of road where their separate routes overlapped was nothing short of a miraculous coincidence. But that made no difference to the evidence. Sid's description tallied on most points with that of Tom Biggins, the landlord of the "Loaded Wain". There was no shadow of doubt left that the man who had set out from Brook Cottage was the same man who had turned up the lane to Chalklands and later murdered poor William Rother. He had taken a fair time for the journey, but doubtless he had stopped on the way for a cigarette.

Meredith lost no time back at headquarters in

making his way to Major Forest's office. Unfortunately the Chief was out and would not be back until after lunch. Meredith, curbing his impatience therefore, shut himself in his own office and began to write up his notes. This done he settled down to a piece of personal routine work which he always imposed on himself when dealing with a particularly complex investigation. This was to run through all the documentary matter connected with the case since its outset, and to catalogue all those points which still required elucidation. At the end of half an hour he had drawn up the following list:

POINTS IN THE CASE WHICH REMAIN UNEXPLAINED

1. Why had Janet Rother met John Rother with that suit-case on the lawn at Chalklands a week before the blood-stained Hillman was found under Cissbury Ring?
2. Why were no buttons, cuff-links, studs, or brace-ends found in the lime along with the severed bones, the identity-disc, and the belt-clasps?
3. Who sent the faked telegram from Littlehampton?
4. Who is the Cloaked Man?
5. Where and how exactly had the body of John Rother been cut up?
6. Who placed the portions of the body on the kiln? Had Janet Rother told the truth about burning that diary?
7. Who killed John and William Rother? What motive?
8. Who typed the false confession purporting to have been written by William Rother?
9. Where was John Rother's skull?

10. Why had John Rother spent a number of week-ends in Bramber disguised as Jeremy Reed the naturalist?

Satisfied that no important point had been omitted, Meredith decided to talk over this list with Major Forest after lunch. New links in a chain of evidence were often forged when two people put all the clues of a case under the microscope.

Over the cold beef and salad back at Arundel Road Tony asked his father with a false air of innocence:

'Have you seen Slippery Sid, Dad?'

'Perhaps,' smiled Meredith.

'Oh, come on, Dad, you might tell the truth. He was able to tell you something, wasn't he?'

'As a matter of fact, Tony, he was – quite a lot.'

'I thought he might,' crowed Tony, feeling in his pocket and drawing out a crumpled brochure. He handed it across to his father.

'What the devil's this?'

'Illustrated catalogue of those wireless sets I was talking about. I thought you might be interested,' said Tony slickly, adding with commendable cunning, 'now.'

'Such persistence deserves some sort of reward, eh? What time do you leave work today? Six o'clock? All right. If I'm not called away I'll meet you outside Green's at ten past. And mind you're punctual.'

'You needn't worry about that, Dad,' grinned Tony. 'Can I have another slice of beef, Mother, please?'

'You're smart,' barked Major Forest as Meredith entered his office. 'Just finished this report you left on my desk. Good work, eh? Moving – what? Sit down and talk. Smoke? Right. Now where exactly are we going to start?'

Meredith thrust his questionnaire under the Chief's nose. 'With number one, sir, if you agree – and work down.'

Major Forest scooped up the paper and glanced quickly down it.

'Eh? What's this? Oh, I see. Catalogue of the outstanding snags. All right, Meredith, we'll deal with 'em one by one as you suggest. First – "Why had Janet Rother met John Rother?" etc. Well – why?'

'Can't say, sir. All through this case I've been puzzled by the relationship existing between the girl and her brother-in-law. Barnet reckoned that he was head-over-heels, and that the girl was just play-acting. When I questioned her later about that visit to the kiln she suggested the same thing. Playing up to John Rother just for the fun of it. But if that were the case it seems a bit odd that she should risk sneaking out of the house in the dead of night to meet him.'

'Did you question her about it?'

'Yes – she denied ever having met him at night.'

'Witness reliable?'

'Very.'

'So we've really got no answer to number one? Right. Number two – "Why were no buttons, cuff-links..." etc. Ah, yes. A strange point this, Meredith. We discussed the matter before, I remember, but didn't get very far. I suppose we must take it for granted that the clothes *were* thrown into the kiln?'

'I think so,' answered Meredith slowly. 'You see there must have been blood-stains, and the chap wouldn't want to leave evidence like that lying around.'

'Quite. It certainly looks as if the best thing for him to have done was to chuck the clothes on the kiln and destroy them. Point is he doesn't seem to have done so. Your men combed through the lime thoroughly, I take it?'

'Sifted every inch.'

'Umph!' The Chief rubbed his chin and pondered for a moment. Then: 'I suppose you realize, Meredith, that before he dissected the body he would have to undress it? Quite – you did. Well, supposing our man decided for some reason not to burn the clothes, could he have taken them with him when he trekked over the downs?'

Meredith slapped his thigh.

'Good heavens! The attaché-case! I reckoned, of course, that he might have a rubber-sheet and surgical saw in the case. I hadn't thought of the clothes. Yes – he could have got 'em away in that all right.'

'Was he carrying an attaché-case when Wimble the carrier saw him in Bramber?'

'No – a suit-case. So Wimble declared. I took it that he had hidden that case up on the downs above Steyning with his Jeremy Reed disguise in it. Perhaps the attaché-case was inside the suit-case.'

'Very possibly. Anyway, I suggest you hunt around for Rother's clothes. We'll assume that they

235

weren't burnt, eh? Might have buried 'em in the garden at Brook Cottage. All right – number three, then. "Who sent the faked telegram?"'

'The Cloaked Man, of course,' snapped Meredith at once. 'That telegram was mentioned in detail in that faked confession which we found on William's body. We've got to assume now that the Cloaked Man wrote that confession; therefore he *must* have sent the telegram, or caused it to be sent, otherwise he wouldn't have known anything about it.'

'Q.E.D.,' grinned the Chief. 'We'll accept that. Number four. A stinger this, Meredith. "Who is the Cloaked Man?"'

'Give it up, sir. No idea at the moment.'

'Same here. Well – number five. "Where and how exactly had the body of John Rother been cut up?" You still stick to your earlier theory, I suppose – that the dissection was done on a large rubber sheet or tarpaulin in those gorse bushes under Cissbury by means of a surgical knife and saw?' Meredith nodded. 'And that the remains were then wrapped in the sheet, driven to Chalklands in Rother's own car by the Cloaked Man, and there hidden away in a metal-lined cabin-trunk, probably in the car inspection-pit?'

'That's it, sir.'

'Any reason to alter your opinion?'

'None, sir, at the moment.'

'Six,' went on Major Forest. '"Who placed the portions of the body on the kiln? Was Janet Rother..." etc. Well?'

'Oh, Mrs. Rother did that part of the job right enough,' asserted Meredith. 'This Continental flight of hers proves, more or less, that she's guilty. The evidence I gathered from the chalk on her shoes suggested that she visited the kiln more than once during the week following John's murder. She explained this fact away by saying that the farmhouse was on a mountain of chalk. But I noticed that my own shoes during my investigations up there never once showed chalk scratches on the upper part of the toe-cap. Just a rime of chalk round the welt – that's all. No – I reckon that her confederate left her to carry out that gruesome act in the tragedy.'

'Which brings us,' said Major Forest, 'to the crux of the whole matter – your main question: "Who killed John and William Rother? What motive?" Far as I can see – if you answer that you ought to be able to answer all the other problems.'

'Not necessarily, sir,' pointed out Meredith politely. 'It's quite possible to *know* who committed a murder without being able to prove a single one of the circumstantial facts surrounding the case. This case, for example. I think we're more or less justified in supposing that the same man committed both murders. That faked confession incorporated so many of the *discovered* details in the first murder that we can't help but think that the man who placed that document in William's pocket knew as much, if not more, than we did about John's death. All our evidence points to the fact that the Cloaked Man did both jobs. But when it comes to substantiating this claim by proving up to the hilt certain problematic features connected with the two cases, we're up a tree. Half these questions still remain unanswerable.

237

We're not even in a position to advance a theory. See how I mean, sir?'

The Chief chuckled at Meredith's emphatic exposition.

'We'll have you lecturing at the Yard yet, you know. The Problems and Principles of Criminal Investigation. How's that for a title? But I quite see your point, Meredith. This next question about the faked confession rather illustrates what you were saying. Even if we knew for *certain* that the Cloaked Man murdered William we should still have to prove that he shoved that confession in the dead man's pocket. Do you think he did?'

Meredith nodded.

'Unless it was Janet Rother, which I'm inclined to doubt. My idea is that the murderer combed through his victim's pockets before he threw him over the pit, to see if the note, which we assume he must have received fixing the rendezvous, was actually on his person. He probably extracted this note, wearing gloves, and substituted the confession. I can't prove that, of course. It's still bound to be pure assumption.'

'Quite. And are you prepared to assume anything as to the whereabouts of John Rother's skull? That's the next query on your list.'

'No, sir. That's one of the questions which is absolutely unanswerable. I haven't the faintest idea where that skull has got to. I've already put forward my theories as to why he didn't pass it through the kiln with the other portions of the body.'

'Which brings us to your final question – "Why had John Rother spent a number of week-ends in

Bramber?" etc. Any clearer now on this subject?'

'Well,' admitted Meredith, 'I've had no reason to abandon my theory of blackmail. I still think that the Cloaked Man knew something about John's behaviour toward Janet, and that he was threatening to tell William. Mrs. Rother may even have been in a plot to egg John on and thus get him under the thumb of the Cloaked Man. After all, that pretty pair of rascals were out for money. John and William were murdered for money. They had to be got out of the way before Janet could inherit. Blackmail would naturally appeal to a mercenary-minded couple like that.'

The Chief Constable nodded an agreement, lit his pipe, leaned back in his chair and stared for a long time at the lazily curling smoke. Meredith, well trained in his superior's idiosyncrasies, knew better than to interrupt, The Old Man was thinking. Suddenly he came out of his reverie, jerked himself upright, and levelled his pipe at Meredith as if it had been an automatic.

'Have you ever thought of this?' he began abruptly. 'That John's murderer never really intended to kill William? Struck me as we were running through those questions. I'm inclined to reason something like this. The Cloaked Man murdered John and then tried to work it that suspicion fell on William. You remember yourself how, at an earlier point in your investigation, you felt pretty sure in your own mind that William was the murderer. First there was that false telegram from Littlehampton. The murderer knew well enough that William would set off to see his aunt. He could anticipate more or less what time

William would leave Littlehampton, and smashed the dashboard clock so that the hands stopped at a plausible time – plausible, that is, where William's movements were concerned. He staged the murder near Findon because he knew that William was bound to pass near that village on his return journey from Littlehampton. Place and time were beautifully gauged, as it happens, because William could easily have been under Cissbury at 9.55 which was the hour at which the clock had stopped.

'To further William's difficulty in proving an alibi Janet Rother walks up on to the down, or at any rate is absent from Chalklands, during the time that William could have been doing the job. She avers that she returned to the farmhouse at 10.15 and that William was not then at Chalklands. In other words, knowing that the Cloaked Man was going to stop that clock at 9.55, she was out to make William's movements appear even more suspicious in our eyes. Even if William had returned before 10.15 he would have been unable to appeal to Janet for corroboration, because she had most annoyingly absented herself. That left us with Kate Abingworth's word alone. An elderly, emotional woman who would be at the mercy of a clever K.C. in a cross-examination. So much for that.

'The motive was obvious. John was alienating his wife's affections. The Cloaked Man knew we shouldn't be long in finding out that particular bit of gossip. To bring the murder home to Chalklands it was necessary to pass the portions of the body through the kiln. Here Janet came in handy. It was natural that we should suspect

William of the murder as soon as we learnt how an attempt had been made to destroy the body on his own door-step, so to speak. This brings me to another very interesting point. That question about the buttons and cuff-links. Suppose the clothes were not passed through the kiln? What then? It was imperative that there should be no question as to the identity of the remains. So what does our murderer do? Gets Janet to drop the identity-disc and John's belt into the kiln along with some portion of the body, knowing quite well that once the bones were discovered these articles would also come to light.

'To strengthen the suspicion that William was responsible for his brother's death was the fact that he was sole heir to John's estate. Unfortunately the Cloaked Man underrated the intelligence of the police, with the result that William was not arrested. An awkward factor when it came to the fulfilment of their scheme to nab the money. So, aware that the police were not prepared to do away with William, our man decided to take on the job himself. Even then he had not lost hope, as that faked confession clearly indicates. He still hoped to throw dust in our eyes by staging a suicide, the apparent reason for which was to be William's knowledge that he was under police suspicion. Honestly, Meredith, that second trick *might* have worked if William had not written that note to Aldous Barnet. That was the unexpected fly in the real murderer's ointment. That note may hang him yet, Meredith. That's my theory for what it's worth. You needn't adopt it, but I think it's worth a good deal of careful consideration.'

241

CHAPTER 17

CLIMAX

On looking back upon the Rother cases, Meredith always upheld that this particular interview with the Old Man marked the turning-point in his investigations. From that moment onward it was all 'main-road progress'. Fresh evidence came to hand, unexpected clues; and the little bits of the puzzle, hitherto unrelated, now suddenly seemed to fit into place without the slightest effort on his part.

'The whole case,' as Meredith put it later, 'seemed to work itself out automatically.'

He had been much impressed, too, by the Chief's theory that William had only been murdered because the police had failed to arrest him on the charge of killing his brother. To a very large extent it accounted for the complex manner in which the first murder had been worked – the actual assault in one place, the destruction of the body in another, and so on. But the main point which Meredith took away from his conversation with Major Forest was the sensible supposition that John Rother's clothes had not been destroyed along with the remains. He determined to comb through every inch of the garden and outhouses at Brook Cottage.

'Well, Hawkins,' said Meredith early the next

morning, 'we're going somewhere this morning where we've never been before.'

'Where's that, sir?' asked Hawkins eagerly.

'Bramber,' grinned Meredith.

Hawkins said a rude word and climbed into the driving-seat of the little blue-black car, on the back seat of which a constable had placed a couple of spades and a sieve. Soon they were clear of the houses and running through the countryside, which was already tinged with the first brown and russet tints of approaching autumn. The rain had cleared and the still heat of early morning promised a really scorching day.

Once at Brook Cottage they set to work.

'We'll take the garden first, Hawkins. There's no need for us to dig unless the ground looks as if it's been recently disturbed. So we'll just run our eye over the place first, see?'

But although at one or two points here and there in the unkempt little garden they found patches of suspiciously loosened earth, their digging operations brought nothing of interest to light. After an hour's strenuous labour Meredith declared himself satisfied as to the innocence of the garden, and switched over his interest to the outhouses. The main building was a brick-and-tile shed such as might be used for storing coal and wood, or hanging garden implements. This particular place had a brick floor, no window, and smelt damp and airless. Meredith carefully examined it by the light which streamed in through the open door. It was cluttered up with all manner of odds and ends – sacks, old newspapers, a pile of rotting potatoes, one or two splintered crates from Fortnum &

Mason, a couple of dozen flowerpots, and a rusty mowing-machine.

Gradually Hawkins, under his superior's instructions, cleared all the movable objects out into the yard until the floor-space was entirely exposed except for the pile of potatoes. Going down on his hands and knees Meredith ran his eye over every inch of the brickwork. It all seemed in order. It was not until Hawkins had shovelled the potato-heap from one corner to another that Meredith hit upon a clue. Despite the grime and dried earth which coated the brickwork under the heap, Meredith noticed that several of the individual bricks had been loosened and cleverly fitted back into place. Prising under one of them with his penknife, he was soon able to uproot a good square yard of the uncemented brickwork.

'Hullo! Hullo!' was his instant exclamation. 'We've hit on something here, m'lad. This earth under the bricks has been newly turned. Here – fetch me that spade. Jump to it!'

Hawkins, lit with an equal excitement, snatched up the spade, and handed it to the Superintendent. With the utmost caution Meredith began to dig. Almost at once his spade came against something that was certainly not plain earth.

'Steady, sir!' ejaculated Hawkins, dropping on to his knees. 'I can see the corner of something sticking up. Looks like material of some sort.' He reached forward and gingerly began to tug. Inch by inch the stuff broke clear of the compressed soil until no doubt remained as to its nature. 'My God! It's the coat, sir. Rother's coat. It matches that tweed cap we found by the Hillman.'

'You've said it!' snapped Meredith, taking the bundle and crossing over to the light by the door. 'The whole darned suit by the look of it. Waist-coat, plus-fours, stockings, coat.'

'Any blood-stains,' asked Hawkins hopefully, as Meredith began to unwrap the closely rolled bundle.

'Blood-stains? No, I don't think–' He stopped dead. 'Well, I'll be jiggered!'

Hawkins stepped forward.

'What is it, sir?'

'This,' said Meredith, withdrawing something from the centre of the clothing. 'Ever seen any-thing like that before?'

'A skull!' cried Hawkins, suffering one of the greatest thrills in his career. 'The missing skull!'

'John Rother's skull,' added Meredith. 'The crowning glory of old Blenkings' skeleton, eh?' Then with a sudden change of expression: 'But what the devil–?'

'Something wrong, sir?'

'Something damnably wrong. There's no hair, no vestige of flesh, rotting or otherwise, on the bonework. Why?'

'Perhaps the chap shoved it on the fire first,' suggested Hawkins. 'Remember, we found the remains of a fire in the hearth.'

'Impossible,' argued Meredith. 'There's no sign of the bones being charred. In fact the skull's got a definitely polished look. Then there's another thing, Hawkins. Why can't we see the fractured bone where Rother was knocked out?' He turned the skull slowly in the sunlight. 'It's more or less intact, isn't it? A few teeth missing, but no sign of

245

any splintering. It strikes me that there's something queer about this particular skull – something we haven't quite realized.'

'Best show it to that old professor chap, eh, sir?'

'I'm going to, Hawkins. We're going to run into Worthing straight away. I'll go through the pockets of the suit on the way.'

But, beyond the tab bearing the maker's name, there was nothing by which the clothes could be definitely identified. The colour and material matched, as far as Meredith could remember, the blood-stained cap. He could easily check up on that. Were there blood-stains on the suit as well? He went over it inch by inch. Yes – a blackish brown patch round the left cuff. Nothing more. That was queer too. These relics would want a bit of explaining away.

Professor Blenkings was delighted to see the police again. He welcomed Meredith with enthusiasm, insisted on a drink, piloted him into the study, and forced a cigar on him.

'Now don't tell me you've found another set of bones, Superintendent. That would be too much to hope for. Most enjoyable that other little job I did for you. Elementary but of practical help, I imagine. What brings you this time?'

Meredith unwrapped the skull from the waistcoat and held it up.

'This, sir.'

The Professor mounted his glasses and peered critically at the exhibit.

Then: 'Most interesting,' he murmured. 'Most interesting. Quite a well-formed cranium, Superintendent. Intact too. May I ask–?'

246

Meredith briefly explained how he had discovered the skull in the shed at Brook Cottage and aired his opinion that it belonged to John Rother.

Professor Blenkings shook his head.

'Oh dear, no,' he contested emphatically. 'That couldn't possibly be Mr. Rother's skull. You told me that he had suffered a severe blow on the head. We should notice signs of that, shouldn't we? Of course we should. But this skull is quite perfect. You must have made a mistake.'

'I rather anticipated that I might have done,' said Meredith dryly. 'Though I can't account for the discrepancy.'

'No. No. Quite so,' burbled the Professor absent-mindedly, as he twisted the skull this way and that the better to examine it. 'By the way,' he added abruptly after a long silence, 'have you got a photograph of Mr. Rother?'

As luck would have it Meredith carried one in his wallet. He handed it over without comment. There was another long silence.

'Well, really,' exclaimed the Professor at length, 'this is a most extraordinary affair! Much as I don't want to disappoint you, Superintendent, I'm bound to point out to you that this isn't Mr. Rother's skull at all. Decidedly not. Most interesting, of course, but annoying where you are concerned.'

'But it must be!' exclaimed Meredith. 'All our evidence points to the fact. Why are you so sure?'

'Have the goodness to look at the photograph. Note Mr. Rother's jaw. A square but not particularly prominent jaw, eh? Now observe the jaw belonging to the skull. It's what we call an undershot jaw. Quite a different formation. Again, if this is a recent photo of Mr. Rother you will observe that he appears to have an excellent set of teeth. The teeth in this skull are very indifferent. Very. Bad teeth in fact. They needed the attentions of a dentist. I'm sorry to upset your expectations, Superintendent, but the facts are quite indisputable.'

'And you think that this skull belongs to the skeleton you made?'

'Well, we can easily make certain of that. Dear me – yes.' The Professor rose and rang the bell. In a few seconds his elderly, stern-faced housekeeper presented herself. 'Ah, Harriet – have the goodness, will you, to fetch that nice little skeleton of mine from the wardrobe. You know where I keep it.'

'Very good, sir,' said Harriet in the level tones of one who has been pottering skeletons from wardrobes for the best part of a lifetime.

In a few minutes the dour-faced lady returned, hugging her macabre and headless companion to her starched apron with an indifference born of utter contempt for the sensational.

'Could do with a dust,' she observed tartly as she dumped her gruesome load in an arm-chair. 'There's a sight of cobwebs atween the ribs, sir.'

'That will be all, Harriet,' concluded the Professor firmly, dismissing her with an imperative wave of his hand. The moment the door had shut, however, he got up eagerly from his chair, picked up the skull and carried it over to the semi-recumbent skeleton. Then, just as if he were trying on a hat, he placed the skull deftly on the shoulders of the framework. At the points where the bones had been severed the fit was perfect.

'You see – there can be no doubt now. Most upsetting I dare say, Superintendent, but I'm forced to point out now that the skeleton doesn't belong to Mr. Rother either! Inexplicable, of course – but there it is.'

'Well, I'll be–' began Meredith.

'Quite. Quite. I appreciate your chagrin. Is there anything further I can do?'

Meredith rose and shook his head. He was so completely dumbfounded that he quite forgot to thank the Professor for his drink. Where had he gone off the rails? If this wasn't Rother's skeleton then who the devil *did* it belong to? And why was the skull wrapped in a plus-four suit that almost certainly belonged to Rother? And how had the flesh been removed from the bone-work so as to leave the skull so clean and polished? It couldn't have rotted off in a bare eight weeks.

For the remainder of the morning, during lunch, and for most of the afternoon, he pondered these questions. On comparing the tweed cap with the plus-four suit he found that the material matched exactly – strong proof, he upheld, that the outfit *did* belong to John Rother. He talked the matter over with the Chief, he re-examined every exhibit and every document connected with the case. He read through statements, advanced new theories and, after analysis, scrapped them. He cursed and smoked, smoked and cursed, and went home to his high-tea in a mood of utter despair. Would the case ever be completed? Was this to be the one outstanding failure in his career? That little job up in the Lake District had been child's play compared with the complexities surrounding this confounded investigation. He was heartily sick of the whole damned case!

Then, half-way through the night, he let out a sharp cry of enlightenment, tapped his wife on the shoulder and drew her complaining from the toils of a deep sleep.

'I've got it, my dear! I've got it! I know what happened under Cissbury on the 20th. My Lord – what a blind–'

'Got what?' snapped his wife in a disgruntled voice.

'The answer to the Rother case,' crowed Meredith triumphantly, ready to accept his wife's congratulations.

'Oh, that,' she said in disinterested tones, promptly turning over and going to sleep again.

But the next morning, after an early breakfast, she had thrown aside her indifference. As she handed Meredith his cap in the hall and brushed down his uniform, she allowed herself to be taken into his arms and fervently kissed.

'Wonderful, eh?' demanded her husband.

'You are,' murmured Mrs. Meredith. 'And you've just been waiting for me to say so. Well, here's luck to you, you stupid boy, and mind you have a good lunch somewhere if you can't get home.'

But on that memorable day Meredith clean forgot lunch, high-tea – everything except the work upon which he was engaged. He did take a hasty drink in the bar-parlour of the 'Chancton Arms', and a cup of tea with the Washington Vicar about half past four. Having obtained the key from Aldous Barnet, he then visited Chalklands and carried off a large picture wrapped in brown paper. He then ordered Hawkins to drain the petrol-tank of the police car, fill up again with exactly two gallons and drive him first of all from Chalklands to Littlehampton. From Littlehampton he drove along the coast via Goring to Worthing, and thus on through Tarring to Findon and Bindings Lane. There Hawkins drew off what petrol remained in the tank, refilled from a spare can and, at Meredith's instructions, returned to headquarters. There the Superintendent went through the same process as before, measuring the petrol which had been drained off from the tank and making a few quick calculations with the aid of his Bartholomew's map. This done he returned, worn out, but utterly satisfied, to a late supper at Arundel Road.

Hardly had he finished supper, however, when the 'phone-bell rang and he was informed by the officer on duty at the station that the Yard wanted an urgent word with him. In a mood of excited anticipation, quite forgetting how tired he was, Meredith set out once again for headquarters. Detective-Inspector Legge was on the other end of the 'phone.

'Ah – there you are. Sorry to drag you out like this, but I've got news that won't keep. Your bearded gentleman was arrested at Dover this afternoon trying to make a get-away. Refuses to make a statement. Gives his name as Jack Renshaw and the address of a London hotel. He's been cautioned, of course, and the Dover lads are bringing him up here tonight on the Guv'nor's instructions. Question is – can you get a train and come up and identify? Better bring a constable, too, as if he's the man you're after you'll have to take him back to Lewes. That O.K.?'

'Half a second,' said Meredith, as he drew the Southern Railway time-table towards him. Then later: 'Yes – that's all right. I'll be along about 10.30. Probably have to stay the night and make the return journey tomorrow.'

'I'll arrange that. Do you reckon it's the end of the case?'

'I don't reckon,' laughed Meredith with justifiable satisfaction. 'I *know!*'

After a quick dash back to his home, where he packed a few things and explained to his wife what had transpired, Meredith legged it to the station and arrived a minute ahead of the train. On the journey he slept like a log. But the moment the train drew into Victoria, he hopped out as briskly as ever, hailed a taxi, and ordered the driver to take him to Scotland Yard. Legge was waiting for him in the ante-room.

'Punctual to the minute,' he grinned. 'Nothing like you County chaps for efficiency. Shall we slip out and have one first, or do you want to see this Mr. Renshaw straight away? There's just time if we step on it.'

'No,' said Meredith decidedly. 'Business first and pleasure when you can – that's my motto. You forget, Legge, that this may be the climax of a two months' investigation for me! Headline stuff, too! You can guess that I feel pretty keyed-up. Where is the fellow?'

'I'll have him sent up,' replied Legge. 'The Sooper has lent me his office. We poor devils have to share a room. A crying disgrace, of course. Have you ever tried to write up a report with a couple of chaps arguing about League football at your elbow? Helpful, I assure you. Here you are – this way.'

A constable was despatched to escort Mr. Jack Renshaw from the detention-cell to the office of Superintendent Hancock.

'Have a cigarette?' asked Legge. 'They're the Sooper's but I can thoroughly recommend 'em.'

Meredith took a cigarette and noticed, much to his astonishment, that, as he lifted the match to light it, his hand was shaking like a leaf. So much depended on the events of the next few minutes. There was a rap on the door. Meredith started.

'Come in,' sang out Legge.

Two constables entered, escorting between them a shortish, stocky man with a dark beard and a bandage round his left wrist. He was dressed as Biggins, the landlord of the 'Loaded Wain' had seen him, in a dark suit, starched collar, and bowler hat. On entering the brilliantly lighted room, however, Renshaw, with an instinctive gesture, reached up and removed his hat, then stepped forward a pace and looked from Meredith to Legge with a questioning expression.

'You wished to see me?' he asked in a cultured voice. 'You sent for me?'

'I'm a police officer investigating the murder of Mr. William Rother. I just wanted to ask you one or two questions. Sit down, won't you?'

With a slight nod of thanks the man sidled into

a chair and sat down, whilst Legge dismissed the constables with a little lift of his hand. Meredith moved across to the front of the desk and leaned back against it, with the light shining over his shoulder full on to Renshaw's features.

'Cigarette?'

'Thanks.'

'Match?' Meredith held out the tiny point of flame. 'Thanks.'

Legge drifted round until he was between Renshaw and the door.

'Well,' began Meredith, 'I won't beat about the bush. You're not bound to answer my questions, but I needn't tell you that it will be for your own good if you do. There are one or two things here I should like you to identify. It's possible you may have seen them before. If you care to make a voluntary statement you may, but I must warn you that anything you may say will be taken down in writing and used as evidence.' Meredith suddenly stooped down and unclasped his suit-case. He drew out the blood-stained tweed cap. 'Ever seen that before, Mr. Renshaw?' The man shook his head. 'No? Very well. Then what about this?' Meredith slowly spread out the three articles of the plus-four suit on the Superintendent's desk. 'Know anything about those?'

'Nothing.'

'Sure?'

'Quite ... sure,' faltered the bearded man with a defensive thrust of his jaw. 'I'm still at a complete loss why I have been detained like this. I was told it was to do with the murder of William Rother. I'm a respectable citizen and I can't see—'

'Quite,' broke in Meredith with a slow smile. Then, after a pause: 'Ever heard of Brook Cottage?' he rapped out sharply. 'Or Jeremy Reed? Well – come on, Mr. Renshaw – what are you hesitating for? Ever heard of 'em? Come on! You've got a tongue in your head, haven't you?'

'No ... of ... course not,' stuttered Mr. Renshaw. 'I mean,' he added with a weak smile, 'that I've naturally never heard of them.'

'Never seen this before, eh?' snapped out Meredith, diving into his suit-case and holding up the skull. 'Come on! Answer! Ever seen it before?'

'I ... don't...' began the bearded man in a shaken voice. 'I ... no ... perhaps–'

'You have seen it before? Haven't you, eh? It's no good lying, Renshaw. We know too much. Come on – out with it! Let's have the truth.'

Suddenly all the fight went out of that stocky figure. His shoulders hunched, his eyes evading Meredith's unflinching stare were fixed on the floor; the colour drained out of his normally ruddy cheeks. He just humped there, twisting his bowler hat, unable at first to utter a single word.

Then: 'My God!' he whispered brokenly, aghast at the position in which he found himself. 'How did you find out? I thought I was safe. In heaven's name how did you find out?'

Meredith smiled faintly.

'Isn't it enough that we have?'

'And you know ... who I am?' demanded the bearded man in a quavering voice.

Meredith swung round on the Inspector.

'Do you, Legge?'

'Well, he gave his name as Jack Renshaw, but

255

I'm quite ready to believe that that was an alibi.'

Meredith nodded.

'You're right. It is. In the same way that Jeremy Reed was an alibi.'

Legge stepped forward and stared at Meredith, bewildered. 'But, good heavens, I thought Jeremy Reed had been identified by you as being one and the same person as–?'

'As John Fosdyke Rother,' concluded Meredith. 'You're right again, Legge. You see...'

Meredith deliberately left his sentence hanging in mid-air. He glanced toward Renshaw. The man nodded slowly.

'You see,' he explained in a choking whisper, *'I am John Fosdyke Rother.'*

CHAPTER 18

RECONSTRUCTION OF THE CRIME

'Mind you,' said Aldous Barnet, 'you've let me have little glimpses of the case, here and there, but frankly, Meredith, I still can't help marvelling. After all, when I'm working out the plots for detective yarns, however complex, I'm in the happy position of knowing as much about the murder as the murderer himself. Even then it's quite easy to trip up on minor details and let your detective utilize some clue which he hasn't even discovered. But you've got to start from scratch. You've got to prove yourself right at every step, test every theory, corroborate if possible every scrap of evidence. How the devil do you do it?'

The two men were seated one afternoon, shortly after the sensational arrest of John Rother, under the gigantic chestnut which towered over the lawns at Lychpole. They were lounging back in deck-chairs in the deep shade, with cooling drinks placed ready at their elbows. At Barnet's invitation Meredith had run out on his first half-day to enlighten the crime writer about the details of his successful investigation.

'He'll respect your confidence,' the Chief had told Meredith. 'I've known Barnet for years. He's longing to get his teeth into the case. Those fellows have got an insatiable appetite for what they politely call "copy", Meredith, and, since he's been a lot of help to you, I think it's only fair to let him into a few of your professional secrets.'

So Meredith had arrived at Lychpole perfectly prepared to give a detailed account of the Rother cases from A to Z. Barnet's honest admiration was very flattering, he felt.

'How the devil do you do it?' asked Barnet.

Meredith laughed.

'You make our work sound very much more sensational and complicated than it actually is. At least seventy per cent of it is pure routine in which, if necessary, we have the co-operation of the whole of the police organization. I reckon one's personal contribution is patience and common sense, aided by a trained observation. Take this case, for example...'

Barnet stretched out his long legs, settled his gaunt frame deeper in his chair, and unobtrusively slipped a notebook out of his breast-pocket.

'That's just what I'd like to do. I'd like to follow your train of reasoning from beginning to end. Would you like to put the whole thing before me?'

'If it won't bore you,' smiled Meredith.

'Bore me! My dear chap – my one hobby is crime. This is a heaven-sent opportunity for me to get a bird's-eye view of an actual murder investigation from the discovery of the crime to the arrest of the murderer. You talk and let me take notes. Perhaps, by altering a few names and details, I could work this case up into a novel. You yourself reckoned that it might make a darned good story.'

'All right. Where shall I start?'

'July 20th,' snapped Barnet without hesitation. 'That's when the whole thing started, wasn't it?'

'Very well then – July 20th – the day that John Rother set out for Harlech. But before we deal with the actual events I think it would be as well to analyse the relationship existing between the three principal figures in the drama: John, William, and Janet Rother. In one respect, Mr. Barnet, you were wrong when we discussed this matter. You had an idea that, although John was wildly in love with Janet, she didn't return the compliment. Personally I think she was even more deeply in love with John than he was with her. She married William, but she could never have really cared for him. They might have hit it off all right if domestic economics hadn't forced them to live at Chalklands. If they could have had a place of their own I dare say this tragedy could have been avoided. Unfortunately they were forced to set out on a married career in a domicile

258

which included John, a man who dominated his brother and, from all accounts, had a very strong attraction for women.

'When John set out, or rather, pretended to set out, for Harlech, things had reached a climax in that unfortunate household. The plot to get rid of William had been hatched, not weeks before, but for the best part of eighteen months. The means by which this was to be accomplished had been thought out to the minutest detail, a scheme in which Janet and John were to play an equal part.

'One of the first essentials in this scheme was for John to work up an unassailable alibi. It was necessary for him to be able to disappear after his supposed murder under Cissbury to a spot where his presence would arouse no comment. Hence the Jeremy Reed trick and the purchase of Brook Cottage. You'll agree with me that it was a stroke of genius to work up this alibi within a few miles of his own doorstep. For one thing, he had to reach his hide-out as soon as possible after he had staged the murder under Cissbury, for another he hadn't the time to travel very far afield over the week-ends. He appeared first in Bramber about January a year ago, where he cleverly suggested that he was an eccentric recluse with an interest in butterflies. His disguise, to my mind, was badly overdone, but it seemed to go down with the more gullible villagers. The old man's arrival was a seven days' wonder, but by the time I went down there to investigate the interest in him had more or less died down. They accepted the fact that he was a queer bird and left it at that. This was due, of course, to John's cunning in introducing Jeremy Reed to Bramber a long time before his scheme was put into operation.

'Now let's return to July 20th. When John left Chalklands that evening there was a perfect understanding between himself and his brother's wife. She knew well enough that he wasn't going to Harlech. She knew that it was the arranged date for John's disappearance. Their initial scheme, curiously enough, did not include the actual murder of William. That was scheme Number Two, only to be put into operation if the first plot went off the rails.

'Briefly their idea was this – John was to so set the stage that it should appear as if he had been attacked and killed at that lonely spot up Bindings Lane. The fake murder was to be so arranged that suspicion would naturally fall on William. They hoped, of course, that the law would bring about William's death without their interference. As a matter of fact, at one point, I was pretty well convinced that William was the guilty party. Everything pointed to the fact. The only snag was that a shepherd up near Hound's Oak had seen a man in a cloak and broad-brimmed hat legging it over the downs just about the time that the "murder" had been committed. This wanted explaining away. We couldn't arrest William until we had a line on the identity of this stranger. For all that, we had practically decided to issue the warrant when we learnt that William had been found dead at the foot of the chalk-pit.

'Before I come to the murder that really *was* a murder I'll run over the details of what transpired on the 20th. As in every murder investigation the time factor is important. So I advise you, Mr. Barnet, to take a careful note of the various times mentioned if you want to get a really comprehensive view of the mystery. John left Chalklands at 6.15. At 6.45 he reached Littlehampton. At 6.50 he went into the post office and sent the following telegram to Chalklands: *Please come at once your aunt seriously injured in accident taken to Littlehampton General Hospital – Wakefield.* With more than commendable cunning he addressed the telegram to himself, knowing quite well that, as he was supposed to be on his way to Harlech, William would naturally open it in his place.

'This telegram reached Chalklands at 7.15. At 7.25 William set off for Littlehampton. A little after 7.30 he stopped at Clark's garage in Findon and had petrol put in his Morris. Clark saw him take the Littlehampton road. John Rother, in the meantime, had set off via Goring to Worthing. Later, when I had anticipated that he had taken this route, I was able to corroborate the fact on the evidence of a farmer who had noticed John Rother sitting in his car on the front at West Worthing.

'William arrived in Littlehampton just after 8 o'clock. He went, just as John anticipated he would, first to the hospital, then to Dr. Wakefield, and then on to his aunt's flat. He left for Chalklands just after nine. This was the only time about which John could not be particularly certain, though he had so planned things to allow himself a fairly wide margin of error on this point. About the same time, as far as I can reason, John left Worthing for Findon and Bindings Lane, arriving under Cissbury some time before 9.30. We know that he was seen by the Findon postman just outside the village shortly after 9. William declared in cross-examination that he had arrived at Chalklands round about the same time, or possibly fifteen minutes later. No matter what time he had left Littlehampton, however, there was no chance of the two cars meeting each other. As you know, the Littlehampton road enters Findon on the north side of the village, whilst John entered from the south side and turned up Bindings Lane before reaching the Littlehampton fork. On the other hand, William could not deny that he had been *near* Findon, and *ipso facto* the scene of the supposed murder about the time when the crime was fixed to take place.

'Now, as to what *really* happened under Cissbury,' went on Meredith, after pausing for a long draught of cider-cup.

'Ah!' breathed Aldous Barnet, his pencil ready poised over his open notebook. 'Exactly.'

'All very simple really. John parked his car among the gorse bushes, splintered his windscreen, broke the glass of the dashboard dials, and stopped the clock at 9.55. He reckoned that we should be smart enough to spot that clock, which was an essential clue if we were to suspect William. I mean if the murder *could* have taken place at six the next morning there was little point in getting William to pass through Findon on the evening before. It was essential to John's scheme that we should notice that clock. As a matter of fact I nearly slipped that. He nearly overrated our intelligence, eh?' Meredith chuckled and went on:

'The blood-stains are easily accounted for. John

made a deep gash in the back of his left fore-arm, allowed the blood to drip on to the upholstery, the running-board, and the tweed cap. He then placed the cap a few feet away from the car to look as though it had fallen off in a struggle. He bandaged his arm just above the wrist, and apparently the place didn't heal too well because he was still wearing that bandage when he set out on the night of August 10th to murder William. Two of the Crown witnesses noticed that bandage.

'Well, John had an attaché-case in the car which contained a long black cloak and a broad-brimmed black hat. These he put on and cut up by Hound's Oak to a point on the downs above Steyning, where he had already hidden his Jeremy Reed disguise in a suit-case. Unfortunately a shepherd named Riddle happened to spot him making up through the woods there. He called out, but John was not such a fool as to stop and pass the time of the day with this very undesirable witness. On the hills he discarded the cloak and hat, noticed that some of the blood had seeped through the bandage on to the cloak, and decided to bury it under some bracken. The hat and cloak were found later by a Steyning child, whose father informed the police. Rother then changed from his plus-four suit into his Jeremy Reed rig and put on his dark glasses. Rather a stupid thing to do in the middle of the night, perhaps, but he couldn't risk being recognized, because in that case his whole scheme of incriminating William would have gone up the spout. After all, you can't have a murder without the murdered man!

'The plus-four suit John placed in the suit-case,

together with the attaché-case which he had taken from the Hillman. He then walked down off the hills into Bramber, where he was seen by Wimble, the carrier, just after midnight. For the next three weeks Rother used Brook Cottage as a hide-out, having already laid in a good supply of food from Fortnum and Mason's. To strengthen the idea that the cottage was uninhabited he pulled down the blinds, closed all the windows, locked the doors, and stole an agent's board from a near-by house that happened to be for sale. With this stuck up in the garden he felt pretty safe from intrusion, I reckon. Moreover, he knew that if anybody did inquire at the agents about the property, the agents would deny having Brook Cottage on their books. So much for the events which transpired on the 20th.

'We now come to the most confusing element in the whole case – the bones. You see, Rother was not going to be content with the discovery of the blood-stained car alone – he wanted to bring the "murder" much nearer to William's doorstep. It was essential to his scheme that an inquest should be held and a verdict of murder brought in, and though it *is* possible to hold an inquest without the remains having been found, it's by no means usual. So John set to work and did the only thing possible ... he supplied the remains! It was on this point that I really blew up. It was not until nearly two months after I had started my investigations that I began to suspect that the bones were other than John Rother's. It was a chance remark of yours, Mr. Barnet, at an early interview which first put the idea into my head.'

'Of mine? I don't remember ever having—'

'Oh, you've probably forgotten by now,' broke in Meredith. 'But as luck would have it I'd incorporated that little remark of yours in my written report of that particular day's work. We were discussing the Rother family in a general sort of way, the day after William's death, and you happened to mention that John Rother was supposed to bear a remarkable resemblance to his great-grandfather, Sir Percival Rother, who was the last of the family to be buried in the family vault. You mentioned a portrait of the old man which hung in the Chalklands sitting-room.

'My original suspicions were aroused when we discovered the missing skull wrapped in Rother's plus-four suit out at Brook Cottage. Professor Blenkings pointed out that this could not possibly be John Rother's skull, and mentioned, among other things, that the skull had an undershot jaw. The next day, therefore, I came out to you, if you remember, borrowed the Chalklands key, and went and had a look at that portrait. Well, to cut a long story short, Sir Percival *had* got an undershot jaw, although in build he exactly resembled his great-grandson. That was good enough for me! I drove down to the Vicarage and explained matters to the Vicar, who gave me permission to investigate the Rother family vault. It was just as I had anticipated – Sir Percival's bones were missing!'

'Good Lord!' exclaimed Barnet with a shudder. 'What a horrible idea!'

'Yes – it's curious, isn't it, how far a man's infatuation for a woman will drive him? At any rate there was that part of the mystery solved. I then recalled Kate Abingworth's evidence about that strange meeting of John and Janet on the lawn at Chalklands a week before the supposed murder. Janet had been carrying a suit-case. Why? Because they were spending the night together somewhere? Not a bit of it. Because they were going down to the church to collect poor old Sir Percival's skeleton.

'I reckon now that John severed the bone frame-work so that it could all be stuffed into the suit-case and hid the case itself until he could get to work with his surgical saw in his own time. This severing of the bones into smaller pieces was one of John's many strokes of genius. It suggested to us, at once, that an attempt had been made to pass the body through the kiln so as to avoid discovery. Large portions of the skeleton in the lime would have suggested carelessness. John's scheme was full of these little touches of reality. For instance, it had been his habit when going on long journeys to empty his tank so that he could check up the miles-per-gallon of his Hillman. When he was setting out on his pretended journey to Harlech he had gone to the extent of carrying out this cor-roborative detail. As a matter of fact, in that case, it helped me in my investigation because I was able to deduce from the residue in his tank that Rother had covered just on thirty miles before he reached Bindings Lane. Consequently when I suspected that he sent off the telegram from Littlehampton and that he would have gone on to Worthing to avoid meeting William on the road, I was able to make a test run and more or less satisfy myself as to the route he had taken on the 20th.

'In the case of the bones, however, this damnable piece of foresight did actually strengthen the case against William. The use of the kiln, too, was devilishly clever because we naturally associated the kiln with William. As to the way in which the bones were smuggled into the kiln – well, there can be no doubt that Janet was responsible. Before the 20th I dare say the bones had been made up into smallish parcels and hidden in Janet's room. The skull, which it was necessary to conceal because of its undershot jaw was probably left at Brook Cottage before the 20th, or even hidden with the cloak and broad-brimmed hat in that attaché-case. All Janet had to do was to slip out each night, scatter a few of the bones in the kiln, cover them with a layer of coal and chalk, and carry on until the whole of the skeleton had been disposed of.

'One vital point, however, had not escaped John's notice. It is very difficult to identify a victim when only the bones remain – and, in this case, charred bones at that. So what does Rother do? Gets Janet to chuck in his actual identity-disc, which he always wore, and his own belt, which had a specially designed clasp. Here, unfortunately for him, his genius didn't take him far enough – he forgot that the murderer would also want to rid himself of his victim's clothes, with the consequence that when we came to look for buttons, cuff-links, and so on we couldn't find 'em. Because of this we searched Brook Cottage for the suit and stumbled upon the skull! So much for the bones. Now we come to the real murder. You're sure I'm not boring you, sir?'

'On the contrary,' Barnet assured him, 'you're

267

hypnotizing me. Already I'm casting round to find a good locale into which to fit this case. There's a first-class story in this tragedy, Meredith – heaven-sent I might say – particularly the plot!'

'Just as I said,' agreed Meredith. 'There's nothing queerer than reality. Your one trouble will be to make your readers *believe* in your yarn. Strange – but a fact.' Meredith stretched himself contentedly, took another drink, relit his pipe and went on: 'Well, let's deal with William Rother's death. You know, of course, how he was found at the foot of the chalk-pit on August 10th. You were present at the inquest. So it's more than possible that I shall be running over ground that you've already traversed.

'One thing still puzzles me – how did John get to know that William had not been arrested? No newspapers were delivered at Brook Cottage while he was using it as a hide-out. No letters arrived from Janet Rother, for the simple reason that John was supposed to be dead after July 20th. Yet in some way those two must have got in touch with each other. Janet must have kept him informed as to the progress of my investigations. The only way in which this could have been worked, to my mind, was for Janet to have taken a bus to Bramber during the day and hidden a note in some prearranged spot. John then crept out in the early hours and collected this very necessary information. That's only guesswork – but it's certain that John must have realized some days before August 10th the exact direction in which the wind was blowing.

'I don't for a moment suspect that the plot to

268

do away with William was hatched in a few days. The scheme which was to be put into operation if we failed to make an arrest, as I suggested before, was probably worked out at the same time as scheme Number One. It is quite possible that the faked confession which was planted in the dead man's pocket was drafted at least a year before it was utilized.

'The general plan of scheme Number Two was to stage William's death in such a way that it looked like suicide. For example, the wires above the pit were to be deliberately cut and the pliers left in such a position that the police were bound to find them. John reckoned that if his first scheme ran according to schedule the police were bound to place William on their suspect list. He knew his brother had a highly strung, nervous sort of temperament. What more natural that William, fearful of what might eventually befall him, should anticipate justice and take his own life? One must realize that William had a very powerful reason for wanting to do away with John. We realized that at once. In the same way we could clearly understand his reason for wanting to commit suicide.

'Unfortunately John made one or two minor errors in the staging of this tragedy. He was over-cautious. When he typed that faked confession he took care that no finger-print should give him away. He obviously took the precaution of wearing gloves. The same with Janet when she placed the confession in William's pocket – with the result that we hit upon the curious and suspicious fact that the sheets and envelope bore no finger-prints at all! Again, the wound in William's temple was uppermost when he lay at the base of the pit, although the medical evidence insisted that it would have been impossible for him to have turned over on his own accord. It was this, you may remember, which suggested to me that William had suffered that wound *before* he fell over the cliff. The rest of our evidence you heard at the inquest.

'Now for an actual reconstruction of the murder. Naturally all the evidence I have got against Rother is purely circumstantial. It's for the jury to decide whether he really did kill his brother in the way in which I'm just going to describe.

'At any rate we know that on the night of August 10th John Rother set off from Brook Cottage on a bicycle. He was seen mounting the machine by Biggins, the landlord of the "Loaded Wain". He had once more adopted a new disguise. He had used his three weeks' concealment to grow a beard, and he was now wearing a respectable black suit and a bowler hat. I imagine that this disguise had been specially chosen for his flit to London directly after the murder. It was just the sort of disguise which would pass without comment in Town. He was seen again that same night, turning up off the main road on the cart-track which led up past the kilns to Chalklands. I suspect that he hid his bicycle in some bushes and proceeded on foot to the point where he had arranged his rendezvous with William.

'I happen to know now just how the note arranging that fateful meeting was worded, for the simple reason that we found it stuffed into a wallet, which we took from John Rother when he was searched after arrest. Careless, you'll admit –

but quite understandable. It's very easy for a criminal to be lulled into a false sense of security when he is not arrested or suspected directly after the crime. As a matter of fact I've got that note with me – perhaps you'd care to see it? A genuine period piece for a criminal museum, eh? Any offers, Mr. Barnet?'

Barnet smiled and stretched out his hand for the note. The address he noted was typewritten.

'Were you able to decipher this post-mark?' he asked Meredith as one connoisseur in crime to another.

'Yes – London. Janet, I happened to learn from Kate Abingworth, went up to Town a few days before William's death. That's what we call a significant fact!'

Barnet chuckled.

'You don't miss much, do you? Thank heaven I haven't decided to commit a murder yet.' He carefully extracted the single typewritten sheet from the crumpled envelope.

If you want to know who murdered your brother [he read] *I can give you precise information which will lead to an arrest. Make no mention of this letter to the police. I will meet you on High Meadow at 2. a.m. on August 10th, provided that you come alone and make no mention of my part in the solution of this crime.*

'And very cleverly worded too,' was Aldous Barnet's comment as he handed back the note to the Superintendent. 'If I had been in William's shoes I'm quite certain that I shouldn't have failed to keep the appointment.'

'Quite.' Meredith kept silent for a space, then asked quietly: 'Notice anything peculiar about that note? Or should I say characteristic?'

'Characteristic? I don't quite follow.'

'Do you remember that evening you called on me at Arundel Road with William's note?' Barnet nodded. 'Well, we had a discussion then about typescript. I explained how it was possible to recognize work from the same machine and, in most cases, work which has been typed by the same pair of hands.'

'I recall that perfectly. It was this knowledge which enabled you to mark down that confession as a fake.'

'Yes, and since then it has told me something more. Something so vital that Rother's life may depend upon it. This note, Mr. Barnet – it has been typed upon the Chalklands portable Remington, and the manner in which the keys have been struck bears a very strong resemblance to that in the case of the confession. I was never able to get hold of a sample of John's typewriting, curiously enough – but I'm beginning to think now that he typed not only this note but the confession as well. We're now trying to trace down a business letter sent out by John Rother to one of their lime customers and if that letter shows the same type characteristics as this note and the confession ... well, I guess we've got him by the short hairs! I have an idea that John took the precaution of destroying every sample of his typewriting before he set out on that pretended journey to Harlech. Pity he was so careless over that note, eh?'

'And as to the actual way in which William was murdered?'

'Assumption only,' acknowledged Meredith. 'I reckon John used a flint. The type of wound rather suggested this. He then dragged the body to the edge of the cliff and swung it out so that it would drop clear of the base.'

There was a long silence, threaded only by the drowsy hum of industrious bees and the sleepy twitter of sparrows in the cool branches of the chestnut. Suddenly Barnet leaned forward and asked abruptly:

'Will he hang?'

'Maybe,' said Meredith with a non-committal shrug. 'That part of the case is out of my hands: I can only display the Crown evidence in the best possible light and leave the rest to the barristers and the jury. Witnesses are an unreliable race. They're like some cricket teams – all right on paper! Many's the time I've been in court when the pet witness for the prosecution has proved to be the star witness for the defence and vice versa. That may well happen in this case.'

'And Janet Rother?'

'I doubt if we'll ever lay our hands on her. We've been in touch with the Continental police, but of course they can't help. Too long a start, I reckon. No, as my son Tony would put it, she's "gone over the side". In other words, got clear.'

'Are you sorry?'

Meredith rubbed his chin with the stem of his pipe.

'Well, you've put me a bit of a poser there, sir. According to regulations, a detective should have

273

about as much feeling as a bed-post. But it's been my experience that the completely official machine never makes a really good detective. You see, Mr. Barnet, crime is bound up with human weakness, human greed, human misery – at every turn in an investigation you come up against the human element. As a "minion of the law", as the newspapers have it, I should look upon Mrs. Rother's escape as a misfortune. But sometimes the law is at war with the man, and if you asked me in the second capacity well, here's luck to her! We're all of us misguided sometimes in life, but I reckon she was more misguided than most – that's all!'

CHAPTER 19

THE OPENING OF A PROBLEM

Aldous Barnet took up his pen and began to write: *Dominating that part of the Sussex Downs with which this story is concerned is Chanctonbury Ring. This oval cap of gigantic beeches may be seen, on fine days, from almost any point in the little parish of Washington. It is a typical village...*

This Large Print Book for the partially sighted, who cannot read normal print, is published under the auspices of

THE ULVERSCROFT FOUNDATION